P9-CNH-178

All Families are Psychotic

A Novel

Douglas Coupland

BLOOMSBURY

 For information address: Bloomsbury, 175 Fifth Avenue, New York, N. Y. 10010.

Published by Bloomsbury, New York and London
Distributed to the trade by St. Martin's Press

Library of Congress Cataloguing-in-Publication Data

Coupland, Douglas.
All families are psychotic / Douglas Coupland.
p. cm.
ISBN 1-58234-165-6
1. Women astronauts -- Fiction. 2. Problem families -- Fiction.
3. Florida -- Fiction. I. Title.

PS3553.0855 A78 2001
813'.54--dc21
2001025707

First U.S. Edition

10 9 8 7 6 5 4 3 2 1

Typeset by Hewer Text Ltd, Edinburgh, Scotland
Printed and bound in the USA by RR Donnelley & Sons, Crawfordsville

IN A DREAM YOU SAW
A WAY TO SURVIVE
AND YOU WERE FULL OF JOY
– Jenny Holzer

01

Janet opened her eyes – Florida's prehistoric glare dazzled outside the motel window. A dog barked; a car honked; a man was singing a snatch of a Spanish song. She absentmindedly touched the scar from the bullet wound beneath her left rib cage, a scar that had healed over, bumpy and formless and hard, like a piece of gum stuck beneath a tabletop. She hadn't expected her flesh to have healed so blandly – *What was I expecting, a scar shaped like an American flag?*

Janet's forehead flushed: *My children – where are they?* She did a rapid-fire tally of the whereabouts of her three children, a ritual she'd enacted daily since the birth of Wade back in 1958. Once she'd mentally placed her offspring in their geographic slots, she remembered to breathe: *They're all going to be here in Orlando today.*

She looked at the motel's bedside clock: 7:03 A.M. *Pill o'clock.* She took two capsules from her prescription pill caddie and swallowed them with tap water gone flat overnight, which now tasted like nickels and pennies. It registered on her that motel rooms now came equipped with coffee makers. *What a sensible idea, so bloody sensible – why didn't they do this years ago? Why is all the good stuff happening now?*

A few days back, on the phone, her daughter, Sarah, had said, 'Mom, at least buy Evian, OK? The tap water in that heap is probably laced with crack. I can't be*lieve* you chose to stay there.'

'But dear, I don't mind it here.'

'Go stay at the Peabody with the rest of the family. I've told you a hundred times I'll pay.'

'That's not the point, dear. A hotel really ought not cost more than this.'

'Mom, NASA cuts deals with the hotels, and . . .' Sarah made a puff of air, acknowledging defeat. 'Forget it. But I think you're too well off to be pulling your Third World routine.'

Sarah – *so cavalier with money!* – as were the two others. None had known poverty, and they'd never known war, but the advantage hadn't made them golden, and Janet had never gotten over this fact. A life of abundance had turned her two boys into an element other than gold – lead? – silicon? – bismuth? But then *Sarah* – Sarah was an element finer than gold – carbon crystallized as diamond – a bolt of lightning frozen in midflash, sliced into strips, and stored in a vault.

Janet's phone rang and she answered it: Wade, calling from an Orange County lock-up facility. Janet imagined Wade in a drab concrete hallway, unshaven and disheveled, yet still radiating 'the glint' – the spark in the eye he'd inherited from his father. Bryan didn't have it and Sarah didn't need it, but Wade had glinted his way through life, and maybe it hadn't been the best attribute to inherit after all.

Wade: Janet remembered being back home, and driving along Marine Drive in the morning, watching a certain type of man waiting for a bus to take him downtown. He'd be slightly seedy and one or two notches short of respectability; it was always patently clear he'd lost his driver's license after a DWI, but this only made him more interesting, and whenever Janet smiled at one of these men from her car, they fired a smile right back. And that was Wade and, in some unflossed cranny of her memory, her ex-husband, Ted.

'Dear, aren't you too old to be calling me from – *jail?* Even saying the word "jail" feels silly.'

'Mom, I don't do bad stuff any more. This was a fluke.'

'Okay then, what happened – did you accidentally drive a busload of Girl Guides into the Everglades?'

'It was a bar brawl, Mom.'

Janet repeated this: '*A bar brawl.*'

'I know, I know – you think I don't know how idiotic that sounds? I'm phoning because I need a ride away from this dump. My rental car's back at the bar.'

'Where's Beth? Why doesn't she drive you?'

'She gets in early this afternoon.'

'OK. Well, let's go back a step, dear. How exactly does one get into a bar brawl?'

'You wouldn't believe me if I told you.'

'You'd be amazed what I'm believing these days. Try me.'

There was a pause on the other end. 'I got in a fight because this guy – this *jerk* – was making fun of God.'

'God.' *He can't be serious.*

'Yeah, well, he was.'

'In what way?'

'He was being so nasty about it, saying, "God's an asshole," and "God doesn't care about squat," and he kept on going on and on, and I had to put a stop to it. I think he got fired that day.'

'You were defending God's honor?'

'Yeah. I was.'

Tread carefully here, Janet. 'Wade, I know Beth is very religious. Are you becoming religious, too?'

'Me? Maybe. Nah. Yes. No. It depends on how you define religious. It keeps Beth calm, and maybe . . .' Wade paused. 'Maybe it can calm me, too.'

'So you spent the night in jail, then?'

'Safely in the arms of a four-hundred-pound convenience store thief named Bubba.'

'Wade, I can't pick you up. I think it's going to be one of those no-energy days. And besides, the car I rented smells like a carpet in a frat house – and the roads down here, they're *white*, and the glare makes me sleepy.'

'Mom, come *on* . . .'

'Don't be such a baby. You're forty-two. Act it. You couldn't even get to the hotel in time yesterday.'

'I was making a quick detour to visit a friend in Tampa. I stopped for a drink. Hey – don't treat me like I'm Bryan. It wasn't like I started the fight or . . .'

'Stop! Stop right there. Call a cab.'

'I'm short on cash.'

'Simple cab fare? Then how are you paying for the hotel?'

Wade was silent.

'Wade?'

'Sarah's covering it for us until we can pay it back.' An awkward silence followed.

'Mom, you could pick me up if you really wanted to. I know you could.'

'Yes, I suppose I could. But I think you should phone your father down in . . . what's that place called?'

'Kissimmee – and I already did call him.'

'And?'

'He's gone marlin fishing with Nickie.'

'*Marlin* fishing? People still do that?'

'I don't know. I guess. I thought they were extinct. They probably have a guy in a wet suit who attaches a big plastic marlin onto their line.'

'Marlins are so ugly. They remind me of basement rec rooms that people built in 1958 and never used again.'

'I know. It's hard to imagine they ever existed in the first place.'

'So he's out marlin fishing with Nickie then?'

'Yeah. With Nickie.'

'That cheesy slut.'

'Mom?'

'Wade, I'm not a saint. I've been holding stuff inside me for decades – girls my age were trained to do that, and it's why we all have colitis. Besides, a dash of spicy language is refreshing every so often. Just yesterday I was hunting for information on vitamin D derivatives on the Internet, and suddenly, *doink*! I land in the Anal Love website. I'm looking at a cheerleader in a leather harness on the—'

'*Mom*, how can you visit sites like that?'

'Wade, may I remind you that *you* are standing in a human Dumpster somewhere in Orlando, yet hearing a sixty-five-year-old woman discuss the Internet over a pay phone shocks you? You wouldn't believe the sites I've visited. And the chat rooms, too. I'm not *always* Janet Drummond, you know.'

'Mom, why are you telling me this?'

'Oh, forget it. And your stepmother, Nickie, is still a cheesy slut. Phone Howie – maybe he can come fetch you.'

'Howie's so boring he makes me almost pass out. I can't believe Sarah married such a blank.'

'I'm the one who gave birth to her, and I'm the one who has to drive with him to Cape Canaveral today.'

'Ooh – bummer. Another NASA do?'

'Yes. And you're welcome to come along.'

'Wait a second, Mom – why aren't you at the Peabody with everybody else? What are you staying in a motel for? By the way, it took thirty rings for the clerk – who, I might add, sounded like a kidney thief – to answer the phone.'

'Wade, you're changing the subject. Phone Howie. Oh wait – I think I hear somebody at the door.' Janet held the phone at arm's length from her head, and said, '*Knock knock knock knock*.'

'Very funny, Mom.'

'I have to answer the door, Wade.'

'That's really funny. I—'

Click

The motel room made her feel slightly too transient, but it was a bargain, and that turned the minuses into pluses. Nonetheless, Janet missed her morning waking-up rituals in her own bedroom. She touched her body gently and methodically, as though she were at the bank counting a stack of twenties. She gently rubbed a set of ulcers on her lips' insides, still there, same as the day before, not just a dream. Her hands probed further downward – no lumps in her breasts, not today – but then what had Sarah told her? *We've all had cancer thousands of times, Mom, but in all those thousands of times your body removed it. It's lazy bookkeeping to only count the cancers that stick. You and I could have cancer right now, but tomorrow it might be gone.*

The motel room smelled like a lifetime of cigarettes. She looked at Sarah's photo in the *Miami Herald* beside the phone, a standard NASA PR crew photo: an upper body shot against a navy ice-cream swirl background and complexion-flattering lighting that made one suspect a noble, scientific disdain for cosmetics. Sarah clutched a helmet underneath her right arm. Her left arm, handless, rested by her side: *Space knows no limitations*.

Janet sighed. She twiddled her toes. Ten minutes later her phone rang again: Sarah calling from the Cape.

'Hi, Mom. I just spoke to Howie. He'll go pick up Wade.'

'Good morning, Sarah. How's *your* day?'

'This morning we had a zero-G evacuation test, but what I really wanted to do was sit in a nice quiet bathroom and test out a new brand of pore-cleansing strips. The humidity in these suits is giving me killer blackheads. They never talked about that in those old *Life* magazine photo essays. Have you eaten yet?'

'No.'

'Come eat at the Cape with me. We can have dehydrated astronaut's ice cream out of a shiny Mylar bag.'

Janet sat up on her bed and pulled her legs over the side. She felt her skin – her *meat* – hanging from her bones as though it were so much water-logged clothing. She needed to pee. She began to meter her words as she eyed the bathroom door. 'I don't think so, dear. The only time they ever allow me to have with you are three seconds for a photo op.'

Sarah asked, 'Is Beth arriving today?'

Beth was Wade's wife. 'Later this afternoon. I think I'm going to dinner with the two of them.'

'How far along is she?'

'I think this is her fourth month. It may even be a Christmas baby.'

'Huh. I see.'

'Something wrong, Sarah?'

'It's just that—'

'What?'

'Mom, how could Wade marry . . . *her*. She's so priggish and born-again. I always thought Wade would marry Miss Roller Derby. Beth is so frigging sanctimonious.'

'She keeps him alive.'

'I guess she does. When does Bryan arrive?'

'He and his girlfriend are already here. He called from the Peabody.'

'*Girlfriend? Bryan?* What's her name?'

'If I tell you, you won't believe me.'

'It can't be that bad. Is it one of those made-up names like DawnElle or Kerrissa or CindaJo?'

'Worse.'

'What could be worse?'

'Shw.'

'I beg your pardon?'

'Shw. That's her name: *Shw*.'

'Spell that for me.'

'S. H. W.'

'And?'

'There's no vowel, if that's what you're waiting for.'

'What – her name is *Shw*? Am I pronouncing that properly?'

'I'm afraid so.'

'That is the most . . . *impractical* name I've ever heard. Is she from Sri Lanka or Finland or something?'

Janet's eye lingered on the bathroom door and the toilet

beyond. 'As far as I know she's from Alberta. Bryan worships her, and she's also knocked up like a prom queen.'

'*Bryan's* pregnant? How come I don't know any of this?'

'I just met her last week myself, dear. She seems to rather like me, though she treats everybody else like dirt. So I don't mind her at all, really.'

'Bryan is such a freak. I'm not going to be able to keep a straight face, you know – when she tells me her name, that is.'

Janet said, '*Shw!*'

Sarah giggled.

'*Shw! Shw! Shw!*'

Sarah laughed. 'Is she pretty?'

'Sort of. She's also about eighteen and an angry little hornet. In the fifties we would have called her a pixie. Nowadays we'd call her hyperthyroid. She's bug-eyed.'

'Where'd they meet?'

'Seattle. She helped Bryan set fire – I believe – to a stack of pastel-colored waffle-knit T-shirts in a Gap – back during the World Trade Organization riots. They were separated, then a few months ago they met again destroying a test facility growing genetically modified runner beans.'

Janet could sense Sarah changing gears; she was finished discussing the family. Next would come business-like matters: 'Well, good for Bryan. You're OK for today's NASA gig?'

'Still.'

'Howie will pick you up at 9:30, after he picks up my darling brother. By the way, Dad's broke.'

'That doesn't surprise me. I'd heard he'd lost his job.'

'I tried to loan him some money, but he, of course, said no. Not that there's much to loan. Howie lost the bulk of our savings in some website that sells products for pets. I could strangle him.'

'Oh dear.' *It's so easy to fall into the mother mode.*

'Tell me about it. Hey, when was the last time you even saw Dad?'

'Half a year ago. By accident at Super-Valu.'

'Tense?'

'I can handle him.'

'Good. See you there.'

'Yes, dear.'

Click

On the walkway outside her room, Janet heard children mewling as they set off to Walt Disney World with their families. She walked to the bathroom across a floor made lunar from eons of cigarette burns and various stains better left uninvestigated. She thought of serial murderers using acids to dissolve the teeth and jawbones of their victims.

She unsuspectingly caught sight of herself in a floor-length mirror by the sink and the sight stopped her cold. *Yes, Janet, that's correct: you are shrinking – sinew by sinew, protein molecule by protein molecule you are turning into an . . . an elf, yes, you, Janet Drummond, once voted 'Girl We'd Rob a Bank For.'*

She was transfixed by the view of herself in a blue nightie, as if she were once again young and this image had been delivered to her from the future as a warning – *If I squint I can still see the cool immaculate housewife I once dreamed of becoming. I'm Elizabeth Montgomery starring in* Bewitched. *I'm Dina Merrill lunching at the Museum of Modern Art with Christina Ford.*

Oh forget it. She peed, showered, dried and then modified those traces of time's passage on her face that she could.

There. I'm not so bad after all. A man might still rob a bank for me, and men still do flirt – not too frequently – and older men perhaps – but the look in the eyes never changes.

She dressed, and five minutes later she was a block away sitting in a Denny's reading a paper. The North American weather map on the rear page was a rich, unhealthy crimson, with only a small strip of cool green running up the coast from Seattle to Alaska. Outside the restaurant window the sun on the parking lot made the area seem like a science experiment. She realized she no longer cared about the weather. *Next.*

Back in her motel room, she lay down on the bed haunted by a thousand sex acts. *OK – this place is creepy but at least I'm not throwing away money.* Her lips were sore to the point that speech was painful, and it hurt to exhale. Her pill buzzer buzzed; she sat up. She reached into her purse and removed a prescription bottle. She turned on the TV, and there was Sarah being interviewed on CNN. As always, her daughter looked glowingly pretty on TV, like a nun who'd never touched make-up.

– Do you think you and children like you, born with damage caused by thalidomide, have other messages to tell the world?

– Of course. We were the canaries in the coal mine. We were the first children born in which it was proved that chemicals from the outside world – in our case thalidomide – could severely damage the human embryo. These days, most mothers don't smoke or drink during pregnancy. They know that the outer world can enter their babies and cause damage. But in my mother's generation, they didn't know this. They smoked and drank and took any number of medications without thinking twice. Now we know better, and as a species we're smarter as a result – we're aware of teratogens.

– Teratogens?

– Yes. It means 'monster forming'. A horrible word, but then the world can be a horrible place. They're the chemicals that cross the placenta and affect a child's growth in utero.

The host turned to the camera: 'Time for a quick break. I've been speaking with Sarah Drummond-Fournier, a one-handed woman, and one heck of a fighter, who'll be on Friday's shuttle flight. We'll be right back.'

How on earth did I give birth to such a child? I understand nothing about her life. Nothing. And yet she's the spitting image of me, and she's gallivanting up into space. Janet remembered how much she'd wanted to help the young Sarah with her homework, and Sarah's polite-but-resigned invitations to come do so when Janet popped her head into Sarah's doorway. Invariably Janet would look down at the papers that might as well have been in Chinese. Janet would ask a few concerned questions about Sarah's teachers, and then plead kitchen duty, beating a hasty retreat.

She turned off the TV.

She once cared about everything, and if she couldn't muster genuine concern, she could easily fake it: too much rain stunting the petunias; her children's scrapes; stick figure Africans; the plight of marine mammals. She considered herself one of the surviving members of a lost generation, the last generation raised to care about appearances or doing the right thing – to care about caring. She had been born in 1934 in Toronto, a city then much like Chicago or Rochester or Detroit – bland, methodical, thrifty and rules-playing. Her father, William Truro, managed the furniture and household appliance department of the downtown Eaton's department store. William's wife, Kaye, was, well . . . William's wife.

The two raised Janet and her older brother, Gerald, on $29.50 a week until 1938, when a salary decrease lowered William's pay to $27 a week, and jam vanished from the Truro breakfast table, the absence of which became Janet's first memory. After the jam, the rest of Janet's life seemed to have been an ongoing reduction – things that had once been essential vanishing without discussion, or even worse, with too much discussion.

Seasons changed. Sweaters became ragged, were patched up and became ragged again, and were grudgingly thrown out. A few flowers were grown in the thin band of dirt in front of the brick row house, species scavenged by Kaye for their value as dried flowers, which scrimped an extra few months' worth of utility from them. Life seemed to be entirely about *scrimping*. In fall of 1938, Gerald died of polio. In 1939 the war began and Canada was in it from the start, and scrimping kicked into overdrive: bacon fat, tin cans, rubber – all material objects – were scrimp-worthy. Janet's most enjoyable childhood memories were of sorting neighborhood trash in the alleys, in search of crown jewels, metal fragments and love notes from dying princes. During the war, houses in her neighborhood grew dingy – paint became a luxury. When she was six, Janet walked into the kitchen and found her father kissing her mother passionately. They saw Janet standing there, a small, chubby, fuddled Campbell's Soup kid, and they broke apart, blushed, and the incident was never spoken of again. The glimpse was her only evidence of passion until womanhood.

An hour passed and Janet looked at the bedside clock: almost 9:30, and Howie would have already picked up Wade by now. Janet walked down to the hotel's covered breezeway to wait for her son-in-law. A day of boredom loomed.

Then, *pow!* she was angry all of a sudden. She was angry because she was unable to remember and reexperience her life as a continuous movie-like event. There were only bits of punctuation here and there – the kiss, the jam, the dried flowers – which, when assembled, made Janet who she was – yet there seemed to be no divine logic behind the assemblage. Or any flow. All those bits were merely . . . bits. But there had to be logic. How could the small, chubby child of 1940 imagine that one day she'd be in Florida seeing her own daughter launched into outer space? Tiny little Sarah, who was set to circle the Earth hundreds of times. *We didn't even think about outer space in 1939. Space didn't exist yet.*

She removed a black felt Sharpie pen from her purse, and wrote the word 'laryngitis' on a folded piece of paper. For the remainder of the day she wouldn't have to speak to anybody she didn't want to.

I wonder if Howie is going to be late? No – Howie's not the late type.

02

Wade sat on the lock-up's sunburnt concrete stoop sifting through the grab bag of possessions returned to him from his overnight captors: sunglasses a size too small so they never fell from his head – a wallet containing four IDs (two real: Nevada and British Columbia; two fakes: Missouri and Quebec) along with a badly photocopied U.S. hundred; a Pittsburgh Steelers Bic lighter (*Where did that come from?*) and the keys to a rental Pontiac Sunfire, still in the lot of the previous evening's bar. His clothes were more blood-splattered than not. At first the blood had been syrupy and had made his clothes turn clammy, rubbery. Then, when Wade was asleep in his cell, the blood converted his denim pants and cotton shirt into a skin of beef jerky.

This is not a state in which one defends God lightly.

Where's Howie?

Wade removed a smooth rock he'd found a decade before while hitchhiking on a Kansas freeway – his good luck charm; three minutes after he'd found it he was picked up by the disenchanted wife of a major league baseball player, who went on to be his meal ticket for the latter years of his thirties.

Honk-honk

'Hey there, brother-in-law!'

Howie called from across the lot where he'd parked his orange VW microbus beside a chain-link fence and a flowering pink oleander hedge.

Christ. Howie's going to be chipper. I hate chipper. Wade walked toward him. 'Yeah, hi, Howie. Get me out of this dump.'

'Right, pardner. Hey, I see a bit of mess on your shirt.'

'Blood, Howie. It's harmless. And it's not mine – it's from the meathead who hassled me last night.'

Inside the vehicle, hot like a bakery, Howie turned on the ignition. The air-conditioning blasted on full, shooting a freezing moldy fist into the car interior. Wade slapped the button down. 'Christ, Howie, I don't want to get Legionnaire's disease from your bloody *van*.'

'Just trying to help, *mon frère, mon frère*. Nothing lurking in the vents of this baby.'

'Also, Howie, I'm not going to walk into some swank hotel looking like a tampon. I have to clean up first. Drive me to the Brunswicks' place.' Howie was staying with the family of Sarah's Mission Commander, Gordon Brunswick.

'I can wash up there and you can lend me some clothes.'

Howie was taken aback. 'The Brunswicks' – what? Sarah didn't say anything about driving you to the Brunswicks.'

'You have a problem?'

'Problem? No. Not at all.' Howie looked panged.

'Howie, just take me there, I'll shower, I'll borrow some clothes, then you can drop me off at my car. You have to pick up my mother at 9:30.'

'No need to be testy, Wade.'

'Have you ever spent a night in jail, Howie?'

Howie seemed almost flattered to be asked this. 'Well, I can't say that I . . .'

'*Drive*, Howie.'

They drove for fifteen minutes and arrived at the subdivision home of the Brunswick family – an astronaut clan as different from the Drummond family as heaven is from earth. Children in NASA T-shirts were on the front lawn looking at the moon, visible in the daytime, through a telescope. The front door had a window shaped like a crescent moon. Behind the door stood Alanna Brunswick, wife of Mission Commander Gordon Brunswick, in a *Star Trek* T-shirt and holding a platter of Tollhouse cookies, smiling like a perfume counter saleswoman.

The doorbell was still playing the *Close Encounters* theme song as she spoke, with a trace of tightly concealed surprise in her voice: 'Howie, this must be your . . . brother-in-law, Wade.'

'In the flesh.'

Wade sensed he'd been much discussed. 'Hi. I'm just going to wash up before I head to the Peabody. Upstairs?'

Alanna's face betrayed deep misgivings, but Wade knew he had a fifteen-second window during which she would be immobilized by his looks, slightly enhanced by rakish night-in-jail stubble. He turned on the smile (*add another five seconds*), then bounded up the stairs.

'Uh – you just make yourself at home,' she shouted after him.

'Yeah, thanks. Howie, find me some duds, okay?'

'Okey dokey.'

Wade saw photos of planes and jets. Training certificates. Black and white 1960s celebrity pilot photos. Saturn 5 rocket models – even the ceiling was peppered with glow-in-the-dark stars, a yellow margarine color in the daylight. Wade could understand why Howie would want to stay here instead of a hotel. These people *lived* for the program; the Drummond family, comparatively, treated Sarah's imminent flight like a display at a local science fair.

He located the bathroom and stripped. His clothing was a write-off; even his shoes were leathery with blood. He wrapped up the garments as best he could and squished them into the trashcan. Once in the shower, yesterday's crud rinsed off and he began to feel new again. Howie stuck his arm through the door and placed some clothes on the counter, and through the water and steam, Wade heard him say, 'Try these on. Take your time.'

Wade toweled dry and inspected the clothing, clownishly small. Only the socks fit. *What the—?* Then Wade remembered Sarah explaining that astronauts are always tiny, chosen for their lack of body mass; there's no such thing as a beefy astronaut. *Trust Howie not to loan me some of his own clothes. Weasel.*

With the towel wrapped around his waist, he stepped into the hallway, the carpet thick and bouncy. He tried various doors. *Gotta find some better adult clothing. What's that – kids' room? No. Over there? Den. Wait – over there – an indisputably adult bedroom.* He walked into the room, bright with fluttery morning sun passing through the surrounding oaks. He turned a corner to where he supposed the cupboard might be, to find Howie and Alanna barnacled together in an embrace. They didn't see him at first. 'Shit. *Sorry.*' Wade retreated to the bathroom.

'Wade—'

'The clothes are too small, Howie. I need stretchy stuff – sweats maybe. And a big T-shirt. And flip-flops for my feet.'

'I can explain.'

'Just find me clothes, Howie.' Wade slammed the bathroom door. Outside there was a freighted silence, followed by the sound of shuffling feet. Wade wasn't quite sure what to think. His breathing was underwater-like, his thinking fogged.

There was a rap on the door: 'Clothes for you, pardner.'

Wade grabbed them and slammed the door.

'We can talk on the way to pick up your car,' said Howie through the door.

Wade got dressed. He looked like a gym teacher on his day off. He opened the door and barreled down to the car. He had no interest in seeing Alanna. Howie trailed behind him.

'Wade—'

Wade looked out the window.

'If you'd just let me explain, Wade. Alanna and I understand each other – the pressure of being married to—'

Wade turned to look at him: 'There's always an explanation, Howie, and I wrote most of them – which in turn makes me understand all too well that there's never an explanation. So shut the fuck up and drive.'

Surprisingly soon they were at the bar.

'That's my car over there.'

'Nice car.'

'Shut the fuck up, Howie.'

'I only meant to say—'

Wade unleashed the cloud of hornets inside his head: 'If you think for one second that I'm going to even breathe a word of this to my baby sister, you're off your fucking rocker. Ditto Commander Brunswick. Nothing on this planet is going to fuck up their mission in even the slightest way. This is between you and me, Howie, and I have no idea where it's going to go. In the meantime we have to sit together at this frigging banquet tonight. You piss me off in any way, and I'll make your life a goddamn living hell for as long as I breathe.'

'No need to be nasty.'

Wade stepped out of the van, exhaling his disgust. 'You just don't understand, do you, you shitty little space martyr?' He slammed the door.

03

In 1970, Sarah attended a summer science camp a hundred miles east of Vancouver, in a gently mountainous spot called Cultus Lake, a very lake-y looking lake, then in the high season of mosquitoes, stinging nettle and drunks manning noisy recreational crafts. Sarah had been looking forward to the camp, and Janet, who'd found it for her, was very pleased indeed, even though Ted shanghaied the event. He'd organized the preparation of supplies, the packing, bought numerous books on the wilds of British Columbia, and then drove Sarah out to the camp himself, rather than allowing her to take the minibus that picked up her fellow campers.

What the Drummond family, Sarah included, hadn't expected was that Sarah would become profoundly and violently homesick at the camp, paralyzed with fear, vomiting out in the reeds and the irises beside the bunkhouse, immobilized and unable to eat or sleep. The family might not have found out about the homesickness had Sarah not pried her way into the owner's private area and made a tearful, pleading long-distance call home around dinnertime, a call Ted answered and which Wade eavesdropped on from the den extension.

'Please, Daddy, I'm so homesick here I think I'm going to die. I can't eat or sleep or concentrate or anything. I want to come home so badly.'

'Hey, Sunshine, camp is good for you. You'll meet smart new kids – breathe fresh air – use that big brain of yours.'

'Daddy, I don't want any of that. I just want to be there in the kitchen with all of you. I feel so far away. I feel so . . . *sick*.'

Wade could hear his mother standing beside his father,

wondering aloud what was happening. 'Ted? What's wrong? Tell me.'

'Nothing's wrong, Jan. Sarah's just becoming used to camp life.'

'I'm *not* getting used to camp life, Daddy. I want to die. I don't want to be here. I want to come *home*.' More tears.

'Ted,' said Janet, 'let me speak to her.'

'Jan, calm down. She's fine. Why should she hate camp? I loved camp when I was a kid.'

'I'm *not* fine, Daddy.'

'You're going to love camp, sweetheart, I wouldn't say that if I didn't believe it. Camp was the best experience of my life.'

There was a clicking on the other end of the line; a woman's voice came on: 'Hello? Hello? Young lady, who have you been calling?' On the line was the camp's director, a Mrs. Wallace.

Ted said, 'I'm sorry Sarah interrupted your dinner, Mrs. Wallace. This isn't her typical behavior.'

In the background, Sarah was wailing.

'Some campers get homesick, Mr. Drummond. This is natural. Your Sarah will be fine.'

Sarah's crying in the background intensified. Ted signed off, yet again apologizing for his daughter's out-of-character behavior. Wade innocently sashayed into the kitchen, where Janet said, 'You have to go fetch her, Ted. She can barely even function, let alone learn about science. It's cruel.'

'It's not. You're overreacting. All kids love camp. She just needs to get used to it. She'll *love* it there. Mrs. Wallace told me that tomorrow they're studying jet propulsion and having Kentucky Fried Chicken for dinner.'

'I don't feel good about this, Ted.'

'Stop mollycoddling her. She's a trouper.'

The next morning, Wade woke up early and sneaked out of the house. Such an absence was in no way unusual and attracted no attention. He took the bus to his bank and withdrew his savings, about $340.00, and hired a taxi, his first, by the stand near the bus loop's Mexican fast-food place. The cab driver was a Crisco-complexioned fortysomething who Wade could tell, even at his early age, was well along life's downward slope. When Wade told him he wanted to go to Cultus Lake and back, the driver made him pony up the money; Wade's only worry was that the driver would be talkative, which proved not to be the case. After the driver blurted out, 'I could use a drive in the country,' he was silent the rest of the way.

By eleven A.M. they were at the camp's gate. 'You park way down there,' Wade said, his genius for orchestrating maneuvers already in evidence. 'I don't want the RCMP looking for a cab.'

'Right, pardner.'

Wade walked up to the main house and asked to speak to the person in charge. The only remotely authoritative figure available was a teenage girl shucking counselor duty to fire up a cigarette. He smiled. Inside a minute he heard what he'd needed to hear: 'The jet propulsion group? That's the Madame Curie bunkhouse. They're down by the boat ramp.' Wade duly went to the boat ramp, where a flock of girls surrounded a launch apparatus, all save for Sarah, off to the side, her knees pulled up to her chest, her stomach cramping, as she hadn't eaten or slept in forty-eight hours.

Wade threw a pebble that landed at her feet. Sarah looked up and caught sight of her brother, and Wade was impressed at how she maintained her cool. Sarah waited until the rocket was on the cusp of detonation before she casually walked towards Wade. He asked her, 'You set to leave?'

'Right now.'

'Follow me. We have to keep quiet.' Wade led Sarah through a second-growth forest, about a century old, and treacherously bumpy with stumps and logs still barely even decayed after all that time. A few minutes later they emerged from the woods directly by the taxi. 'Hop in, little sister, and keep your head down. Step on it, Carl.'

'You're the boss.'

Minutes later they were on the Trans-Canada highway, and Sarah was holding tightly on to Wade's arm. 'It's OK, baby sister, we're going home. Home sweet home.' He patted her on the head. 'You hungry?'

Sarah squealed out a 'yes'.

'Carl, let's stop at that gas station up ahead.'

'Your wish is my command, boss.'

The two of them drank Cokes and ate chocolate bars. Years later, Sarah would say they were the most delicious things she could ever remember having eaten. Just over two hours later they were home. Carl accepted only a hundred dollars for the job, saying, 'It's probably the last nice thing I'll ever do.'

Wade stopped at the bottom of the driveway. He hadn't given the homecoming much thought. 'What are we going to tell Dad?'

Sarah said, 'I'll handle him.'

And she did. It was a Saturday, and Ted was in the kitchen eating an egg salad sandwich. Sarah walked into the kitchen and said, 'I escaped that prison and I'm not returning, so please don't try and make me. My decision's made and I'm not the least bit ashamed of it. I'm ready for any punishment you want to throw my way.'

Wade, listening in, was chilled to hear rebellious words he himself might have spoken. Both he and Janet, who was standing by the sink, waited for one long, held-in breath expecting Ted's nuclear detonation, but instead Ted bellowed out, 'That's my girl! What spunk to escape from that hellhole. Jan! Make our little jailbreaker an egg salad sandwich!'

04

Three years before his arrival in Florida to join his family, Wade had been living in Kansas City having an on-again/off-again (but mostly on-again) relationship with the wife of a major league baseball player. News of his affair with the baseball wife had leaked out and was splashed about the pages of the local daily tabloid. The baseball player and three of his buddies had entered Wade's favorite bar armed with Louisville Sluggers, fortunately while Wade was in the john, from which he scrambled out a rear door, then into the parking lot, then a further few thousand miles west. In Las Vegas, through a friend, he'd quickly landed a job as a hockey player in a trashy casino. He was paid more to fight with the other players than he was to play hockey, and as the coach handed him his thousand-dollar signing bonus, he'd said to Wade, 'A good rink is a red rink. Nothing makes guys double up on bets more than blood. Not even tits. If you have a freakish blood type like Rh-negative, I'd advise you to stock up a bit of it beforehand. The people who sell blood in this city – you don't want to know. And hands off the waitresses. I don't need you jerk-offs in the Hamburger League spreading broken hearts and the clap. Be back on Monday night. Seven o'clock. No helmet.'

That night Wade won 30,000 frequent flyer points in a poker game. The next day, feeling powerful, nostalgic and flush, he flew home to Vancouver. A storm pushed the plane to the west, and he watched the cities along Interstate 5 sweep below him. Drinking a beer and looking at the ground, he tried remembering the last time he'd seen a family member – it was Sarah, briefly, at a Holiday Inn by the University of Kansas in

Lawrence. Everybody else he'd dealt with through infrequent phone calls, often made from airport waiting lounges or on cell phones on the freeway where an easy way out was built into the call. Wade had read about Sarah's impending Kansas visit by accident in the newspaper while searching for the weekend sports scores. She was to be a keynote speaker at a symposium on gene splicing and Wade had arranged to meet her in the lounge of her hotel before her speech.

'Wade.'

'Little sister.'

They kissed and then talked about the family. Wade hadn't known any of the recent family news Sarah brought with her, and could only drink more and more quickly as he learned the details of their parents' divorce, Bryan's third suicide attempt, and Sarah's wall of degrees, Ph.Ds.

'What about you and Howie?'

'Howie? He's fine.'

A silence followed this, which Wade took as the signal to stop probing. Instead he asked what she'd been up to job-wise recently.

'Well, last week I logged in my two hundredth hour of reduced gravity flight aboard parabolic aircraft. And I've been deep sea diving, too, in a customized suit to prepare me for a spacewalk.'

'Really?'

'Part of the job description.' Sarah sipped a ginger ale.

'Mom said a few months ago that you'd become a captain in military jet flight.'

'She did?'

'Is it true?'

'Yeah, but it sounds so grandiose when you say it that way. To me it feels like I'm valet parking NASA's cars.'

Wade was overwhelmed by her accomplishments and rubbed his forehead. Sarah said, 'You know, big brother, doing all this stuff isn't the big deal it seems like.'

'It isn't, is it?'

'You know, Wade. In a weird way I think doing things is easier than *not* doing things.'

'Right.'

They hit a lull where it was easier to jiggle their ice cubes with swizzle sticks than speak. Sarah then asked Wade what he was doing in a voice Wade could tell was working hard not to sound patronizing, Wade lied and said he was working as a computer programmer. He thought it sounded smart. Sarah asked a simple question about LINUX coding and he knew he'd been caught, but she didn't push it.

'OK, so here's the truth. I've got myself a bit of a . . . sugar momma.'

'Well, at least that's more in character, Wade. Why are you so hard on yourself? Nobody else is. Or ever *was*, for that matter. I've never understood that about you. You're your own worst enemy.'

'My life's a joke, Sarah. I disappoint people. And I don't even care when people stop caring about me. And I leave, and I leave no traces behind me.'

'You're life is *not* a joke, Wade.'

'Then what is it?'

Just as Sarah was about to answer, a university don in a cap and gown came to retrieve her for her speech. In a moment she was gone, and in her absence Wade needed to make his brain go quiet immediately. He ordered three double vodka rocks and began a weeklong blackout-drinking binge. *That* was the last time he'd seen another family member.

The flight attendant took his empty beer can away for landing. Within an hour, around two o'clock in the afternoon, as the rain drizzled out in the parking lot, he was in his old drinking haunt, the Avalon.

Down the bar, Wade noticed a cute blond with a whiff of a mean streak about her pantomiming a 1950s starlet sneaking peeks at John Wayne in her powder compact. He laughed in spite of himself, and mimed a *Who me?* response. She wagged a naughty-naughty finger at him through her mirror. Wade moved over to the stool beside her, whereupon she said, 'Oh my, the *wolves* in this city.'

'Geez, you movie stars.'

'You have a thing against us hard-working girls of stage and screen?'

'Excuse me for interrupting your beauty cocktail.'

She snapped her compact shut and turned to him, saying, 'I'll have you know, I had two lines in a motion picture just this morning.'

'Oh, excuse me again. What motion picture might this have been?'

She placed her hands on his knees, looked him in the face and said, 'A godawful hunka shit for some junky American cable network. Mind if I sip your scotch?'

'Go right ahead.'

She downed it. 'You live here?'

'Used to. Not any more.'

'Where now then?'

'Las Vegas.'

'Mmm. Charming. So tell me . . .'

'Wade.'

'So tell me, *Wade*, what are you addicted to?'

'What do you mean?'

'You know what I mean.'

'Do I?'

'You live in Las Vegas, your eyes are bloodshot and I saw you diddling around with coins on the counter like John Q. Barfly. You don't shave regularly, because if you did, your skin would be tougher and you wouldn't have the' – one, two, three, four, she counted them – 'nicks on your neck. You're also in a pub in the middle of a weekday and you're jittery, but your drinks aren't really quenching the jitters. So I'd hazard a guess you're into a thing or two.'

'Pussy-*pussy*, don't be so *negative*. Let's focus on the good stuff, like the six million twelve-step meetings I've seen in my time.'

'You mean, let's find the *joy* in your situation.'

'Yes. The joy.'

'Are you staying at the hotel here?'

'Yeah.'

Without another word they went up to Wade's room. Two hours later the blond was gone, her cell phone number penned onto the base of Wade's right thumb. She was a decorator. Stoked by sex, Wade felt strong enough to call his family. He dialed his mother and got her machine: *Hi, this is Janet. I'm not in right now, so please leave a message and I'll get back to you in a jiffy.* It was her polite voice, the one she used when speaking with checkout clerks and the insurance man, never with the family.

Beep

'Mom, Wade here. Yes, your firstborn male child. Guess what – I'm in town. Yes, that's correct, the stranger returns. I'll call you later tonight or maybe I could just stop by and say hello. And, uh, Mom – it's not too good an idea to leave your name on a machine like that. The world's full of creeps. See you soon. Love ya.'

He hung up: *I'm a bad son, a bad, bad son.* He looked up his father's number, *Drummond, Edward B.*, apparently living a few miles away from Janet in Eagleridge, doubtless in one of that neighborhood's gee-whiz cliffside houses. 'Dad?'

'Wade? Hello!'

'Hey, Dad.'

'Wade, where are you – wait, you're not in trouble, are you?'

'No. No trouble. I just got into town and thought I'd come visit. I'm not *always* on the lam.'

'Come on over. Where are you staying?'

'In North Van. With friends.' Best keep an excuse within arm's reach.

'Come visit. I'm over in Eagleridge these days. Meet the wife.

Highway exit number two. It's a no-brainer. You got the address from the phone book. Come on over.'

'Now? Sure. I guess.'

'We're having Chinese tonight.'

'I'll be there in twenty minutes.'

'Wade—'

'Yeah, Dad?'

'Nice to hear your voice again.'

'You, too, Dad.'

Wade left for his father's house in a rental car. His driving was lazy and he had a mild hangover from earlier on. Sheets of rain kept dumping, intense at times, never stopping.

Dad – oh, man. Still the hypocritical prick acting out some corny 1960s idea of manhood. Wade knew that his father had dropped his mother quite cruelly and was now living the life of Mr. Salt-and-Pepper Chest Hair, with his shirts wide open, his golf clubs leaned just inside the front door, and a trophy wife somewhere in the near distance plopping a Gipsy Kings CD into a slot.

Wade felt that at a certain point in their lives, most people passionlessly assess what they have and what they lack – and then go about making the best of it – like an actor who goes from playing leads to playing character roles; like a party girl who goes from being a zany kook to being a cautionary tale for the younger girls. Wade believed that the adult world is a world of Ted Drummonds, and Wade hoped his father would be proud that his son understood this.

He arrived at the house, which was an event in itself – glass and steel and concrete blocks inset into a cliff overlooking the Pacific. Wade half expected to find his father in an eye-patch overlooking a backlit map of the world, stroking a white Persian cat and planning ICBM attacks on New York. Instead Ted opened the door, shouted 'Wade,' and hugged his son so hard Wade thought blood would squeeze out of his pores like juice. 'Come on in. Have a look around. Quite a place, eh? I got sick of that suburbia crap.'

Ted poured generous drinks for them. He'd obviously been to a gym and somebody hip was shopping for his wardrobe. And then Wade saw a flash in his father's eyes. The flash said, *It's all shit, Wade, just don't say the words out loud, because then even the shit goes away and we're left with nothing.*

Drinks in hand they took a tour of the main floor, high ceilinged and enclosed in glass, on which the rain continued to drum. The fact that Ted had yet to mention any other family member was leaving Wade feeling a touch disoriented. *Who is this old guy? What am I doing in his James Bond living room?*

Wade asked, 'Where's, uh, your wife?'

If Ted was awkward about Wade meeting her, he didn't let on.

'Nickie? She'll be downstairs in a second. She's just in from work.'

'She works, huh?'

'You know these modern young ponies. Keep them in the corral and they get testy. They've just gotta have their jobs.'

'Huh. You don't say.'

An awkward silence draped them. Ted asked when Wade's flight had arrived.

'Around noon. I'd have called sooner, but I got waylaid with a piece of action from the bar down at the Av.' This seemed to arouse his father's conversational energy, and Wade found himself needing to please his father, so he gave him a soft-core version of the events. Ted hit him on the shoulder with a that's-my-boy slap.

From the kitchen there came a tinkling sound.

'Nickie!' said Ted. 'Come on in and meet your son.'

Nickie came in, carrying a tray of martinis, an ironic smile on her face parodying the demure wifeliness of the 1950s that Janet had once believed in. Wade quickly saw that Nickie was the afternoon's blond; the insight was reciprocal. Their faces blanched; the martini tray lurched sideways, glasses toppling onto the polished slate floor. Ted and Wade stepped forward and awkwardly helped Nickie pick up glass shards, whereupon Ted saw Nickie's cell number penned onto Wade's hand.

Wade walked straight to the front door, got into his car and drove off, heading for home – Janet's house. Janet was in the driveway removing groceries from her car in the rain. *Mom – ditched by her ingrate family, mateless and brave*. Wade's brain rifled through a billion images, selecting those that spoke of his mother – Janet using canned mushrooms to enliven a pot of spaghetti sauce and enculturate her brutes, only to see her family pick them out and mock them; Janet sneaking a twenty-dollar bill into Wade's electric guitar fund; Janet feeding the backyard sparrows crumbled-up melba toast when she thought nobody was looking – *Mom!*

Janet saw Wade, shouted his name and cried. Wade held her close to him.

'Mom, just so you know, Dad's going to be pretty pissed off with me, and he might well come looking for me.'

'Did you steal from him – or do you owe him money?'

'Neither.'

'Then why should he – oh, who *cares*? He deserves whatever you throw him. Have you eaten yet? Come in! Have you had dinner? Oh there's so *much* I want to ask you about, and there's so much for you to catch up on.'

She made a delicious pasta primavera – *God, I miss home cooking* – and Wade fell quite effortlessly into his version of Wade Ten Years Ago. But throughout the jokes and fun and memories, he had the sensation that within the past few hours his life had morphed into a horror movie, and that this was the sequence where the axe murderer is outside the house, scoping out the patsies, while the audience squirms and shouts, '*Leave*, you idiots!'

The doorbell rang and Wade nearly jumped out of his skin. It was Bryan, his depressed brother, in drenched thrift store clothing – *still, at his age* – in need of a shave, his eyes bloodshot, all crowned with a finely maintained mullet hairdo.

'Bryan, you ring the doorbell at Mom's house?'

'It was locked.'

'OK. Hi.'

'Hi.'

An awkward silence followed as Bryan removed his soaked pea coat and threw it onto a chair. 'So much for formalities,' said Wade. 'Are you hungry? There's tons of food.'

'Nah. Wine would be nice, though.'

Bryan seemed to be in good enough spirits and had a glass of white wine with Janet and Wade. Wade had the impression that none of the three was being particularly truthful, and the lack of truth was making the conversation wooden. They stuck to neighborhood gossip and Sarah's career, yet Wade was aware of the deeper, unasked questions: *Is Mom imploding with loneliness? Is Bryan on the verge of another meltdown? And you'd think Dad never existed. And why don't they ask me about my life? Not that I'd tell them but geez –*

Wade broke the conspiracy of silence. 'Bryan,' he said, 'you've tried to off yourself, what – three times? – and never got it right. Are you sure you really *do* want to off yourself?'

Janet said, 'Wade! Don't go giving him fresh impetus.'

'No, Mom – it's good to be talking about it like this,' Bryan said. 'Everybody pretends I never did anything, but I did.' He registered the looks his mother and brother gave him. 'I can see that you're wondering if I'm going to try it again. And the answer is no. But then these *moods* hit me. Shit. I don't know any more.' He sloshed around what little wine remained in his glass. 'It's depressing to think that my moods aren't even remotely cosmic, that all they are is the result of lazy little seratonin receptors in my brain.'

'Are you taking anything for it – your depression?'

'I've taken everything. I don't think I'll ever reset my brain back to zero again.'

Janet said, 'Bryan is working.'

'Really? Where?' Wade asked.

'I play bass in bar bands, and the TV commercial work is pretty steady. I get by. A nine-to-five job would *really* do me in.'

The doorbell rang. The three of them stared down the hall at the front door as though the next few seconds were beyond their control, like an eclipse. Bryan went to answer it. *Whoomp!* Ted charged past Bryan, booming, 'Where is that sleazy little fuck?' Nickie burst through the door moments after him, her Nissan Pathfinder parked akimbo on the front lawn just outside the door. She was shouting, 'Ted, don't be a moron. It's not as big a deal as you're making it. *Shit.*'

Ted's face was bruise-colored in fury. Wade had dealt with Ted's anger more times than he could count. His instinct was to protect his mother. He stood up and placed himself between the two. He said, 'Dad, calm down!' but instead Ted raised a .233 and shot Wade through the side of his stomach. The bullet passed through him and lodged inside Janet's right lung, entering just below the ribcage.

'Jesus, Ted!' Nickie came toward Wade, who was clutching his side, his blood puddling freely there in the kitchen.

Wade was incredulous. 'Ten years in the States and nothing happens. I'm in Canada for eight hours and—'

He heard a *thunk* and turned around to see Janet on the floor. 'You shot Mom, you goddamn freak! Jesus – Bryan, call 911. Dad, you're gonna bake in prison the rest of your life. I hope it was worth it.' He bent down to cradle Janet.

Sirens were audible almost instantly. Ted slumped on a plastic kitchen chair, swaying, white as paper.

Wade screamed out, 'OK it was an accident – everyone got that? An *accident*. He was trying to show us his Clint-fucking-Eastwood gun moves, and he didn't know the gun was loaded. End of story.' He looked down at Janet, saying, 'Sorry, Mom – it's my fault. I'm sorry.'

Nickie forced Ted to remain seated. He was stuttering, his

head between his knees. Bryan put down the phone and came over to Wade and his mother. He squatted on the floor beside them. 'God, Wade,' he said, 'I'd *kill* to be murdered.'

Paramedics banged through the door.

05

Howie drove up to the front of Janet's motel, looking angry and distracted. As far as Janet could remember, this lack of spaniel good cheer was a first. For a quick moment she hoped that the drive to NASA could be interesting. She wouldn't have to hear about lively meals with the space-crazy Brunswick family, or the weather, or string or pebbles or lint or starlings or regular sugar versus sugar cubes – or just about anything that popped through Howie's brain.

'Good morning, Janet – another beautiful day in F.L.A.'

So much for that notion. He's talking about weather already – in clichés no less – and he's determined to be perky. 'Yes, good morning, Howie.'

'Hop in for a ride in the Howmobile. Cape Canaveral ho!'

'Howie . . .' Janet stood beside Howie's open window. 'I'm not feeling too well today. I don't think I can manage another NASA dog-and-pony show – all that walking and . . . *smiling*.' Janet waited for Howie to protest.

'You're *sure* you don't want to come?' he asked.

'I'm sure.'

'OK, I'll see you soon enough.'

'OK.'

'Fare thee well.' And, *vroom!* Howie was gone.

For the first time since Janet had met him, years ago, she was mildly curious about what might be going on inside his mind.

Her rental car wouldn't start. She walked into the motel office and asked the kidney thief to order a taxi, and soon an ancient Chrysler, seemingly bound together by rubber bands and masking tape, thumped up to the curb. Janet got in and asked to be taken to an Internet café she'd seen listed in a tourist flyer.

The science fiction planet of Florida passed by the cab window: pastel-toned and smooth, one image dissolving into the next. The palmetto scrub landscape would, for no apparent reason, burst into a cluster of wealthy superhomes here, then a burst of lower-middle class discount stores there – followed by a business park, followed by a tourist attraction. All of these money-driven *bursts*.

When she arrived at the Internet café, godless children in black outfits up near the front casually sipped elaborate coffees that in the Toronto of her youth would surely have been banned as threats to society. The shop's background music was a popular song apparently called 'Boompboompboompboomp-boompboomp'. Janet walked to the back of the café to find an empty seat in front of a computer screen.

Thank God I can finally read my e-mail. Thank God I can be in a place with a few people who aren't scared by technology and who don't fear the future.

Janet had thirteen e-mails, most of them from members of her medical list groups. She replied to Ursula, an ex-prostitute in Dortmund, and entered an online discussion about a potential Mexican source of thalidomide to relieve the ulcers in her mouth. Janet and Ursula's old source had moved into the more lucrative field of banned diet medications, and there was gossip that a British firm, Buckminster, was going to have legal supplies available shortly.

Janet's pocket buzzer vibrated; she downed her medication plus a Pepto-Bismol as unthinkingly as movie popcorn. The world outside – cars and signage and electrical wires – was almost too smothered in light to read properly, like objects in the movies being sucked into a glowing UFO.

She stood up for a stretch. Around her, she saw a few Bryan-ish loser types furtively glued to their screens, doubtlessly ferreting out porn. Some of them bothered to hide their screens as she neared them; others couldn't care less. Janet saw images that to her were more gynecological than pornographic; she could only wonder how it was that men craved these identical, repetitive snapshots, as though one day these men were going to hit upon the ultimate shot that would render all the others unnecessary. Some years back, when she'd first begun tromping about the Internet, she'd been flustered at how even the most innocent of words placed into a search engine triggered an immediate cascade of filth. Apparently there existed no unsexed word in the language.

She sat down again . . . *ahhhhh* . . . Janet's computer made her feel connected in a manner TV never did. TV made her feel she was a member of society, but it also made her feel like just another ant in an anthill. She massaged her fingers and noticed the girl behind the counter giving her the stare. Janet decided that she really ought to buy some more coffee or a snack; she'd been hogging a terminal for hours, not that there was a huge demand for them. The counter girl was wearing what appeared to be a blue nightie, and her eyes were smeared with mascara. Janet had given up on youth fashions with the Sex Pistols in 1976. Young people could wear green plastic trash bags for all she cared, and apparently some of them did.

Janet requested a café Americano, which the counter girl made at a snail's crawl and slopped across the counter. When Janet asked for ice cubes to cool down the coffee, she received the same look she might have got had she been in a chain gang holding a dented tin cup. Janet looked at the girl sweetly, paid her money, and as if she were cresting the top of a roller coaster, added, 'Screw you, *too*, dear,' with bright, sugary eyes. Until recently she would never have had the nerve to act on such a thought, but she was a *new* Janet now. She went to sit back down at her terminal. The hard drive purred. Time vanished. She looked up and wondered, *Where am I again? . . . Florida. Orlando, Florida. Cape Canaveral is an hour away. My daughter is going into space on Friday.*

Suddenly it was the afternoon. Where did the morning go? She paid her bill with the chippy clerk, then phoned a cab and went outside to wait. Goggle-like sunglasses protected her eyes, now photosensitive from her medications. She stood in a thicket of dry, unmowed grass in which lizards frolicked about. The grass gave her shins tiny paper burns. She heard a honk and looked up, expecting a taxi, but instead it was . . . *Bryan*? It was, in his hockey hair and signature worn-out black leather jacket, simmering silently like a disgruntled pre-rampage employee, his face as stressed and lined as a trussed-up pork roast.

'Mom – geez, what are you doing out in the middle of nowhere?'

Janet got into the rear passenger seat. 'I was in the Internet café, Bryan. When did you arrive in Orlando? Have you checked into the Peabody? And why are you wearing a leather jacket on the hottest day in the history of weather?'

'Well, what are *you* doing in the backseat? I'm not a limo service.'

'I feel like being treated like a queen today. Did you check into the hotel?'

Bryan growled.

'I'll take that as a yes. What's put you into such a pissy mood, buster?'

'Had a huge fight with Shw. Knock down, drag out.'

'Hmmm.' Janet decided to remain noncommittal.

'Aren't you going to ask me what about?'

'A few years ago, yes. These days? No.'

'She's a witch.'

'Can you turn up the A/C?'

Bryan cranked the air-conditioning. 'She's going to abort our baby.'

'Really now.' *Under no circumstances become involved in this. Hey – wait – me, a grandmother at last!*

'She didn't even bother to ask me what I thought.'

'And what *do* you think?' *Janet, this is not your business.*

'The baby is the first good thing that's ever happened to me. My life's always been about nothing, and now I finally have something, and she's going to go and *kill* it.'

There was a silence. 'My motel's the third right after this light, Bryan.'

'You're not staying at the Peabody?'

'Too expensive.'

'I should have guessed. Why do you always have to pull your "I'm destitute" routine?'

'Bryan, how do you even know Shw's planning to do this?'

'She kept on being weird whenever I'd talk about cribs and Lamaze classes. Then I caught her in a lie with the phone's messaging system. A clinic appointment.'

'You're certain, then.'

'Yeah.' A stoplight turned green. 'Forget it. How are *you* feeling, Mom?'

'Fair enough. Nothing too astounding. But you're trying to change the subject.'

'I am. It's just – *hard* for me.'

Janet and her son sat quietly in their respective emotional worlds. As they neared the motel, she asked him where he was headed next.

'Nowhere. Just driving.'

'Why don't we just drive around for a while then?'

'Really?'

'Why not?'

Bryan's face lit up, as though Janet had allowed him to lick chocolate cake batter from a pair of electric beaters. He relaxed. 'Do you want to know a funny thing about Shw?'

'Amuse me.'

'She was never toilet-trained.'

'I beg your pardon?'

'Just what I said. Her parents never trained her. They considered toilet training "patriarchal and bourgeois" – a way of "suppressing personal freedom in the name of sanitation." They say sanitation is very middle-class and very to-be-loathed.'

'You're joking.'

'Nah. They're these leftover sixties lefties. You wouldn't believe the junk they have in their heads.'

'Does Shw use a toilet these days?'

'Yeah. She said that when she was five she looked around and saw that nobody else was wearing diapers and she just kind of figured it out on her own.'

Janet said, 'Something like that could seriously mess up a child.' Now was as good a time as any to ask the following question: 'Bryan, what exactly is the history behind Shw's, er, *name*?'

'Oh, *that*. When she turned sixteen, her parents told her she should choose her own name, and that the name she was given at birth was limiting and perhaps socially crippling.'

'What, then, is Shw?'

'It stands for Sogetsu Hernando Watanabe – a martyred hero of the Peruvian Shining Light terrorist faction.'

'She couldn't just choose Lisa or Kelly?'

'Not Shw.'

Janet mulled this over. 'What's her real name?'

'She won't tell me.'

'Bryan, if you could have chosen a name at fourteen, what name would you have chosen?'

'Me? I'd have chosen Wade. I was always jealous of his name.'

'Maybe we ought to go to the hotel,' Janet said. 'And maybe meet Wade for lunch. He's there now.'

'He was supposed to get in last night, but he didn't.'

'That's another story altogether.' And Janet told Bryan about the bar brawl.

The Peabody was a deluxe high rise of the sort Janet associated with post-World War II movies in which virtuous women lunched with friends and resisted overtures to go upstairs with dark, mysterious men. Beneath the entranceway's front canopy was a small crowd, at the head of which Janet saw Sarah and another astronaut – *Commander Brunswick?*

Sarah saw the two of them and waved them over. Bryan gave the car to a valet, and then he and Janet navigated across a tangle of feed cables and then through a throng of broiling, rubbernecking tourists. Oblivious to the crowds and noise and heat, Sarah said, 'Hi, Mom. Hi, Bryan. This is Commander Brunswick. I don't think you've met yet.'

Janet stuck out her hand to what seemed to her to be a tiny, perfect Great Dane, a man as small as Sarah. *Wait – that would mean he's not a Great Dane at all, but a Weimaraner – and yet he –*

Commander Brunswick said, 'Hi there,' but didn't stick out his hand. He said, 'Sorry – we can't touch people this close to takeoff. Colds and flus and all that stuff.'

'I understand.'

'Sarah, what's going on here? This wasn't in the schedule,' said Bryan.

'It's a quickie press conference – a fundraiser for the March of Dimes. We're waiting for some kids to get here for a photo op – we were going to do it at the Cape, but some of the kids got too sick. We'll be heading back to the tin in about' – she looked at her watch – 'seven minutes.'

'The tin?'

'The shuttle.'

A radio person asked Commander Brunswick a question, which grabbed all of his attention. Wade emerged from the throng of heads and bodies. Sarah grabbed him by the shoulder and said to Janet, 'Mom, I hear Wade visited the Brunswicks' place this morning. What did you think of *them* – the Brunswick clan?'

Wade said, 'It was like going to a Trekkie convention – all these kids on the front lawn.'

'I know. Aren't they a trip?' Sarah looked to Janet and

giggled. 'They're appalled by our family, you know. They really are. I was there last week, and it reminded me of all those science fairs I used to go to when I was young. I thought Alanna Brunswick was going to bring around a tray of Ritz crackers garnished with fetal pigs.'

Janet asked Wade where Beth was.

'She'll be here in a sec. She wanted to change and look nice for Sarah.'

Janet took a swig from an Evian bottle filled with motel tapwater. Carrying a bottle around with her made her feel faintly chic. She then saw Shw cut through the crowd, as itty-bitty as an astronaut, dressed in Lycra and aging black motorcycle leathers. She looked as if she'd groomed herself entirely with moistened fingertips.

Bryan, quite pleased to be able to introduce a girlfriend – any girlfriend – said, 'Wade – this is . . .' But he never got a chance to finish. Shw scootched past, giving Janet a quick greeting, and then jockeyed right up to Sarah and began barraging her with personal questions. 'So, how much can you bench press? Do you know your IQ? Aside from your hand, do you have any other medical conditions that might, er, affect your being an astronaut? Do you think you'll ever have kids? Is there any reason you might not be able to?'

'Jesus,' said Bryan, 'leave my sister alone.'

Shw turned around, fuming: 'No, you leave *me* alone. This is a free country, and your sister and me are talking. Got it?'

Janet and Wade made eyes at each other, which Bryan noticed, and which caused him to flush. Meanwhile, the crowd continued growing, and electrical testing noises sounded like large angry bugs.

Ted and Nickie appeared, and Janet hadn't been prepared for the moment. Her body twitched as though she'd suddenly been asked to come onstage to sing a karaoke song. She knew her face would be reddening just like Bryan's.

'Oh, hello, Jan,' said Ted. 'Rather a funny place to meet again.'

'Hello, Ted.'

Ted's signature eye twinkle had mutated since she'd seen him last, having now become the bland politician's smile – the smile of someone who knows that the bodies in the car trunk are indeed dead. But he was tanned and wearing garments that were flattering in a younger way than Janet might have selected. *That would be the influence of Nickie.* Janet thought Ted looked better than he had any right to; his inner corrosion was well-hidden, whereas Nickie, at his side, looked anything but relaxed, quite drained of blood and oblivious to the goings on with the astronauts and the crowd. And once Nickie had caught Janet's eyes, she zeroed in directly on Janet's very core and said hello in a way that was too genuine to ignore. Janet was as terse as she could muster, and tried to pay more attention to Sarah, who was still being pestered by Shw. Wade had vanished, and thus had precluded an even more awkward social situation. *Thank you, Wade. I owe you one.*

Sarah was looking for a way out of talking to Shw. Janet wondered if she had a secret cue to alert security to come and fend off people who had become too clingy – the way the queen used her handbag to semaphore messages to her staff. Janet was going to come to her daughter's rescue when Sarah looked up, smiled and said, 'Oh hello, Beth.'

Beth? Janet turned around, and there was Beth in one of her best Sunday church outfits, seemingly lifted from a museum diorama depicting Kansas life in the year 1907. Shw was not happy at being eclipsed. She said to Beth, 'So, *you're* Wade's wife, huh? What's with the prairie schoolmarm dress, eh? You look like a fridge magnet.'

Beth said, 'And you must be Shw. Hello.' Two cats handcuffed together would radiate more warmth.

Sarah said to Shw, 'Shw, Beth is religious. Respect each other's boundaries.' Sarah looked up and saw Ted and Nickie. 'Hi, Dad.'

Ted said to Bryan, 'Hey, Bryan, introduce me to your little lady.'

Shw heard this. '"Your little lady?" What planet are *you* from?'

'Excuse me, then,' said Ted. 'Madame has a name?'

'Yeah. It's *Shw*.'

'Huh? Sorry, I didn't hear that.'

'Shw, bozo. S-H-W.'

Ted was genuinely perplexed. 'Let me understand this – your name is spelled S-H-W – and that's all?'

'That's right.'

'I've never met anybody named Shw before.'

'So now you have. I chose it myself.'

'Hey, Bryan – if you've got a few extra vowels, why don't you sell one to the little firecracker here?'

Shw's posture went rigid. She locked her eyes at Ted and said, 'You're a total asswipe. I didn't believe Bryan, but now I do. You're a shitty person, Ted Drummond. And you screwed up your family so badly they'll never be fixed. You must be really proud of yourself.'

'Trust Bryan to hook up with a disaster like you.'

'Don't talk that way about Shw,' Bryan said. 'She's pregnant and I don't want you stressing her out and hurting the baby.'

'Oh, Bryan, ferchrissake,' said Shw, 'I'm dumping the thing, OK? So don't get all high hat.'

'You are *not* getting rid of our baby.'

'Yes, I *am*, and you can't do anything to stop me. What are you going to do – strap sheet-metal around my vagina?'

The crowd witnessing all of this was riveted. Beth cut through the bickering and asked Sarah, 'Tell me, Sarah – do you believe in extraterrestrial beings?' Beth's smile was ominously sweet.

Sarah looked at her sister-in-law. 'I think life and living beings are strewn about the universe as generously and as commonly as pollen in a July breeze.'

'So then tell me, do you believe in God?'

'Let me put it this way: If God is dead, or if God never existed in the first place, then anything would be permitted, wouldn't it? But not everything *is* permitted.' Sarah stopped. That was her full reply.

'I see.'

'Hey—' Shw said to Beth, 'is God a vegetarian? You look like one of those people who knows everything.'

'I don't understand your question.'

'Look at it this way – say there's a snake out in the desert, and the snake eats a rat. It's the food chain, and so it's no big deal. God isn't involved. And then say you're in Africa and a lion eats a gazelle or something. Same thing: food chain; God's not there either. But then say that same lion one week later kills a human being and then eats that human being. What – suddenly God's involved in it? – like we're the only divine link in the food chain or something?'

Janet began to withdraw from the rather stagy conversation. Sarah could hold her own with anyone. She then felt a gentle tap on her shoulder. She looked around and saw Nickie. *Huh*?

'Janet, can we talk for a minute?'

'Talk?'

'Yes. I think it's important.'

Janet became wary. 'I don't think there's anything you and I could—'

'Two things have happened,' Nickie said. 'You need to know about them.'

Curiosity won out. 'What the hell. Sure.'

'Come into the lounge. It's a zoo out here.'

Janet was happy to be able to go inside. The heat had been wiping her out, and walking into the Peabody was like walking into a brisk autumn day. The two women made their way to a small lounge – a tasteful rattan and sea foam dream, like something from an upmarket outdoor wear catalog. The moment they sat down, the waiter took their orders – two club sodas.

'So then what's up,' Janet said.

'I have AIDS, too.'

Janet thought about this. 'OK, I'm sorry you had to join the club, but what do you want me to do about it?'

Nickie was about to say something, thought the better of it, and stopped herself.

Janet asked, 'From Wade?'

Nickie nodded. 'Pretty sure.'

'Does Ted know?'

'No. I've only known for three days. I told him I was having a woman's problem, and that shut him up pretty good.'

'With Ted it would.'

Their sodas arrived. Janet briefly considered a toast, and then realized it would seem like a sick joke, so she sipped quietly. 'You said there were two things. What was the other?'

'It's about Helena.'

'Helena?' Janet put down her glass. Helena was her oldest friend with whom there had been a terrible falling out. 'What *about* Helena?'

Nickie said, 'I don't know the whole story of what happened between the two of you, but for what it's worth, just before the end she said she was sorry for everything she did to you. She said it was her craziness that did it, and not her. She said there was some other person who took over her body and that her explosion with you – her word: *explosion* – was her one regret in life.'

Janet didn't move. 'How could you possibly know any of this?'

'Her sister is my dad's second wife. She took me out to the mental facility or whatever it is they call those things these days. We got to see her on the day they were trying a new medication on her. It gave her this small window of clarity where she said all these things. And then the medication stopped working, and then a day later she killed herself. I guess the medication went wrong. I'm sorry. But she did apologize. She really did miss you. She really did care about you.'

Helena . . .

'Janet?'

Across the lobby, extremely sick children hooked to machines and tubes were being wheeled out into the sunlight.

06

Janet had one memory of Helena that shone brighter than all others. It was from September 1956 – Janet and Helena, young coeds, were walking in downtown Toronto, en route to lunch with Janet's father at Eaton's. The air was tinged with the sugar of yellowing leaves and the sun was palpably lower on the horizon. Helena was teasing Janet about her blossoming romance with Ted: 'It's those big American teeth, isn't it? *That's* what you like. Those big American teeth, and that thing he does with his eyes.'

'What thing?'

'Don't go *what-thing?*ing me. You know *exactly* what I mean.'

'So what if his eyes are nice.' Janet fished around in her dutiful brain to find something bad to cancel out the good: 'But that wreck of a car of his farts blue smoke like crazy.'

'You are *so* repressed, Janet Truro. And Ted is *such* a Yankee.'

'Helena, you should see the packages his mother sends him – they make me dizzy. *Heaps* of sweaters and shirts – monogrammed, and inside a bundle of shirts there was, get this, a bottle of rye! From his *mother*! I can't imagine what his father sends him.'

'A box of hookers.'

'Oh, Helena, stop!' Janet's nose exploded. 'My gee-dee nostrils are flapping.'

'Maybe a box of *dead* hookers. You know those Americans.'

Janet gasped for breath.

'So, Troo, does he want you to be a goody-goody or his slut?' Troo was Janet's nickname, an abbreviation of Truro.

'Helena!'

'Answer my question, which is it?'

'Why – I can't *tell* you.'

'Yes, you can.'

Janet knew quite well what Helena meant, but Helena's question scared her, in both its obvious and indirect implications. 'He wants me to be a nice girl.'

'My, what a satisfying answer *that* was.' A concrete mixer rumbled past. 'So if Ted is Mister American Hotshot, why's he going to school up in Canada? Why aren't the folks from Yale coming with buggy whips to chase him home?'

'Americans think Canada is sort of glamorous. Mysterious.'

A snort: 'Kee-*riste*. You *must* be joking.'

Janet couldn't quite believe it herself – a city of porridge, bricks and sensible rain garments – but she had to defend her suitor. 'Well, we *do* worship the queen, you know. And to Americans, royalty's as weird and foreign as communism. Communism with jewels and missing chins.'

They stopped and were looking at Mexican sombreros and a papier maché cactus inside a travel agency's window display. Behind these, a scale model airliner aimed toward the future. Janet ran down the street. 'Try and catch me, Helena.'

'Troo, slow *down*.' Helena was slightly overweight. 'You'd think this was the gee-dee Kentucky Derby.' She puffed her way to the corner where a Don't Walk signal had stopped Janet in her tracks. 'Come on, Troo – let's cross.'

'But it says don't walk.'

'You are such a chickenshit, Troo. Live dangerously and jaywalk. C'mon!' Helena was across the street now. 'Yoo hoo!' she taunted. 'I'm on the other side of the street, and it's *lovely* over here.'

Janet decided to cross the street just as a constable walked around a corner, blew his whistle, called her over to him and gave her a jaywalking ticket. Helena was in stitches. Janet was mortified – another 1950s word. *My permanent record . . . a blemish!*

Mr. Truro missed lunch in the Eaton's cafeteria – shepherd's pie, carrots, rice pudding and Cokes – but instead offered to drive Janet and Helena home. William had become stout with middle age, and with it came a sort of handsomeness. Helena was in the front seat saying outrageous things to bait him: 'Women are *much* better than men at hammering out details. I bet you anything women take over the legal profession by 1975.'

'Janet, where'd you hook up with this suffragette? Soon she'll have you taking over my job at Eaton's.'

'And what would be wrong with that?' Helena demanded.

'My little Janet in a job-job? She'd be . . . swamped.'

Helena rose to the bait. 'Swamped? Why *swamped*?'

'The world's a hard place, Helena,' William said.

'So what?'

'So *what*? You're *young*. That's what.'

'Oh, brother!'

Janet said, 'You guys are talking about me like I'm not even here.'

Her father had ears only for Helena.

'You don't know,' said William. 'Life is boring. People are vengeful. Good things always end. We do so many things and we don't know why, and if we do find out why, it's decades later and knowing why doesn't matter any more.'

'You want to keep your little Janet in an ivory tower?'

'Yes, I *do*.' The Impala was at a red light; the quieted engine made this last word of William's sound as if an ogre had belched it out. The moment was charged and needed defusing. 'Helena, turn on the radio,' Janet piped up. 'I feel like hearing Dean Martin.'

William said, 'That wop?'

'Daddy, he's *not a wop*.'

William accelerated through the newly green light. Invisible hands pulled Janet into the rear seat's foam. Helena asked to be dropped off at home, near the corner of Bloor and St. George, so William had to make a detour. Once there, Helena pointed out the house in which she was renting an upper floor. 'What a dump, eh, Mr. Troo?'

'You're the arty type, Helena. It suits you.'

'Ciao then,' and off she sauntered. *Ciao? What on earth does that mean?* Janet felt like the one bird left behind after the rest of the flock had migrated. She couldn't shake the feeling, and when Ted proposed in a Hungarian restaurant on the next Friday night, she accepted. For the months prior to the wedding, not a day passed without moments of remorse, as though she'd spent all of her carefully saved money on a dress she had no place to wear. *But Ted's so handsome and mysterious! But what have I done? I barely know the man. What if he snores? What if we don't get along? What if—*

The next what-if was hard to even think of, let alone put into words, the what-if of the flesh. *Our bodies – his body – I've never even seen . . .* all *of him. Oh dear. Oh dear. What am I going to do?*

It was at this point where magazine articles, Doris Day films and her mother went silent. *There's something wrong going on here, but what?*

A hand shook Janet's shoulder. 'Janet? Janet? Are you OK?' It was Nickie, and Janet was back in the Peabody hotel.

'I'm fine. Please. Fine.'

'Are you sure?'

Janet looked at Nickie. Any hostility she'd been harboring against the woman had left. 'Sure.'

Both women then heard footsteps coming close to them – cowboy boots on marble: Wade walked around the corner, right into Janet and Nickie's table, obviously expecting neither of them. 'Oh – hi – I . . .'

'Hello, Wade.'

'Nickie. Hey. I—'

Janet said, 'Relax. Sit down with us.'

'Why? What's up?'

'Just sit.'

'Is it news?'

'Yes, it is.'

'Bad news?'

Nickie said, 'Yes, Wade, it's bad news.'

'It's not . . . ?'

Nickie nodded. 'Yes, it is.'

Wade slumped down into a rattan chair. 'Shit. Sorry. What can I—' Wade suddenly looked at his mother, but something else was now in his eyes.

Something is wrong.

Wade reached over to her with a napkin. 'Mom—'

'What? *What?*'

'You're doing a Dracula all over your shirt. Don't panic. It'll clean up just fine.'

'I'm bleeding?' Janet reached for another napkin and blotted her chest, pulling the cloth, which evidenced a fair amount of blood coming from her mouth. 'Oh dear.'

'Mom,' Wade said, 'I'm going to check you into this hotel and then I'm going to go get your things at your motel, OK?'

Janet felt confused. 'Yes, dear. Yes. Of course.'

'Don't worry. Things are going to be just fine. Can you stand up? There. Stand up. I'll take you up to my room and you can lie down there. Things'll be just fine. Just you wait and see.'

They walked toward the elevators, Nickie carrying some extra napkins, which she handed to Wade. Janet and Wade got in and Nickie said, 'I'll call you later, Janet.' The door closed.

07

Wade put Janet to rest on the bed in his room, and then grabbed the keys to the sedan rented with Beth's credit card. He went downstairs only to find that Sarah, the sick children and the crowd had all vanished. The media trucks were just pulling away, their wires snapped in as crisply as if into a measuring tape's chromed handle. But some of his family was still there – Bryan and Shw were in the throes of a fight – ostensibly over a set of car keys, which Bryan apparently wouldn't give up. The other guests in the lobby were unable to ignore the embarrassing set-to, and Wade tried to skulk past them, but he was noticed. Shw loudly said, 'Ha! Your brother'll drive me.'

'No, he won't.'

Wade didn't want to get involved. 'I'm looking for Beth.' He realized he was dangling the car's keys.

'She went out shopping,' said Bryan.

'I hope she doesn't spend much,' Wade said. 'We're flat broke.'

'Wade, give me a ride,' Shw said.

'I'm only going to pick up Mom's stuff at that shitbox motel she's staying in. She should be here with us.'

'How *is* Mom?' Bryan asked. 'I ask her all the time, and she always says she's "just fine", which is completely suspicious.'

'Bryan,' said Shw, 'she's got AIDS. She is not "fine". Some sons you two are. You should be laying flowers at her feet and instead all you do is give her grief. Wade, I'll come help you get her stuff.'

'Shw, I'm not sure if I need any—'

'Oh, shut up. Yes, you do – all her frilly scary women's stuff. After that you can drive me to the gun range.'

'Gun range?' Wade looked at his brother.

'I know,' Bryan said, 'talk about a sure-fire way to screw up a fetus – all those shots'll make the kid deaf. And you should check out the heavy metal content in the air and soil around those ranges. It's like instant Minamata disease.'

Shw said, 'Florida is freaking me out. I need firearms to reempower myself.'

Both men did a double take: *Reempower myself*? Curiosity about the mother of his future niece or nephew outweighed Wade's reservations. 'Tell you what – I'm parked right out here and I'm leaving right away. If you're going to come, then come.' He walked out into the north parking lot, brazier hot, and was about to reverse out of his slot when Shw opened the door and got in.

'Bryan is such a scaredy-cat.'

Janet's motel wasn't far away, but it was situated in a realtor's purgatory, neither residential nor upscale retail nor – nor anything really. It looked like a correctional facility gone bankrupt and converted into the most cheerlessly utilitarian of lodgings. 'Jesus, Mom,' said Wade under his breath, 'what a dump.'

Wade and Shw got out and went to Janet's room. Once inside, Shw said, 'It's like time stood still in here. Can you imagine how many people must have banged away on that mattress? It looks like a satellite dish.'

'I'll pack the big clothes,' Wade said. 'You pack the, er, smaller stuff.'

'Her dainties? Ooh, milord is so squeamish.'

'Just pack.'

The suitcases were full in a few minutes, Shw tossing in the underwear. Wade asked, 'Is it true that you two guys met while setting fire to a Gap?'

'Yeah. I just wanted to set fire to things and destroy shit.

Bryan was down there because his musician friends were there, and he's such a follower that he'd probably follow them to Dachau if that's where they were going. But in general? I hate corporations. They're fucked. I'd like to blow them all up, and Bryan, to his credit, probably would, too.'

Wade coughed out a noncommittal noise: 'Huh.'

They headed into the bathroom to fetch toiletries. Shw looked at Janet's fiesta of pills. 'Shit, look at Willy Wonka's factory.' She picked up a bottle and looked at the label. 'It's not even English.'

Wade said that it didn't look like English because it was technical terminology. 'It all comes from Latin roots.'

'Blow it out your ass. I can out-vocabulary you any day of the week. The label's not *in* English. It's in Spanish.'

Wade looked over. 'Portuguese – from Brazil.'

'What's your mother doing with Brazilian drugs?'

Wade looked more closely. 'Well, what do you know—'

'Know what?'

'Those pills you're holding.'

'What about them?'

'Thalidomide. I guess Mom's using them for her mouth ulcers.'

'What's so "oh-wow" about that?'

'You don't know what thalidomide is?'

'No, I don't.'

'It's this drug they used in the early 1960s for morning sickness – but it turned out the stuff caused severe deformities in babies – stillbirths and spontaneous abortions, too. That's why Sarah only has one hand. Didn't Bryan tell you? Here – let me see that . . .' Wade reached for the bottle, but the blood had drained out of Shw's face. 'What's wrong?'

Shw picked up a full plastic bottle of Evian and began violently bashing Wade on the head and face. 'You moron – you let me touch that shit? Are you out of your mind? How could you do that to me?'

Wade fended off the blows, surprisingly powerful for someone of Shw's size. 'I didn't even know it was there until you showed me. Shit. Stop that.' Wade grabbed the bottle; Shw was quaking. She ran into the shower stall and hopped in fully clothed, and cranked the faucet at full blast.

Wade asked, 'What's all *this* about?'

'I'm rinsing that shit off me.'

'It was in a blister-pack. Nothing touched you.' Something clicked: 'Hey, I thought you were getting an abortion.'

'Well, maybe I'm *not*.'

'OK then.' Wade swept items from the countertop into his mother's traveling case and said, 'Ready when you are. I'll be down in the car.'

Shw stayed in the shower five more minutes, then came out only because the hot water had run out. The gun range was a half mile away and Shw, wet as a dog, was quiet for the ride. He dropped her off, and she said, 'I'm being a real hag today. Thanks for the ride.'

08

On a hot, sunny August afternoon, 1973, Wade said to Bryan, 'Bryan, don't touch the plastic. You'll only screw it up.'

'Wade, be nice to Bryan. He only wants to help.' Sarah turned to Bryan: 'Even still, Bryan, don't touch things, OK? Because you probably *will* muck them up.'

'Maybe I should just *go*.'

'Don't go,' Sarah said, 'Just don't touch things, OK?'

The trio was out on the baking driveway with a trove of plastic dry-cleaning bags and bent coat hangers. Their mission was to build a hot air balloon by taping the bags into a large, lightweight condom attached to a metal ring at the bottom. In the middle of the ring was a wire X onto which was attached a Miracle Whip lid bearing white barbecue fire-starting bricks. Sarah was a tiny fern among her two sequoia brothers – even with Bryan younger than her – but she was definitely the one running the show.

'I'm thirsty,' said Bryan.

Wade looked at him. 'Bryan, I'm holding a Do-I-give-a-shit?-ometer in my hand and the needle's not moving. Shut up.'

'We'll get a pop later,' Sarah said. 'We're almost ready for liftoff.'

Wade was holding the wispy plastic balloon. Sarah used a Bic lighter to ignite the fuel. 'It'll take a minute for the hot air to fill the balloon,' she said, then stood up and watched.

'It looks like a big dildo,' said Wade, as the balloon began filling with air much hotter than that of the August afternoon.

'What's a dildo?' Bryan asked.

Sarah looked at Wade. 'He's too young for that stuff, Wade.'

'What, *you* know what a dildo is?'

'Of course I do.'

'What is it then?'

'It's a plastic replica of a man's dink used by women when they're by themselves.'

'What do you mean "used by"?' asked Wade.

'You know *exactly* what I mean by "used by", Wade. And *now* Bryan's probably going to use the word in front of Mom or Dad – and he'll most likely use it wrongly – and *you'll* be the one who gets in shit.'

'No, Bryan's the one who always gets in shit.'

'I do *not*, Wade. Dad beats *you* up way more than he beats *me* up. And besides, I'm not a baby. I'm two years younger than Sarah.'

Sarah changed the topic slightly. 'Wade, does it hurt when Dad hits you? I've never actually been hit.'

Wade found it hard to imagine never having been hit. 'Hurt? *Huh*. I never thought of it that way. I suppose so. But when Dad hits me, it's not like he wants to hurt my outside. He wants to hurt me on the *inside*. He thinks he's King Shit, and he wants to let me know it.' The bag was almost full enough with warm gassiness to rise. 'Hey – it's ready.' All eyes watched as the balloon hovered inches above the driveway.

'Let 'er go,' said Sarah.

Wade let the balloon rise up into the air, silent, clean and jiggly. There was just enough wind coming from the west to blow it towards the Capilano river and over toward North Vancouver. The trio ran to the top of the street, Sarah carrying the binoculars, to monitor its progress.

'I bet it goes all the way into North Van,' Bryan said.

'Unlikely,' said Sarah, payload specialist in training. 'The fuel's only going to burn for about fifteen minutes tops.'

'What if it lands in the forest?' Bryan asked.

'Well then,' said Wade, 'it lands in the forest.'

'But the forest is dried out. It could start, like, a forest fire.'

'Bryan, stop wrecking the fun.'

A car approached from behind – Janet in the station wagon. She pulled up beside them. 'Hey, gang – whatcha up to?'

'We made a balloon,' said Sarah. 'We're watching its progress.'

'Aren't you all clever.'

Sarah asked, 'Do you have any pop there, Mom?'

'Pop? I think I do.' She reached behind her and pulled three cans of ginger ale from a bag.

'Bryan,' Sarah said, 'you take them, okay?'

Janet drove off, her final words being, 'Barbecue hamburgers tonight. Be good.'

Once she was out of hearing range, Sarah said, 'Uh-oh. I think I took the last of the barbecue lighter bricks for balloon fuel.'

'Don't sweat it,' Wade said. 'I'll say I took them.'

Bryan opened up the ginger ales and passed them around. The three sat as the balloon wafted away, taking turns with the binoculars. 'It's sinking,' said Sarah.

'No, it's not,' Wade said. 'Let me see.' He took the binoculars. 'Oh – it *is* sinking.'

'Where?' asked Bryan.

'Down in Glenmore. Near the school.'

'Wade, let me see.' Sarah grabbed the binoculars and Wade yielded. 'Ooh. You're right.' She watched as the balloon descended onto a subdivision. 'Uh-oh . . .'

'What?'

'It's going to touch down on the Beattys' house.'

Wade grabbed the binoculars. 'Oh, *crap*.'

The balloon landed on the shingled roof of a ranch house, which quickly ignited. Sarah said to call the fire department, but Wade said to wait, that a guy next door to the Beattys' was hosing off their roof already, and that passersby had stopped to watch. Next they heard sirens; the fire seemed to have migrated across the roof underneath the shingles, popping out of the rightmost side like a cat's tongue. Then, *whoosh*, the whole roof was ablaze and the fire engines arrived and a major scene unfolded.

'We are in deepest shit,' said Wade.

'I told you it could start a fire,' Bryan said.

'Bryan, so *what*,' said Sarah, 'accidents happen.' She put down the binoculars, and they watched as a small tornado of smoke rose from the house down the hill. 'Do you think they'll figure out it was us?'

There was no need to answer this, as Mrs. Breznek from across the street walked onto the road in her apron, saw the fire and then turned around and began screaming at the three children. 'You little monsters! Who the hell do you think you are? I'm calling the police right now. You're all going to get a thorough licking on this one. Jail, too.'

'Blow it out your ass,' said Wade. Mrs. Breznek snorted in disgust.

'Wade—' Sarah giggled.

'How can you giggle?' Bryan asked.

Wade said, 'Shut up, loser. I'll take the blame.'

'Wade, don't do it. I'll take the blame. I'll say it's a science project that went wrong. The tether line snapped. If you take the blame you'll be shipped to military school.'

'I think the fire's out,' Bryan said. 'It's just steam now.'

Indeed the fire was almost extinguished. A minute later a police cruiser showed up at the house; Janet came out, curious and worried. 'Officers?'

'Can we speak to your children, Mrs. Drummond?'

'The children? I—'

Sarah spoke up. 'I had an accident, Mom. My science experiment escaped.'

'Science experiment?'

An hour of confusion and technicalities ensued.

'It was my fault,' Wade kept saying. 'I should have been watching more closely.'

'Wade,' Sarah shouted at him, 'stop trying to cover for me. The fire was *my* fault.'

When Ted got home from work, he was careful to get Sarah's story first.

'Dad, I was looking at your old technical journals, from university when you were studying propulsion. I wanted to do something like that. It was a challenge.'

'You sent a fiery payload up into the sky during peak forest fire season just because I used to study it in college?'

'Yeah.'

Ted grabbed her. 'You are the greatest little princess in the world!' He squeezed her and made her giggle. 'Jan – what's for dinner tonight?'

'I was going to barbecue . . .'

'Let's order in pizza for once. And Wade, why don't you choose what kind.' He tickled Sarah's feet. 'You're so lucky to have a big brother to help you on your projects, young lady.'

09

Wade returned to the hotel to check in Janet, but there was no vacancy. 'Mom, share the room here with me and Beth.'

'Dear, I don't want to be a pest.' Janet was lying on the bed, the curtains drawn.

'Mom, you've never been a pest. And it's a good chance for the two of you to get to know each other.'

'I suppose I could.'

Wade sucked in some air: 'Mom, I saw the thalidomide in the bathroom.'

Janet looked up at him. 'Oh?'

'It's OK. I know it's for mouth ulcers.'

'It is.' Janet raised her body and craned her head towards Wade.

Wade sat down on a chair beside the minibar. 'What I'm wondering is where does a person even *find* thalidomide these days? Do scientists have garage sales? It's – freakish – that anybody's even making the stuff any more. It's creepy.'

'I get it from Brazil, through an underground network. Usually it comes FedEx. Or sometimes through Mexico, but Mexico's a disaster, so Brazil's better. They use it down there for treating leprosy.'

'Leprosy? Seriously?'

'I know. The irony is too rich to ignore. Now they're using thalidomide to *prevent* people from losing limbs and digits.'

'Huh.' The room was quiet. 'What about Nickie, then?'

'Her being infected?' Janet asked.

'It sounds so bad when you say it like that. But yeah.'

'I have no idea what to say about it, Wade.'

He tossed a foil-wrapped complimentary sachet of decaf coffee grinds back and forth between his hands. 'So are you two friends now?'

'Friends? No. But I don't hate her any more. She's actually a very nice woman.' Janet slumped back onto the bed.

'You OK?'

'Yes, but I need some sleep. The sun here wipes me out. When is Beth returning?'

'No idea. You rest. I'm going to look at the view.'

Wade took the phone out onto the balcony. He sucked in some air and made a call he'd hoped he wouldn't have to make. He dialed an old business acquaintance.

'This is Norm.'

'Norm – it's Wade.'

'Wade Drummond? Well, *well* – what's up, my man?'

'This and that. I'm a married guy now, Norm. Pretty soon I'll have a kid and a minivan and the whole works.'

'You – a family man?'

'*Pffft* – all the snowmen in hell melt in a puff of steam.'

'Family's a good thing, Wade.'

'You should see my family. Every single one of us is psychotic.'

'All families are psychotic, Wade. Everybody has basically the same family – it's just reconfigured slightly different from one to the next. Meet my in-laws one of these nights. Where are you phoning from?'

'Orlando.'

'You're in Orlando? Oh, right – your sister's the astronaut. She's amazing.'

They caught up for a few minutes and then came an awkward manly silence.

'Norm. I need money.'

A pause. 'Well, don't we all.'

'I had to get a loan from Tony the Tiger in Carson City, for this fertility clinic that cost a bomb. My wife and me had to go to Europe for this new procedure. Fifty K.'

'Fifty K? What could cost fifty K?'

Might as well jump right in. 'Norm, I'm HIV. This place in Milan takes ejaculate and places it into a centrifuge and the lighter viral particles rise to the top, leaving what remains on the bottom clean.'

Norm was silent. 'OK. Sure. I've heard lots of stories before. That's a pretty good one.'

'It's not a story – it's the truth.'

'But the point remains that you need dough.'

'Yeah.'

'You know how it works, Wade – the greater the risk, the greater the reward.'

'Like I don't know that.'

'How much you need?'

'The fifty K plus another fifty for Tony's interest.'

'That's some risk.'

'It's what I need.'

There was a long silence on Norm's end followed by 'You've actually phoned at a very opportune moment, my man. I could use a courier right about now.'

'Courier?' Wade knew that in the underground labor economy, this was the lowest, most dangerous job level. 'Why not.'

'Tell you what – I'm having a fling with Cheryl. She's in a Pocahontas dance number on Main Street USA over in Disney World.'

'Cheryl?'

'Yes, little Cheryl, and she's still young enough to like older men. Meet me outside the monorail exit at Main Street USA – tomorrow morning, ten on the nose.'

'Disney World? You?'

'Wade, Wade, *Wade* – nothing bad ever happens in Disney World. It's the only safe place in this fucked-up state. I've had many a meeting there.'

They signed off. Wade stepped back into the room as Beth got in from shopping. After a nap they all ate a calm dinner in the hotel dining room, Janet's treat. Afterwards they went for a walk along International Boulevard, a frustrating experience for Wade, as everything, even the most casual trinket, was so expensive. They went back to the room to watch TV, and Wade once again took the phone out onto the balcony, and this time he rallied all of his nerve and all of his guilty feelings about being a vagrant, useless son, and called his father down in Kissimmee.

'Yeah, hello?'

'Hey, Dad, it's me, Wade.'

Ted's reply gave away nothing: 'Wade.'

'I didn't get much of a chance to talk with you today at Sarah's thing downstairs.'

'Buncha media clowns.'

'It was busy all right.'

'So you're out of jail,' said Ted. 'Good. You're too old for jail. Something kind of sad about a man being jailed after forty, like he's incapable of seeing the big picture.'

'You're looking good.'

'Well, it's not like I deserve to. But Nix tells me I have fortunate bone structure. And I have regular bowel movements, and I have free use of the Y's tanning bed.'

'So, Dad – I heard through the grapevine that maybe you might need some money.'

'What grapevine? My grapevine's my own frigging business.'

'Just thought you might be interested in a scheme I've got to make some quick pocket change.'

Ted went silent.

I notice he's not hanging up.

'Easy come, easy go,' said Ted. 'The house I can live without – the damn thing leaked. Nix can bring home the bacon until I locate a new gig, can't you, Nix?' Nickie, doubtless, was rolling her eyes in the background.

'Hey, Dad, why don't you come with us to Disney World tomorrow? We can have fun. I'll pay.' *No turning back now.*

'Disney World? Are you out of your mind?'

'Dad, you see, there's this guy – Norm . . .' Wade realized how bad that last sentence fragment sounded: *There's this guy, Norm . . .*

'And?'

'He needs some help on a project . . .'

'And?'

'I was going to help him and I thought maybe you could, you know, help, too.'

'Doing what? And how much do I get?'

He sounds almost ruthless. 'For you? Ten K, and it'll be nothing more than a quick day trip to somewhere nearby.'

A pause: 'OK.'

'What – you don't want to know the details?'

'I want the money. I'll leave the details to you.' There was a pause. 'It was very kind of you to think of me, Wade.'

The two men arranged a pickup time the next morning and hung up. Feeling like Santa Claus, Wade went inside the room where he, Beth and Janet fell asleep watching the History Channel. Around three, he woke up and couldn't get back to sleep. He went out onto the balcony, swaddled in the bored, muggy remains of a Gulf wind. He looked up at the moon, either full or nearly full. *If human beings had never happened, that same moon would still have been in that very same position, and nothing about it would be different than it is now.* Wade tried to imagine Florida before the advent of man, but couldn't. The landscape seemed too thoroughly colonized – the trailers, factory outlets and cocktail shacks of the world below. He decided that if human beings took over the moon, they'd probably just turn it into Florida. It was probably for the best it was so far away, unreachable.

Wade then thought about his mother, seemingly ebbing away before his eyes – and yet she was also somehow younger than ever – *she knows about things now, stuff even I didn't know about until recently: scary sex shit – she's opened up so many doors* – and again he felt one of the countless bolts of shame he felt whenever he thought of his father's behavior, his own behavior, and what it had done to his mother – his womanizing and stupidity.

At least tomorrow there would be money, and maybe *now* Wade could keep away those goons from Carson City, the ones parking outside his and Beth's condo flashing their high beams at one A.M. And maybe a bit left over to try some new anti-HIV drug combinations. *And the ten K for Dad? Peanuts. For once I can do him a sizeable favor.*

Life was simple, really: a wife to care for and a baby on the way – a little nest to protect, and this enormous world just waiting to pounce and shred the whole shebang. Wade thought about his blood flowing through his veins – his legs and toes and fingertips and scalp – and he tried to keep totally still to see if he could feel the blood moving within him, but no go. *We're no more allowed to feel our blood than the rotation of the earth.* He thought about his AIDS. When he'd told Sarah, he'd said, 'It's a time machine, baby sister.'

'Don't be so flippant, Wade.'

'I'm not being flip, Sarah. The truth is the truth.'

'In what *way* is it the truth?'

'Like this: If it were a hundred years ago instead of right now, both of us would be dead. You from that burst appendix in grade three – or an infected cut.'

Sarah had said, 'Or they'd have drowned me at birth.'

'Blink, you're alive; blink, you're dead. Me? Hell, I'd be dead a hundred different ways by now. So I figure that this virus is merely resetting the clocks to where they ought to be reset. Senior citizens are unnatural.'

'You honestly believe that?'

'I do.'

'Excuse me if I have trouble agreeing with you.'

Wade had heard the hardness in Sarah's voice. She'd asked him, 'Are you able to get a job and work?'

'Sort of. I have this part-time job dealing cards in this shitty club off Fremont Street. No booze, either – these livers are picky little fuckers.'

'Medication?'

'Yeah, but let's leave it at that. I have to take a pill every time I blink. Pills are driving me mental.'

Out on the hotel balcony, fire ants had discovered Wade. He went inside. Beth was snoring. It was 4:00 A.M. and time for a 3TC capsule and a sip of pineapple juice. *Where did the past six minutes go? When time is used up, does it go to some kind of place like a junkyard? Or down a river like the waters beneath Niagara Falls? Does time evaporate and turn into rain and start all over again?*

Wade took his pill, sipped his juice and went to look out the window at the hotels and roads and cars covering Florida. *Talk about a time machine.* Of all the states – even Nevada – yet again Florida struck Wade as being the one most firmly locked in the primordial past. The plants seemed cruder here, the animals more cruel and the air more dank and bacterial. He felt as if the whole landscape were resigned to the fact that in a billion more years it'd all probably be squished into petroleum.

Janet was sleeping on the rollaway couch, her breath slight, like a finger brushing against paper.

Wade opened the sliding doors onto the balcony, still hot, even at this hour, and lit a cigarette. If he couldn't drink, he'd smoke. Forget the fire ants. *Wade,* his doctor had told him, *your liver has the metabolizing capacity of a two-year-old girl's. I don't know when it was you had your last drink, but whenever it was, it was your last.*

He turned around and looked into the bedroom. For no reason, the red message light on the phone started blinking. *Huh?* He went inside, picked up the cordless phone and pushed the message button – Sarah:

'Wade, hi, it's your baby sister. You won't be awake – we're on these funny hours that have to do with orbiting schedules. I'm on a break. Doesn't that sound goofy? *Hi, I'm an astronaut and I'm on a coffee break*. But it's the truth, and today has been a long haul, so I gladly welcome some feet-up time. The Russians have tissue regeneration experiments on this flight, and I swear, their whole zero-G research program is being run by a McDonald's crew chief. Remember when the Soviets used to have their act together? We should be so lucky again. How's Mom? How are *you*? Beth and I only had maybe seventeen seconds together. Bryan's girlfriend is – oh, God – well, at least she has two X chromosomes. If you wake up early enough, give me a call. I'll be hitting the sack at 8:00 civilian time.'

She left a number, which Wade went onto the balcony and dialed. 'Baby sister?'

'Wade! Oh, this *is* yummy. What are you up to? What are you doing up at . . . *4:15 in the morning?*'

'Way too much weird family juju. Can't sleep. Sometimes I wish we were the way real estate salespeople look in those little newspaper ads – with nice parted hair, optimistic attitudes and perfect little lives – and that we'd all had our reptile cortexes surgically removed.'

'How's Mom?'

'OK. Tired.'

Wade told her about Shw. And Bryan. And Nickie. Sarah listened, rapt, and then asked, 'What are you guys going to do about Nickie and Dad?'

'No idea. Sarah—?'

'Yeah, big brother?'

'Tell me something – how do you *deal* with so many responsibilities? *How*? I really mean it. We've sort of talked about this before – when you visited me in Kansas. I can barely arrange dinner reservations at Jessie's Catfish Grill, and I can't even order Disney World tickets over the phone. I've never had to actually *do* things before. I never had any reason to. And I finally want to accomplish things, but don't have a clue how. Meanwhile, you're orchestrating DNA strands in outer space, fostering world peace and landing the single most complex artifact ever made by the human species out in the desert.'

Sarah took a second. 'I never think about it like that, Wade. There are simply these things that need to be done, and it's simpler to do them than to not do them.'

'You're amazing.'

'You give me too much credit.'

'Wade—' Sarah cut Wade off. 'Sorry, but my break's nearly over, and I really need to ask you one thing.'

'Shoot.' Wade braced himself.

'How is your health in measurable scientific terms?'

'*Jesus*, Sarah.'

'Just tell me, Wade.'

Wade took a deep breath. 'OK then. Not too hot.'

'That's what I thought. You didn't look too groovy today.'

'My cell count numbers are falling bit by bit. My numbers just won't stay steady.'

'How do you feel on a day-to-day basis?'

'A bit tired-ish. Otherwise OK. I had a rash, and some days I feel fluey. Anything more than this is complaining, so I don't want to go any further on that subject.'

The acid in Wade's stomach gurgled. He remembered back when he was eight and Sarah was six, out in the backyard trees, him puncturing a hole on the inside of his wrist with a safety pin, and Sarah unsqueamishly poking a hole in the end of her left arm, and the two of them then mixing their blood amid the sound of buzzing flies and rustling alder leaves. There had been a lot of aphids that year, and the wind was whistling through the holes they'd eaten in the leaves.

'Wade, I have to go. The Russkies are beckoning me – small

vanilla shake, six-pack of McNuggets and a Happy Meal plastic toy. Call me tomorrow, same time, OK? – if you're awake. What plans do you have for the day?'

'Disney World.'

'You looking forward to it?'

Wade paused. 'You know what? I *am*.'

'Have fun, big brother.'

'G'night, baby sister.'

10

'Wade, what the hell are you doing?' Ted came in the back door from work to find Janet and Wade watching TV.

'Mom and me are watching the *Sonny and Cher Show.*'

'It's a funny show, Ted.'

'You're not watching TV,' said Ted, 'you were *dancing.*' Ted spat this last word out like it was a pubic hair.

'Leave him alone, Ted. We're enjoying the show. How was your day? You're late again.'

Wade said, 'So what if I *was* dancing?'

Ted said, 'Jan, you're going to turn him into a pantywaist.'

Wade didn't know what a pantywaist was, but he didn't like the way his father was blaming his mother. 'Hey, *Dad*, how was work today?'

'Like you care.' Behind this talk was a laugh track completely out of sync with their words. The cat, Haiku, sensed a squall and leapt from the top of its alpine perch on the TV.

'Hey, *Dad*, when was the last time *you* ever danced?'

'Wade, stop bothering your father. I really do want to watch this show.'

Bryan, his radar attuned to free entertainment, poked his head into the room from the hallway. Sarah was nowhere to be seen.

'Hey, *Dad*, I asked you a question. When was the last time you ever danced?'

Ted spoke to Janet. 'Time to buy our boy leotards, dear.'

'I bet the last time you danced was with a bunch of your frat buddies when you were in college,' Wade said, pushing buttons like mad. 'You were all probably naked and rubbing each other with shaving cream.'

Janet said, '*Wade*—' A song came on TV, a fast song with a strong beat.

'*Ooh*. This is my favorite song. Hey, Dad, come in and join the fun.' Wade began dancing in his awkward fifteen-year-old way, ad-libbing lyrics along the lines of, *Ted Drummond is a pantywaist. In his clothes he has no taste. He likes to be naked and he likes to dance in a circle with men.*

Wade saw Bryan's eyes widen and dilate. Good – this meant Ted was going to zoom in for the kill, and he did. He stormed over to Wade, who was by now adept at ducking his father's swings. Wade jumped onto the Naugahyde couch screaming, *pantywaist, pantywaist*, and Ted lunged after him, sending the sofa toppling, eliciting a (predictable) scream from Janet.

'You're a pantywaist and you can't even catch me . . .'

Just then the power died, and to Wade it felt as if the entire house had been clubbed on the head. The night was dark and rainy, and nobody could see anything. Ted twisted his ankle, shouted, 'Oh fuck—' and Wade ran off crying a victory whoop. But victorious or not, he knew he needed to hide out for an hour or so until Ted cooled down. He fumbled his way toward the basement door and headed down the stairs where, with a candle, stood Sarah by the fusebox. Upon seeing Wade, she flipped the power on.

Hours later Ted had simmered down and gone to bed. Wade was watching the news with Janet and Sarah. He said, 'You and Dad should get divorced.'

'Wade! Don't talk like that. And you shouldn't taunt your father so much, either. He has to give a speech tomorrow, and his leg is all pranged.'

'Gee. What a tragedy.' The news went on about inflation and Gerald Ford. 'So why'd you marry him in the first place?'

'Wade, *stop it*.'

'No, I mean it. I did the math and I was born thirteen months after you were married, so it's not like you *had* to.'

'I don't have a clue. Or – *I don't know*. He was *American*. He was studying rocket fuel systems and it was so sexy at the time. He was going to take us to the moon.'

'And?'

'And then – he started designing oil pipelines and we moved west and the moon got lost along the way, and I can't believe I'm telling this to my own child.'

'You're always stopping yourself the moment you start saying something good.'

'I know I do.'

'You have this whole secret world that nobody knows about, don't you?'

'Wade! Jesus, not even Helena cuts to the quick like you.'

'You should get divorced. He doesn't deserve you.' Wade didn't mention that the week before he'd been playing hooky to search for illegal fireworks over on Lonsdale Boulevard, and he'd seen his father lunching with his secretary in a schnitzel restaurant.

'Wade – the man is your father. Show him some respect.'

Wade noticed his mother didn't deny his suggestion of divorce. 'You know what Dad told me when I asked him why he married you?'

Resistance was futile; Janet pretended she didn't care. 'OK then, what?'

'I'm not telling you.'

'Wade!'

'OK, OK. He told me he liked you because he can never tell what you're thinking about.'

'Did he now?'

'That's what he said.'

'Really now?'

'Yup.'

He could see that his mother enjoyed being mysterious.

11

The next morning Nickie was on the phone to Janet, who had the room to herself. She was luxuriating on the bed, twiddling her toes and enjoying the blanket's softness. 'How's your mouth?'

'Better than yesterday.'

'Good. You know what? I'm going bonkers down here in Kissimmee. The place is like a mortuary. Ted went to Disney World with the others. The very idea of Disney World makes me retch.'

'So—' began Janet, 'would you like to . . . go out for an early lunch, perhaps?'

'Yeah. I would. I'll come by there in Ted's car. What about Her Holiness – we should ask her, too.'

Beth was vomiting in the bathroom. 'Morning sickness. Not a good idea.' Janet paused. 'I ought to call Shw, too.'

'What on *earth* for?'

'Protocol, I guess. She may or may not be the mother of my grandchild.'

'I don't know . . . she strikes me as bonkers. And that name of hers . . .'

Janet called Shw's room. 'Shw, it's Janet. Have you eaten anything today?'

Shw's reply was almost silent. 'No.'

'Nickie and I are going out for coffee. Slap on some makeup, throw on some clean clothes and I'll meet you downstairs in a half hour. Can you do that?'

'I don't wear makeup.'

'But you'll still join us?'

A pause. 'Yes.'

Click

A half hour later Nickie picked up Janet at the hotel's main entranceway, like Pennsylvania Station with its comings and goings. Janet was wearing black wraparound sunglasses of the style favored by rock stars and seventysomething Hollywood agents, and young, Gappy clothing. *By wardrobe alone I could pass as a twenty-five-year-old male coffee clerk in St. Paul, Minnesota.*

Nickie asked, 'Is Gwendolyn coming?'

'Gwendolyn?'

'Shw just sounds so stupid.'

'There she is now.'

Shw hopped into the rear seat, offering an efficient little grunt as a greeting.

'I'm actually in a really OK mood,' Shw said. 'Don't take my grunt the wrong way.'

'So – what's new today?' Nickie asked her.

'Bryan wanted me to go to Mauschwitz with him. He begged. I was disgusted.'

Janet changed the subject. 'That valet parker is so handsome.'

Nickie said, 'Nah, you're just horny. That's all.'

'Finally! Somebody who treats me as a sexual being!'

They drove. Janet watched the landscape melt by. Nickie asked, 'Is there any NASA stuff on today?'

'Nope. A clear slate.'

'Huh.' The car became immobilized at a red light amid a crowd of mobile homes and red and white rental cars. 'Sarah's really smart, isn't she?' Shw asked.

'I suppose she'd have to be.'

'Is she street smart?'

Janet considered this. 'Even if you're an astronaut I suppose there'd have to be *some* degree of treachery and backstabbing you'd have to confront. If nothing else, think of the hundreds of people who *weren't* picked for the shuttle flight.' She lapsed into her familiar educational mode. 'But you know, they choose astronauts for evenness of personality the way breeders choose dogs – astronauts are like the black labs of the aerospace world.'

Shw asked, 'Do you think they chose Sarah only because she's handicapped?'

'You're the only person who's ever said those words out loud,' Janet said.

'It's a natural enough question.'

'I know it is. I'm so tired of people never saying things. Silence reminds me of when I was growing up. Stifling.'

'What was it like?' Nickie asked.

'What was *what* like?'

'Sarah. The missing hand and all of that.'

Janet concentrated on giving an accurate answer. 'Growing up I was always told to be a good girl and to look good. All of my notions of self-worth were based on my appearance and demeanor. I don't think I ever really *knew* a person during my youth. And then with Sarah I'd be out shopping or at the playground and people would see her hand missing and in a flash, through their reactions, I was able to see their cores – whether they were kind or bad or stupid or what have you. I didn't even know what I was seeing for such a long time. All of this new type of information being thrown at me – I didn't want it – I didn't ask for it! And yet the information was still thrown at me. I tried to ignore it, and I never discussed it with anyone. In spite of what you hear, the 1960s were very *very* backward.'

'When were you born, Shw?' Nickie interrupted.

'1982.' Shw's silence after this reply seemed to negate further probing.

Nickie asked, 'So, Janet, what's the deal with Bryan? I don't understand why he's not, like, a stockbroker or something. He has the looks, if he'd just lose the hockey hair.'

Shw shot Nickie a pissy glare through the rearview mirror, and Janet answered that Bryan had always marched to his own drummer. She turned her head back and asked, 'What's *your* story, Shw?'

'My story?'

'Yes. Where are you from? Your family. That kind of thing.'

'I'm from Lethbridge.'

'Lethbridge – that's a lovely part of Alberta. Is all your family there?'

'My father is. My mother lives in Nova Scotia with a guy who makes model ships. I never see her.'

'What does your father do?'

'He's a Marxist theorist at the university there.'

'A Marxist.'

'Yeah. And he's full of crap.'

'I thought you were sort of radical yourself.'

'Maybe. But he's so embarrassing. He still believes all that communist bullshit – these days it's like believing in witch dunking. Globalization's the *real* demon. Globalization mixed with science. Dad's head is so up his ass he can't see past his pathetic disdain for the middle classes – *whoops* – excuse me, the *bourgeoisie*.'

Janet changed the subject. 'How about you, Nickie? What's your story?'

'Nothing big. I'm just a middle-class girl who waited too long to make some of life's big decisions, and the ones I did make weren't all too smart.'

'Such as?'

'Such as I'm really hungry right now.' She pointed to a mundane franchise restaurant. 'Let's go into that restaurant over there. The sign says that extra bacon's only nineteen cents this week.'

'I'm a vegetarian,' said Shw. 'And I've got morning sickness, too.'

Nickie steered into the parking lot. Once inside the restaurant, they claimed a booth. Everything inside the restaurant seemed to be orange, purple or brown.

'Ooh, he's *hot*,' Nickie said as the waiter left.

'Everything in this restaurant has meat in it,' said Shw, wiping her nose – a cold in a formative stage.

'You vegetarians are just a bunch of control freaks,' Nickie said. 'Order a frigging fruit plate.'

'They probably cut up the fruit on the butcher block right after they cut up some cow.'

'In a place like this,' Nickie said, 'your fruit plate would have been manufactured last February in a fruit plate laboratory in Tennessee.'

'Oh look,' said Janet in her chipper 1956 voice, 'scrambled eggs. How lovely.' This motherly tone persuaded the others to properly check out the menu. Janet removed a pill caddie from her purse and plunked it onto the table.

Nickie was agog. 'Christ, your pillbox is the size of a sewing kit. Will I to have to buy one of those?'

Just then the waiter, name-tagged Kevin, returned. 'That's *nothing*,' he said. 'A few of the folks who come in here, their pillboxes are as big as Kimble-Wurlitzer organs.'

Janet nodded at Nickie. 'She and I both have AIDS.'

'Well, so do I,' said the waiter.

Nickie said, 'Well isn't *this* a party.'

'I feel a group hug coming,' said the waiter, 'but my boss is chewing my ass to speed things up here. There's a Trailways busload of French tourists that arrived fifteen minutes ago – France-French – it's your worst table-waiting nightmare come true, so I have to take your orders real quick. Don't worry about tipping.'

The women placed their orders, while much Parisian quacking was heard from the restaurant's other side.

'So, like, what is it with your family?' Shw asked. 'You're like the *disease* family. Are any of you *not* sick?'

Nickie looked at Shw and changed the topic. 'I hear you're not too thrilled with having a kid, eh?'

'Oh look – Trophy Wife can actually talk.'

'Such lovely manners,' Nickie said. 'I've stuck my foot into it as always. If it makes you feel any better, I've done it, like, a half dozen times.'

'It?'

'Abort.'

'I'm going to the toilet.' Shw skulked off.

'I thought that maybe if she saw a shipwreck like me who'd been in the same boat, that maybe she'd think twice about her actions.'

'Do you want kids?'

'I guess. But I'd be a disgraceful mother.'

'You wouldn't.'

'Well, thank *you*, Cindy Brady. Anyway, we couldn't afford kids.'

'I forgot – he's that broke, huh?'

'Oh! We're so screwed ragged it's sick.'

'But you went marlin fishing—'

'Courtesy of one of his so-called friends. And you know what we've been eating down here since we arrived? Nachos and salsa. And hot dogs. That's what. We stopped at some jumbo outlet store on the way in from the airport.' Nickie looked at her nails and found them buffed enough. 'I *hate* being poor. I really do. And it really bugs me that I can't just dump Ted.'

'That's one of the most romantic things I've heard in months.'

Nickie said, 'And the one thing that bugs me about this whole AIDS business is that Ted might leave *me*. Imagine: I care about a person who'd dump me like that.' She sipped her coffee. 'Maybe I'm selling him short. I don't care if I die. And these HIV drug cocktail thingies make you grow fat deposits in the weirdest places – I could end up with six tits.'

Janet asked, 'Do you talk like this around Ted?'

'Basically.'

Janet looked out the window at the brilliant parking lot. 'I sometimes wonder if I'd been more . . . *forward* like you and like her – whether things might have been slightly different between me and Ted?'

'You? Maybe. But probably not. Ted says that you two never fought. He said you "simmered". That's his word – *simmered.*'

'I did. It's an unattractive trait. I no longer simmer.'

Nickie said, 'I should go try to retrieve Gwendolyn. The things we do for family – however twisted the connection.' She stood up, turned around and said, 'Hey, check out those two hunky pilots coming up the walkway.'

'You don't have an off button, do you, Nickie?'

'Nope.'

Nickie walked over toward the ladies' room near the till, just as the pilots walked through the door, dashing and bronzed. She swapped a smile with the less tanned pilot, who then grabbed her around the waist and slapped a piece of duct tape over her mouth. He screamed, 'Everybody. Listen. Listen – *now!* We have ourselves our first hostage. Anybody fucks up even once, and Malibu Barbie here gets her head blown off. No cell phones, no pagers, no 911s, no nothing.'

The other pilot raised a rifle, cocked it, and blasted a pie case, sideswiping Kevin's arm. A blizzard of blood and breakfasts smashed onto the cash counter and floor. Customers screamed; the pilot shot out a plate glass window; two people in the parking lot ducked and ran for a hedge. The less suntanned pilot screamed, 'Shut the fuck up all of you. We're here on business and we *mean* business. My friend Todd here is going to be coming around to take your jewelry. You Frenchies all love jewelry, and no Disney shit – I repeat, *no Disney shit – ne pas de merde à la Disney*. Any crappy little Lion King brooches or Little Mermaid bracelets, and Todd here takes one of your toes as a punishment.'

The French twittered among themselves; the pilot shot one of them, a middle-aged man, square in the chest. The room went silent. Janet saw the metal gun barrel touching Nickie's right ear; she remembered, as a child, her father pretending to pull quarters out of her own ear. Her head felt like a bee sting.

Our lives are geared mainly to deflect the darts thrown at us by the laws of probability. The moment we're able, we insulate ourselves from random acts of hate and destruction. It's always been there – in the neighborhoods we build, the walls between our houses, the wariness with which we treat the unknown. One person in six million will be struck by lightning. Fifteen people in a hundred will experience clinical depression. One woman in sixteen will experience breast cancer. One child in 30,000 will experience a serious limb deformity. One American in five will be victim of a violent crime. A day in which nothing bad happens is a miracle, a day in which all the things that could have gone wrong didn't. The dull day is a triumph of the human spirit, and boredom is a luxury unprecedented in the history of our species.

Janet left her booth and walked toward Kevin.

The gunman at the till said, 'Move back, lady.' Nickie was trying to shout through the duct tape.

'I'm sixty-five, you twerp. Shoot me, but I'm going to help Kevin here. I'm sure your buddies would really respect you for shooting an unarmed sixty-five-year-old lady.' Janet sat down beside Kevin and held his hand.

Pilot Number Two, 'Todd', had turned away and hopped from table to table, making the Europeans dump their jewelry into a cotton sack. When one woman refused, he said, 'Not going to play along then, eh?' *Bang*. He blasted off the toe of the man beside her. Janet heard screams and the gentle clinking of coins and jewels tumbling over one another, into the loot bag.

'It's time,' shouted Nickie's captor. '*Move*.'

Todd returned to the front door just as Shw, oblivious to the restaurant's drama, was exiting the ladies' room near the front door. The pilot reached for her purse, but she pulled it back just enough so that its contents sprayed over the floor, hundreds of fifty-dollar bills.

'Jesus,' said Number Two, stopping briefly to pick up a wad of them.

'There's no time. Go. *Now.*'

In a breath, they were out the door and gone.

Nickie ripped the duct tape from her mouth. She sucked in air as if she'd been deep underwater, fighting for the duration of a dream to rise to the surface.

Janet looked down and the linoleum before her was soaked in blood, a rich, cough-syrupy purple. Nickie was talking to her, but she couldn't hear – *no sound.*

Nobody in the restaurant was moving. The smell of burning breakfasts wafted in from the kitchen, where Janet would later learn the staff had locked themselves in the fridge. A dozen police officers stormed through, bellowing, *Nobody move!* Paramedics hopped over partitions and booths, heading for the traumatized French. Photographers were already documenting the scene, and Kevin's blood looked black in the afterburn of flashbulbs.

Janet looked over to see Shw picking up wads of bills with . . . *doughnut tongs?* A cop bellowed, 'Don't touch that money!'

'It's my money, you prick. Those assholes tried taking it.'

'Jesus, Shw,' said Nickie, 'Where'd you get a load of fifties like that?'

The manager confirmed that the money was Shw's, but the cops still told her not to touch the evidence.

'What? Like I'm gonna want to scrape off the scabs when it dries?'

'Leave it where it is, ma'am, or I'll have to charge you with tampering with a crime scene.'

Shw flung her purse onto the floor. Medics in space suits descended on Kevin, as two officers solicited a description of the two gunmen from Nickie: 'The first one was cute in a Kevin Costner way, but he had mean eyes, like he tortured bugs and small animals when he was a kid. He had really bad skin – too many drugs or an all-candy diet. He had a blue tattoo of a Celtic cross on his right upper hand, and, oh – he was really hung.'

'We can't use that in a report, ma'am.'

Kevin was lifted onto a dolly, Janet holding on to his good hand. The paramedics had covered him up with a rustling sheet of plastic foil – a space blanket. The plastic covered him as he was trollied out the doors and into the sunlight, which turned him and his metal blanket into a glittering, crinkling foil wrap.

Janet spoke to the Orange County police officers, and then it was Nickie's turn again. While the police were interviewing Nickie, another officer was talking to Shw. Janet was maddened to be able to hear only shards of Shw's words . . .

'. . . I'm with them' – Shw pointed at Nickie and Janet – 'but just barely. I used to date the older woman's kid.'

Used to date?

Shw was not the picture of intergenerational warmth. She wanted out of there, and quick. She was finally allowed to gather her remaining bills. The manager pointed her towards the hose behind the restaurant, which was used by staff to rinse out the Dumpsters. Minutes later Janet and Nickie found her there. She'd laid the rinsed bills out to dry on a dazzling white-painted ledge, where ants were now crawling over them, sensing a meal in the traces of blood enzymes.

'We're leaving shortly,' Janet said, adding, 'You don't have to come. Correct me if I'm wrong, but I have a feeling this is the last time we're ever going to be seeing you.'

At this, Shw spritzed her money more forcefully.

'Well, whatever,' said Nickie, 'in two minutes, we're legally divorced, so you might just as well tell us what's the deal with the cash here. It's nosiness pure and simple. If I don't find out, I'm going to have a hollow nagging feeling in me until the day I get hit by a bus.'

'It's *my* body,' said Shw. The hose kinked; she bent down to unkink it.

'You've lost me,' said Janet. 'Can you back up a bit?'

She stopped her rinsing and looked at Nickie. 'Look, Bryan's been telling you I want an abortion, right? He probably would –

he's such a death-obsessed basket case.' She resumed spritzing, and went on. 'This lady in Daytona Beach – her husband's in auto parts. Nice guy, but he shoots blanks and they want a kid. End of story. Thank you, Internet. So this money here is my down payment. Bryan's a moron, but he's good-looking, and his sister's an astronaut – *that's* what got me into the six-figure range. I said I wanted an abortion because I figured he'd go along with the death part of it.'

Janet said, 'Wait, wait, *wait* – you're going to *sell* the baby?'

'Well, *duh!* How was I supposed to know he'd go loopy?' Her spraying continued.

'There *are* laws.'

'Please don't get involved in this, Janet, because I actually like you and I want it to stay that way. And anyway, if you do find me, I'll just say I miscarried in a Tastee-Freeze bathroom.' She looked at Janet's face. 'Oh, don't go looking so high-hat on me. The kid is mine and I can do what I want with it.'

'Does Bryan know about the sale?'

'No. But I imagine he soon will.'

Shw's spraying grew menacingly close to their feet, and Janet could feel droplets on her shins. 'I think we'd best be going.'

Janet and Nickie went to their car, and then realized they didn't know where to head next.

'I think we should go get drunk,' Nickie said, 'I really do. Can we – *do* that in our condition?'

'I think so.'

Silently they prowled the roads in pursuit of a good, eleven A.M. cocktail.

12

The monorail's interior was steaming clambake hot, as Wade, Ted and Bryan whooshed above a Walt Disney World lake. Garish, emotionless music filled the air like the smell of somebody else's shampoo. Ted was already bored, while Wade was feeling flu-ish. *I used to be so good in the heat – even those summers in Kansas City*. Only Bryan seemed to be in a festive mood as he jabbered away. 'Hey, Dad,' Bryan said. 'This is kinda cool, huh? You and your sons at Disney World.'

'Yeah, sure. Right.'

'Makes you kinda proud, huh, Dad?' Bryan wouldn't let up. Ted turned to look at Wade as if to say, *Shut this guy up, will you?*

'And isn't it really neat – us being down here and Sarah going off into space?'

Ted snapped. 'I spent my whole fricking career in engineering so that Sarah and people like her could go up into space and help drag the rest of the species out of the shit. So yes, Bryan, it does seem "kind of neat" that we're all here.' The monorail was full; people stared at them. Whining children stopped whining. Bryan looked taken aback.

Wade thought, *What a geek. Why on earth would Bryan give a rat's ass about Dad's approval? And does he have to be so bloody pathetic about it?*

The loudspeaker's neuter male voice loudly described a Polynesian wonderland off to the left, and a vast Rocky Mountain-style timber lodge off to the right. Wade thought about his father. What *would* the world have to offer Ted Drummond, and the men like him, a man whose usefulness to the culture had vanished somewhere around the time of Windows 95? Golf? Gold? Twenty-four-hour stock readouts? Sailboats? Extra decades of life? Past a certain point, what *is* there for a man's man in this society? Or, for that matter, here in Florida – a land of massive science projects cooked up by people like his father and his golf buddies – a place vividly in decline, yet brashly on the way up. Wade rifled through his mental snapshot index of the region, his images of dumbed-down theme park attractions, crack dens, the space shuttle, malls bursting with doodads, freeways tangled like electric cords and the nightly evening news that felt like a recurring fever dream. He thought of the burning sun and the beautiful, deadly creatures that lurked beneath muddy waters like bruises waiting to surface.

Wade's pocket buzzer went off and he took a 3TC capsule swigged down with the dregs of a can of Orange Crush. He felt seasick and chalked it up to the monorail ride, now entering a large A-frame concrete building he'd seen on TV thirty years before. The hotel had once seemed like the future, and now it looked like . . . just another building. He'd never expected to see the structure in his lifetime, yet here he was.

The monorail stopped at the Magic Kingdom and they disembarked. Wade remembered his conversation with Beth before leaving for Disney World: 'No freaky shit, got it? I don't care what deal you set up for your dad, but *you* are not to be an accomplice. Do you read me? And I don't care how much money we owe the fertility clinic or whoever – I don't want you in the pen or on the lam. Read me?'

'I'll be fine.'

'Don't eat junk food. You know what the clinic said about junk food.'

'I know.'

Ted and Bryan stood in a patch of shade that lowered the temperature not even a smidge. Around them churned a foam of two-parent families. Wade got to thinking: *How many of these fathers whispered like pigs into the ears of temps in the office supply room? How many were spending their noon hours in motels? And the mothers – how many were starting to drink Chardonnay with their lonely lunches in the kitchen? How many felt trapped and unloved? How many were almost sick with jealousy over 'that bright young gal who's just turned the marketing department upside-down with fresh ideas?' – That bright young gal with a future as big as Montana and legs like Bambi's mother's?*

His father's voice interrupted his reverie: 'So where do you know this Norm guy from?'

'Kansas City.'

'What does he do?'

What does Norm do? 'Norm is Norm for a living. He's based in Tampa now.'

'He's late.'

'No, he's not. We're exactly on time – a slightly different thing.'

Pow! A parade burst out of nowhere, like a living room turning into a surprise party.

'Give this place a mute button and it might be OK,' said Ted. His voice picked up. 'Geez, look at the knockers on Miss Mermaid.'

'I never understood the deal with mermaids,' Bryan said. 'I mean, how are you supposed to actually *do it* with one? And I mean, she's got a great rack and all, but she's half *fish*.'

'Bryan, she's a goddamn cartoon, you moron.' Ted was indeed not in a Bryan mood. Soon the two were focused on Beauty, floating by them, seated atop a mobile balcony along with Beast.

Where's Norm?

Wade was feeling dizzy. The glare and the crowds were swamping him. *I'm in Walt Disney World. I never thought I'd be here, yet here I am. No newspapers. No litter. No evidence of the world outside its borders – like a casino, really.*

Endless distractions. It could be 2001, it could be 1986, and it could be 2008. And all these young parents – so much younger than me – no old people save for Dad. A few bored and embarrassed teenagers. This is supposed to be life-affirming? This place is like some cosmic dream crusher. All you can get out of a place like this is a creepy little tingle that lets you know your kid is never going to be anything more than a customer – that the whole world is being turned into a casino.

'Wade.'

It was Norm, a ponytailed beanpole, no child in tow, with skin the pale yellow color of those with overtaxed livers. He was carrying an attaché case, an item that stood out in Disney World like a machine gun. Norm motioned for Wade to follow him into an olde-time restaurant away from the throng. Wade grabbed Ted and Bryan and headed after Norm into the restaurant, where he'd already secured a table in the far corner.

'Norm, this is my dad, Ted, and my brother, Bryan.'

'Charmed.' Norm made no effort to shake hands.

There was an awkward silent moment, and then Ted asked, 'So, Norm, what is it you do?'

'I follow in my father's footsteps.'

'What did your father do?'

Wade cut in, 'Dad, I'm sure Norm doesn't want to be job-interviewed.'

'No, Wade. It's OK,' Norm said. He turned to Ted. 'After World War II, my father made his living returning stolen artwork to its rightful owners.'

'Decent,' said Ted.

'Yes. Very decent. Very noble. And you can just imagine the bargains and temptations and bribes that came my father's way. And you know what? Not once did he ever succumb.'

'Really now?'

'Yes, Ted, really. And because of this nobility, we spent our lives in a two-and-a-half-bedroom Monopoly token of a house in one of Kansas City's lesser suburbs.'

'I see.'

A waitress in period costume broke in and demanded their beverage order. They ordered iced teas and she left.

Norm continued. 'Fortunately, dear old Dad allowed me to escort him on many of his jaunts. I'll never forget the day we returned a Rubens to a camp survivor who once owned a chain of department stores in Baden-Würtemburg. I become warm and *verklempt* every time I think about it. But that's not too often, really.'

Four iced teas were plunked onto the table. From his attaché case Norm removed a flask of peppermint schnapps. 'The favored beverage of teenagers around the world. It rots my gut, but leaves my breath minty fresh. Life is such a collection of little trade-offs.'

'Go on,' said Ted. 'You were talking about your father.'

Norm finished spiking his iced tea. 'Yes, well, dear old Dad let me come along on his trips, and the greatest gift he ever gave me was making a proud moral point of ensuring I knew who among his clientele were the biggest bribers, sleazebags and connections in the business.' He sipped his tea. 'A toast—' The four men raised their glasses. 'To dear old Dad.' They toasted and then Norm's face became almost wistful. 'His Piper Cherokee hit a set of utility lines outside El Paso in 1981, after which I took over the family business. Needless to say, I do not live in a two-and-a-half bedroom Monopoly token house.'

Ted said, 'The war ended over fifty years ago, Norm. You mean you can still do good business finding and returning loot after all these years?'

'The war? *Pffft*. These days my job is to—' He paused. 'Find objects, find people, and then match them up.'

Bryan said, 'So you're not a drug dealer then.'

Norm howled. Ted slapped Bryan on the chest. 'Christ, what a loser, Bryan. Keep your trap shut.'

Norm stopped laughing enough to say, 'No, Bryan, no drugs.'

From across the restaurant came a commotion. '*Ladies and*

gentlemen, we have an important announcement to make. Young Cicely at this table here is eight years old today. Please join us in singing her a very "Happy Birthday".' Young Cicely, flanked by two camera-crazed parents, bravely tried to exhibit enough pleasure to be worthy of the attention thrown her way. The restaurant, like everywhere else in the theme park, burst into song. At the song's end, the patrons clapped, and Ted said to Norm, 'This place is driving me apeshit. Norm, get to the point. Wade says you and he have some kind of caper I can help with.'

Norm cocked an eyebrow, stole a quick glance at Wade and said, 'A caper! I haven't heard that word since the last time I saw Faye Dunaway in a mink stole driving a pink Corvette into Mexico.' He looked squarely at Wade: 'Tell me about this caper, Wade.'

What an asshole. 'You made your point, Norm. Tell my dad about this courier gig, and the sooner we'll be out of here.'

Norm said, 'Very well. Mr. Drummond, allow me to show you and your sons the artifact in question.' From his attaché case he removed a clear, zippable sandwich bag. Inside it was a white greeting card envelope that was in turn protected between two screwed-together sheets of clear plastic. He sighed and handed it over to Ted, whose eyes immediately goggled.

'Holy shit. Is this what I think it is?'

'Yes, Ted, it is.'

Bryan said, 'Lemme see it,' and tried to grab it, but Ted swatted him on the knuckles with a spoon.

'Ow! That hurt. Lemme see.'

'Show some respect, you little twerp.'

Bryan looked at the envelope's front. It read: *Mummy*. 'Big deal. What is it – a map to some stolen Egyptian mummy or something?'

'Oh, *Jesus*.' Ted was stilled with awe. Wade was in a form of shock, too.

'What's going on here?' asked Bryan. 'It's just a Hallmark

envelope with a card in it or something. Just a—' He froze. 'It's from the funeral. It's from the coffin . . . *her* coffin.'

Norm took the letter from Ted and placed it in his attaché case. 'Yes, Bryan, it is.'

'Lemme see it again.'

'No.'

'That *is* the real letter, isn't it?'

'I already told you, Bryan, yes, it really is. People don't spend ten million dollars on fake letters.'

The Drummond men sat speechless as young Cicely across the restaurant sliced her birthday cake. Another song began, and Wade entered a trance. *I shouldn't be tired, but I am, and I have to slog through the rest of the day. And what the hell is Norm doing with a copy of that English William-the-Prince guy's letter from his mother's coffin? And why does Bryan have to be such a goof? And please, God, let Dad make his money and then let him run far, far away. The music in this place – it's so loud and so blank. And my glands are so raw—*

'Wade?' Bryan was shaking Wade by the shoulder. 'You OK?'

'I didn't sleep last night.'

Ted spoke to Norm. 'How do you know the letter's real?'

'Oh, *please*.'

'Has it been opened?'

'No.'

'Why not X-ray it?'

'We do not X-ray it because the envelope is part of the royal family's custom stationery, made of bleached birch cellulose bonded on the inside with a titanium layer that keeps out both X rays and ESP. The letter inside might as well be encased in lead.'

'What sort of person would buy a letter like that?' Wade asked.

'Wade, you of *all* people ought to know that people will pay just about anything for just about anything.'

'What's that supposed to mean?'

'Tetchy, tetchy. The buyer could maybe be a rich class-obsessed Saudi who wants a social lift. The buyer could represent a faction hostile to England who wants to hold the letter ransom in return for a political favor. The buyer could be the heir to a low-end retail outlet chain who once fell in love with an Englishwoman. Who knows? Maybe it's the Franklin Mint, and they want to own it so they can make licensed copies.'

'It's that Kraut in Lyford Cay,' Wade said. 'Isn't it? Florian.'

'You *do* have ESP, today, Wade. Maybe your powers can penetrate the envelope.'

'What's Lyford Cay?' Bryan asked.

'It's the Richie Rich part of the Bahamas,' Wade said.

Bryan wasn't interested in this. He asked Norm, 'Can't you steam it open?'

'No,' said Norm. 'Part of the ten-million-dollar price tag is the confidence that the letter's message be known only to its owner.'

Ted asked, 'How does a person even go about finding a letter like this anyway?'

'She was cremated,' said Norm. 'The local crematorium was borrowed for the evening. There was chaos. Things slip through cracks. And so forth.'

'Why would they cremate her? I thought she was buried on a little island in a lake.'

'Bryan, do you honestly think the royal family wants DNA like hers lying around? The secret service most likely went through her boudoir to find her old toenail clippings to flush down the toilet. As for Prince Charles, well, they're probably cloning *him* like a battery chicken. Royalty is either going to do very well with biotechnology – or it's going to disappear completely. Regardless, we are Americans. Our very roots are nourished at their deepest levels with our disgust for the monarchy.'

'It's so sad,' said Wade.

'Oh, boo *hoo*. Just get it to the Bahamas for me by tomorrow night. You know where he lives.'

'What's our cut?' asked Ted.

'One percent of the take. Cash.'

'We'll do it,' Ted said.

'What do you mean "*we*"?' Wade asked, more irked at how Dad had hijacked the proceedings than anything else. 'Exactly whose gig is this?'

Ted said, 'We're all in on this, Wade.'

'I think I'm feeling love in the air,' said Norm, with a paternal smile.

'Norm, why don't you just take it there yourself?' Wade asked.

'Because, young Wade, the Bahamian gendarmes know me far too well. You know how nasty those Bahamians can become over a stack of, how shall I say, "unpaid parking tickets". You three chaps will be my go-betweens.'

Wade was unimpressed. 'There's something else, isn't there?'

'Actually yes,' Norm said.

'I *thought* so.'

'What is it?'

'Well, the thing is' – Norm lowered his voice an octave – 'I'm not really supposed to *have* this letter.'

'Don't tell me – the people who actually own the letter – if ownership is even the correct word in this case – want it back.'

'You might say that.'

Wade looked at his father and could tell from his eyes that he was already feeling solvent.

'You three lads are going to have *such* fun,' said Norm. 'I gather you don't socialize too often.'

'When was the last time the three of us did anything together – just the three of us?' Bryan asked.

'Oh, geez—' Ted hated this kind of question.

Wade said, 'We went to see *Diamonds Are Forever* at the Odeon.'

Norm said, 'You *must* be kidding. That movie came out in 1973, at *least*.'

Wade said, 'Let's be practical. How are we going to get to the Bahamas? If we're going to go, I suggest we hop to it, because we can only fly there in sunlight. We should be driving to the east coast, pronto.'

'How come you know so much about this stuff?' Ted asked.

Wade said nothing.

'Let's just charter a jet from downtown,' Bryan said.

'Yeah, us and our triple-A credit ratings,' said Ted.

Norm said, 'I need to take Peter Pan to the men's room and give him a severe shaking down.' He stood up. 'Wade, guard the case for me.' Norm began to walk away.

'Boy,' said Ted, 'he trusts you big-time.'

Norm turned around. 'Wade is quite trustworthy, Mr. Drummond. You should give him a chance to display this trait.' Wade smirked and then the power went off. Everybody froze.

Norm said, 'A power failure – in *Disney* World?'

A hive-like chatter began to rise in the restaurant. Outside, the rides went dead.

'You never think of power being a factor in a place like this,' said Ted.

'I know,' Wade said. 'It's like the place is fueled by Tinkerbell's pixie dust.'

'Speaking of which, Peter Pan still needs his shakedown.' Norm went to try and use the men's room at the restaurant's rear, but returned shortly. 'Too dark.'

'You're afraid of the dark?' Ted asked.

'I am.'

'I'm going to try and find a men's room.'

Once he was out the door, Ted said, 'He's a freak.'

'That *freak* is bailing you out of hock,' replied Wade. 'You could be a bit more polite, you know.'

'How far away is the Bahamas?' Bryan asked. 'Is it near Mexico?'

'It's 120 miles east of Miami.'

'That's close,' Bryan said.

The three sat and waited for Norm to return. In silence Wade contemplated the letter. What could it possibly say? *I miss you. I had things to tell you I never said. Come back. Don't leave me like this.*

A waitress said they'd have to wait for power to order food. Minutes passed. Wade was becoming aware of how the three were utterly uninterested in one another's company. Beth had once said that males within a family were never really close with one another; it was only with women that intense family relationships were born. Wade saw what she'd meant.

The power came on and the restaurant's guests clapped. Wade said, 'I'm going to go find him.' In the nearby men's room Wade found only a dad changing a diaper and a teenager washing his hands; the bank of toilet stalls was empty. He asked the dad if there had been a guy with a ponytail in there recently, and the reply was no. He looked for and found the next nearest men's room. No Norm inside. Then, down Main Street USA, he saw a small crowd clustered around something; Wade immediately knew the something would be Norm. He pushed his way through the crowd to find a doctor on holiday with her family, crouched by Norm's body, saying, 'He's dead.'

'Dead?'

The woman looked at him. 'Are you related?'

The last thing Wade wanted was an association with Norm. 'No – it's just that people don't actually *die* in a place like this, do they?'

'This guy did. Cardiac, it looks like.'

Wade quickly scooted back to the restaurant. He sat down with the gravity of a person bearing bad yet interesting news. 'Guys, it would appear we're now on our own.' He grabbed the case and unclasped the lock.

Ted asked, 'What are you talking about?'

Inside the case, sandwiched between the upper and lower lids of the case's foam, were an empty schnapps bottle and the letter.

13

The last time the Drummonds had been together as a family was a warm June night in the 1970s. Ted and Janet Drummond were throwing a party for no other reason than that they owed one to a lot of people. They still had friends then, and they still cared a good deal about what their friends thought. The three kids were in high school, and Ted and Janet still thought of themselves as being younger rather than older.

Sarah later told Wade that she and Bryan had spent a few hours talking with the guests, most of whom had been smashed. They then went and sat at the top of the stairs and ogled the guests below. Mr. Laine, Ted's tax guy and self-styled rogue, was hitting on Janet like crazy. Ted was telling crude jokes to a cluster of people by the stereo console, purchased new that afternoon. Wade had helped his father wire it.

Kitty Henry put a cigarette burn in Mom's favorite couch, and Helena, Mom's best friend, was shamelessly hitting on Russ Hallaway, a single Romeo with a tree-trimming service, who was rumored to have an oval-shaped bed.

All of this was happening as the RCMP car, cherries flashing, with Wade in the backseat, pulled into the driveway. The front door of the house had been open that evening so as to let in both fresh air and confused moths. Guests saw the cruiser's cherries, and they melted away from their respective cliques toward the open door. At this point, the Herb Alpert record finished, and the party's earlier shrill roar became a low and curious buzz.

Ted, along with some of the guests, was out the door. An RCMP officer was unlocking the cruiser's rear door to allow Wade, his long hair covering his face, to slump out of the car.

The officer and his partner spoke to Ted, who then swatted Wade on the neck, using the full heft of his chest and shoulders, which hurled the boy across the lawn. The guests went silent. Wade stood up, shook his head, and dove, tackling Ted onto the lawn, starting a brawl in which a choppy, seedy narrative emerged:

'Stay out of my life, you goddamn Nazi goon.'

'Why don't you keep your pecker in your pants, you little shit?'

'Oh, stuff it. Her father made her get rid of it, Dad, and losing a grandchild means fuck-all to you.'

'And so you had to go and attack him, did you?'

Janet came out shrieking, and a quartet of the guests managed to pull Wade and Ted apart, grass-stained and speckled with blood.

The cops left and guests quickly dribbled away.

Wade came up to Sarah's bedroom and climbed through her window out onto the roof. He heard Ted putting on fresh records, but the music was playing to an empty, still smoky room. Mom was in the TV room downstairs, and Wade could hear her crying, with Helena feeding her sympathy and Kleenex.

Around two, Sarah climbed out across the cedar shingles and joined Wade for a cigarette – her first and last. 'So, how do you feel – about almost being a father?'

'I don't know. The baby was alive. Now she – or he – isn't.'

Later, Sarah placed graham crackers and a bottle of Sprite on the window's ledge. She said good night to Wade. 'I feel like I'm leaving milk and cookies out for Santa Claus.'

'Sleep tight, baby sister.'

Sarah said, 'We're never really going to be a family again.'

Wade said, 'What are you talking about?'

'All of us – together under one roof. It's over.'

Wade considered this. 'I guess it is.'

He left early the next morning.

14

The three men were driving Wade's rental car down a pristine new toll highway, with Ted at the wheel. The highway seemed as if it had been opened only ten minutes ago, the shapes of its bends and curves and hills dictated by the countless untameable lakes and swamps that pocked the state. Highway signs had promised an interchange a few miles down the road that would then connect them to another near-identical road.

They were en route to Cocoa Beach, just south of Cape Canaveral. From there, Wade intended to dump Ted and Bryan in the lap of Connor, an old paramutuel betting friend whose life had been reduced to his thirty-two-foot Chris-Craft plus whatever he could cadge off people witless enough to rent both boat and captain for the afternoon's fisheries. One last phone call before Ted's cell phone's batteries died confirmed that Connor could use a bit of extra cash and would do a Bahamian run for Ted and Bryan. Good. After that, Wade was going to wash his hands of the day's idiocies and return to the hotel and take his pills plus some extra antinauseants. He'd then call his loan sharks and ask for an extension. Dealing with them seemed safer than dealing with his father and brother.

They were apparently the only car driving on the clean white lanes free from even the faintest of tire skids. The only thing marring the experience was Ted, who was in a nasty mood from not having eaten and from having to be around young people far longer than he preferred. He said belligerently, 'So let me understand this, Wade. You two are going to have a kid even though you're going to die any day now.'

Wade would have tackled and strangled anybody else. But

seeing as it was his father, Wade only regretted having broken the news. 'Dad, I'm not about to die, and Beth's negative and so is the kid. We're gonna be just fine.'

'Yeah, right.'

'OK. Be an asshole. See if I care. You can let me out of the car at that tollbooth up ahead and you can kiss your ass-saving jackpot good-bye.'

'Calm down. Jee-*zuzz*. Give me fifty cents.'

Wade rooted about his pockets for coins. He could feel Bryan pulsing with jealousy over Wade's upcoming not-to-be-aborted child. 'Bryan, you can check your pockets, too, you know.' He looked around: Bryan had taken Prince William's letter from within its protective covering of Plexiglas sheets and was fondling it. 'Jesus, Bryan, put the letter back in the bag! I can't believe you even unzipped it.'

'I just wanted to touch the paper. Is that a big crime?'

Bryan slid the letter back in its bag and made a feeble attempt to locate money in his pockets. The car pulled up to the tollbooth; they paid and drove through.

Wade looked at his father. The light in the car was harsh, and Wade suddenly saw a cragginess there that he hadn't seen before. He knew his own face looked shrunken and beleaguered in this same light. 'So, Dad, you honestly think I'm going to be dead next week, don't you?'

'Well – no. Cripes. Sorry I even brought it up. But it just seems to me like you could have thought about who'd take care of the kid a few years down the road.'

'A few years down the road.'

'Yeah.'

'Down the road meaning what – five? Twenty?'

'I don't know. *Two?*'

'So, we have a number on it now. You estimate I'll be dead in two years.'

'Well, yeah. Is that a crime?'

'Stop the car.'

'Don't be so melodramatic. So you may not be dead in two years. So I'm wrong, and you don't die. Big frigging deal.'

'I said stop the goddamn car!'

Bryan snorted from the backseat.

Wade stuck his index finger in his mouth, removed it, tip glistening, and held it out toward his father. 'Stop the car.'

'Don't be a jerk, Wade.'

'Stop, or I'll touch you – and likely *infect* you at that.'

Wade saw a vein in Ted's forehead pop out. He waggled his index finger even closer. 'Stop the car . . . *Dad*.'

Wade touched his father's cheek. Ted screamed and slammed on the brakes, jolting the sedan sideways perpendicular to the lane. There was a squeal, the hiss of gravel, and then the car did a neat double flip, as if in a 1970s cop show. It hopped a tiny roadside fence and landed on the ground beneath an embankment, right side up, amid a thicket of sharp, wild, prickly grasses. The engine still purred calmly. A road map fluttered from the ceiling down onto the center console. There was no noise outside; the empty freeway was out of both sight and mind. Everything was just the same as it had been a few minutes before, but at the same time completely different.

The three sat quietly, as though the smallest of gestures might reactivate the violence. They swore and looked around themselves slowly. Bryan began to whoop. 'Oh, *man*, Dad – this is the most heinous thing you've ever done. You are a *stud*! You *rule*!'

There was no possible way to get the car up and onto the road. The right front tire was sinking into the edge of a drab, unscenic swamp. In a crisp, efficient manner, they had traveled back in time to a nonhuman epoch. Ted turned off the engine and his body went rigid with shock. Wade opened his door, and the car's *ding-ding-ding* warning sounded. He looked at the car's body from the outside. 'You asshole! This car's rented in Beth's name. Do you have any idea how long she worked to regain her fucking credit rating? The roof looks like a goddamn cheese grater.'

Ted thawed slightly, got out, and looked at the car. 'Relax. We're OK.'

'This is *not* OK – we're *fucked*. And I'm the one who told her not to buy maximum insurance. She's going to fucking *freak*.'

Bryan's hormones and enzymes, still in shock, bulleted about his system. 'Dad, you are a total *stud*. Not a single broken window. Even the rearview mirrors are untouched. Man – that was so cool it – ouch! Ow! Oh *shit* . . .'

'Bryan,' asked Wade, 'what is it now?'

'An ant just bit me.'

'A what?'

'A *fire* ant. *Shit*. There's a colony of fire ants right here.' Bryan had placed his right leg squarely into the center hole of a fire ant colony. 'Hey, Bryan – they're swarming all over you – even right up to your neck. Shit.'

Squealing like a braking train, Bryan started brushing himself off with inefficient, powerful windmill strokes. His screaming became almost inaudibly high-pitched.

Ted looked a bit stunned. 'Gee, Dad,' said Wade. 'You could maybe help us out here. Bryan's being eaten alive.' He turned to Bryan, 'Bryan, take off your shirt. The ants are crawling in under the fabric, and your odor is frightening them and they're only going to bite more.'

Bryan went even crazier. Wade ripped Bryan's shirt off and commanded him to doff his jeans. Bryan had been bitten over his entire body; a few dead ants dangled from his pale pectoral skin like blood-colored earrings. Wade swatted them away. 'They're gone now, Bry.'

Bryan ran over to a rock and squatted on top of it, whimpering. He covered his head with his hands and began to rock.

Ted shouted, 'Stop acting like a girl, Bryan, and come over and help us lift the car out of the mud.'

'Like we're going to drive it up the little bluff there and onto the freeway?'

Wade and his father were entering combat mode.

'Enough from *you*, Typhoid Mary. If it hadn't been for you and your infantile game, we'd be on the road still.'

'You're the worst driver in the fucking country. You rolled us off a road to avoid being touched by me.'

'Don't be such a soap opera.'

'This isn't a soap opera, it's real life, and you'd rather kill us all than be touched by me.'

Ted said nothing. Wade began to walk toward him. Ted tried playing it cool, but he began to edge away. Just then Bryan shouted, 'The letter!' He pointed towards the swamp. The wind had blown Prince William's letter, sealed inside its plastic Ziploc sack, out into the swamp and was ferrying it away faster and faster. Ted stood frozen and Wade grabbed him. He summoned his flagging strength and shunted his father into the swamp. 'Get the letter *now*, you asshole. It's the only chance you have to haul your ass out of bankruptcy.'

'I'm covered in mud!'

'Get the letter!'

'There could be alligators in there.'

Wade walked to the side of the swamp and coughed up a ball of phlegm and spat it at his father, just missing him. 'Me or the letter. Take your pick.'

Ted turned and went after the letter, plunging chest-deep into the brown water on his third step. He paddled out several yards, grabbed the letter, gulped in air, and headed toward the shore, but Wade stood there coughing up more spit, shooting it at the ground and saying, 'Now – *apologize* to me.'

'For what?' Ted was holding the letter now.

Wade hocked a loogie that splatted on Ted's forehead like an egg on a windscreen. Ted screamed and went under water, thrashing with his other hand to wipe the loogie away. 'For everything.'

Ted bobbed to the surface. 'I'm sorry. Shit – I'm sorry.'

Wade coughed up another loogie and shot it at his father. 'You don't *mean* it.'

Ted screamed again and plunged, missing the saliva bomb. 'What kind of proof do you want? I'm gonna drown in this swamp.'

'Not unless the leeches suck your blood out first. *Ooh* – leeches – I hadn't thought of that. Plump juicy leeches, sucking your blood, leaving nice big open holes in which my infected spit will fester and multiply.'

'Bryan! You brother's turned into a sick-fuck monster. Keep him away from me.'

Bryan was still on his rock. 'No *way* am I going near that anthill. You're on your own.'

'Fuck. You win,' said Ted.

'How do I win?' Wade asked.

'If you'll stop spitting at me, I promise that when I leave this hellhole of a swamp you can touch a leech hole or scrape or cut or whatever the fuck it is that's cut me down below.'

'How do I know you're not lying?'

'I'm not lying.'

'Promise to me that your mother will go to hell if you're lying.'

'You're so fucking sick.'

'Say it!' Wade knew that Ted's only kryptonite was the memory of his mother, dead some fifteen years.

Ted shouted, 'Shut the fuck up.'

Wade coughed up another loogie – they were coming fast and easily today, not a good health indicator – and prepared to shoot it at his father. He instead spat it at the ground. 'Yes, Dad, your very own mother, Grandma Drummond, drifting around with angels, eating chiffon pies and playing contract bridge with all her friends until she's lassoed down to hell for eternity, burning and rotting for ever because *you'll* have broken your promise to me.'

Ted treaded water.

Wade knew his clause had worked. 'I'm waiting.'

Ted broke: 'You win.' He swam to shore. Wade gave him a

hand to lift him out of the mud, which farted as Ted stepped from it, losing a shoe in the process. Ted moved onto dry land. 'Thank God.' He slapped the letter down onto the car's hood.

Wade made a command: 'Roll up your pants.'

'Oh, shut *up*.'

Wade tackled Ted. Grass crackled on the dirt where they fell. Wade grabbed Ted's squirming leg. He placed his entire weight on Ted's rib cage, pinning him down, and took the leg and rolled up the cuff to find any number of small, bleeding cuts.

'You win. Touch my cuts. *Jesus*, you're a monster. Infect me.'

'Infect you, I will. Here I go, one, two, three.' Wade touched a dry fingertip to a bleeding cut, called his father an ignorant bastard, then fell onto the grass and shut his eyes.

An hour later the three men hobbled along the highway – Ted minus a shoe, Bryan shirtless, swollen and walking with legs apart to prevent chafing, and Wade feeling ever sicker. Wade then registered an off-kilter perception: The sun was in the wrong place, on the left instead of on the right – meaning that Bryan had been navigating them in the wrong direction and that the many miles they'd walked since they'd rolled the car had been pointless. Ted swatted Bryan on the head and called him a cretin, but Wade got in between them and said, 'Dad, don't hit us any more.'

Ted looked peeved. 'He's still Bryan, and he's still a fuckup.'

Wade made a disgusted *pffft* and said, 'Like *you're* not a fuckup?'

'At least I don't—'

'Oh, be quiet. We've stopped listening to you.'

The occasional vehicle, usually a trailer rig, roared past, ignoring them utterly; the usual swarms of highway cops and sundry law enforcement agencies had chosen that day to ignore this lone stretch of highway.

'We should walk to the tollbooth,' Wade said.

Bryan said, 'That's ten miles the other way now.'

'At least we'd be going in the right direction,' said Ted.

A wave of sickness came over Wade, and he knew he couldn't walk further. 'I have to stop here,' he said.

Ted and Bryan exchanged looks.

'Yes, I'm sick. Happy? Now go on without me. You have the numbers and addresses and stuff. Just *go*. A cop'll come and find me soon enough.'

Just then, a white four-door sedan passed by them. It shrieked to a stop a hundred paces away.

'A good Samaritan,' said Bryan, 'Thank God.' A smallish woman got out of the car. It was Shw. Bryan said, 'Oh, shit.'

'What in hell's name are you three losers doing out here on the freeway? *Christ*, Bryan, you look like Porky Pig. What happened to you? Wait, don't tell me – I probably don't want to know.'

'Just give us a ride to the tollbooth.'

'No. I'm leaving you and your freak-show family. I'm retarded for even stopping to ask you three losers what you're doing here. What *are* you three doing here?'

'Dad flipped the car a few miles back. We're on our way to—'

Shw raised her hand and said, 'Stop right there.'

'Hey – where'd you get a car?' Bryan's tone changed considerably.

'I rented it, dipshit.'

'With what money?'

'With my money.'

'You don't have any money.'

'Christ, you are so stupid, Bryan.'

'Do they actually pay people to have their babies killed these days?'

'I'm outta here.' She opened the door.

'Wait!' called Wade. 'I'm sick as a dog. Just take us to a gas station and forget about us.'

'I don't want you three in my car.'

'We'll sit in the trunk.'

This actually seemed to make a kind of sense to Shw. 'Why should I do it?'

Ted spoke up for the first time. 'Maybe just to prove to us you aren't a total see-you-enn-tee.'

'Your honeyed speech moves my soul.'

Shw got into the car and slammed the door.

Bryan said, 'Thanks, Dad – there goes our ride,' but to the surprise of all three, Shw ground the car into reverse and zoomed towards them, making them jump. She popped a button and the trunk lid came open. Through a crack in the window she said, 'You have ten seconds to get in. 10. 9. 8. 7. 6 . . .'

The three climbed in; for whatever reason the trunk smelled of fish and harsh chemicals. As they pulled onto the road, they were squished like puppies in a basket. Wade, on the right side, pulled his head up and vomited over the tail light, making Ted, on the left side, try to squeeze himself as far away as possible. Bryan began to speak to Shw through the wooden panel behind the rear seats. 'I love you, Shw. I don't care what you do with the kid. I love *you*. I love *you*.' Shw replied by cranking up a Gloria Estefan dance song to full volume. Minutes later they pulled into a Citgo gas station where Shw screamed at them to get out. Ted and Wade complied, but Bryan refused.

'Bryan, it's over, OK? Now get out of my car.'

'No.'

'Have it your way.' She did a spectacular reverse donut, and then thrust the sedan at considerable speed into a concrete billboard piling out behind the station, one touting a Universal Studios tour. Bryan catapulted out like a jack-in-the-box. Shw squealed away, and within a few moments she was gone.

Wade was hosing himself off as Bryan hobbled towards him and Ted.

'Your taste in women is flawless, Bryan,' said Ted.

In response Wade spritzed his father with the hose, and Ted said, 'Christ, are you two ever testy.'

At that point Bryan's face screwed up.
'Don't tell me—' said Wade.
'I don't believe it,' said Ted.
Bryan had left the letter inside the trunk.
'I'm just a fuckup.'

15

Janet and Nickie giggled like cartoon mice as they entered a biker bar in pursuit of their post-holdup cocktails. After the morning's disaster, a biker bar was a no-brainer. A half hour later, they'd downed three drinks with a new round on the way, at which point they'd calmed slightly. They watched the billiards table, where men who most likely owned junkyard dogs cracked a rack of balls. Nickie said, 'I wonder if Shw could dominate these louts.' She made a disgusted noise, 'Forget about Shw.' She turned to Janet and said, 'Janet, tell me more about Helena. To be honest I really don't know what happened.'

'Helena, God—' Janet sighed. 'Where to start? She was my best friend. We went to university together in the 1950s. In Toronto. I was the uptight one and she was the bohemian. We were a good match. When I had kids she fell away a bit – she was into 1960s feminism and then New Age and crafts and shawls and sand candles and all that spacey stuff. But when Helena was around I felt like there were so many other things to do in life besides be a housewife. She convinced me that my own narrow little road wasn't some sort of dead-end trap.'

Two screwdrivers arrived. Janet raised her glass: 'To unlikely friends.' The women each took a sip and Janet went on: 'I moved to Vancouver with Ted and the kids, and she moved West around the same time, too – Vancouver was so hippsy-dippsy then – and the kids loved it when Helena came to the house because she was so different from what they were used to. She really turned me on to cooking. Oh – that was one of her big gifts – she could cook like a fiend.'

'What happened?' Nickie asked.

'It was so weird,' Janet said. 'So goddamn weird.'

'Go on.'

Janet told her, even though she was still trying to make sense of it. On a very dull Wednesday afternoon some years earlier she'd looked out the den window and had seen Helena's car pulling up. *Helena's here – what fun!* There had been a recent estrangement – Helena had taken an oddly vinegary disliking to Janet's politics, which, by Janet's own confession, were milquetoast. When she saw the car, Janet figured a truce was in the offing, and her spirits rose. She opened the front to find Helena hopping out of her Chevette wearing blue jeans, Frye boots and . . . nothing else. 'Boobies just flapping in the breeze. It was a chilly day, too.'

'Oh, geez.'

'You better believe it. Clem and Judy Payne next door just about had a seizure. I mean, you just can't *imagine* how odd it is to see a woman – let alone a very full-breasted sixty-year-old woman – walking around in half a birthday suit.'

'I'm trying but—'

'Exactly. The most preposterous thing I ever saw. Maybe in five hundred years all the gals will be going bareback, but in West Vancouver in 1996? Shocking. Shocking. Just *shocking*.'

Janet had opened the front door as if there were nothing untoward about the situation.

'Hi, Jan.'

'*Helena* – what in God's name? Come *in* – come into the house.'

'Not just yet, Jan. The day's so nice. I want to take in the sun.'

'Helena, it is *not* sunny, it's overcast and freezing outside and you are *naked*. Come in the house.'

'You're *so* uptight, Jan.'

'I am *not* uptight.'

'Listen to yourself.'

Nickie was glued to the story, which Janet had never told anyone.

'Of course ten seconds later a police cruiser pulls up the driveway behind Helena's car. It's a recurring theme in my life – police cruisers pulling up the driveway – it's how periods in my life begin and end.'

'What happened?'

Janet ran the movie in her head: the police officers – a man and a woman – approached the front door in a bland, official manner. Janet was miming a *What-can-I-do?* gesture as she watched the police approach Helena. They asked if everybody could step inside, but Helena didn't see why that might be necessary.

The officers spoke to Helena: 'If we could just step inside, ma'am—'

Helena didn't reply.

'Ma'am? Please.'

'No. I like it out here. I'm going to sit on this stoop and enjoy the day.'

The Kim family's teenage boys were out on their deck watching things develop. Binoculars were quickly produced. The Paynes weren't going to budge from their perch, either.

Helena said, 'If sitting in the sun and enjoying nature is a crime, I stand accused. Arrest me. Otherwise, leave me alone. Janet – please ask these people to leave your property.'

Janet and Nickie sipped their drinks. Janet continued, 'The cops tried being rational, but of course it wasn't a rational situation, and things went nowhere. The Kim kids, meanwhile, had called their pals on their cell phones, so out of nowhere there were maybe a dozen teenage boys across the street staring at my front stoop. One of them was taping the episode on a camcorder. It felt so – *underwater and dreamy*. The woman officer told Helena she was going to have to arrest her, and Helena said, "Fine." I mean, the officers bent backwards giving her every chance to save face, but no.'

'Yikes.'

'I know. So the woman officer tried to handcuff Helena, and

Helena went nuts and tried biting her, so the other one came to help her, and her boobs were flying around and suddenly she was screaming "*Rape!*" I could only stand there aghast. Then Helena noticed that I wasn't trying to stop the police, and she began screaming just the vilest names at me. Have teenage boys and you get used to being called names – but then she started talking about . . .'

'About what?'

'She started talking about how she'd been having an affair with my father – for decades, it turns out. I didn't believe her, but it's amazing how many names, dates and places a mad-woman can scream out while evading arrest – a huge list of wheres and whens – as well as where my mother had been while the trysts were occurring – worst of all, she screamed out things my father had said about me.'

'Oh, Christ.'

'There aren't words to describe the feeling. There just aren't. Then the teenage boys joined in on the bull herding – like Pamplona. It was October – there was still dew on the lawn. Such a *mess*.'

It's all your fault, Janet Drummond. You're a traitor to your sex. You're a traitor to your family and to me, your only true friend in the world. You're a scab. You're dried up. That's what your father said about you – you're a dried-up goody two-shoes party-pooper scab.

'It took a few minutes to get Helena into the cruiser, and I was so relieved the windows were rolled up so I couldn't hear her filth any more. The cops drove away, the neighbors evaporated, and there I was at my front doorstep. My life could never be the same again, and I was just standing at my door. I got cramps it was so awful.'

Janet finished her drink. 'Very shortly I'm going to be over-the-top drunk. We should go back to the hotel.' She got out her card to pay. 'You know, after Helena went nuts, the divorce was a complete anticlimax. I never minded the divorce as much as it seemed on the outside. We probably shouldn't have married to begin with. Live and learn.' She paid the bill. 'Shall we go?'

They went back to the hotel and both fell asleep on the king-size bed. Around sunset, they were awakened from their slightly drunken sleeps by fireworks neatly framed by their window: blisteringly pink and white chrysanthemums blooming and dying.

Nickie said, 'I bet this is how rich people get to wake up – with fireworks displays. I bet they probably have rich-people-only fireworks that we'll never get to see – ones that work during daylight.'

Janet briefly couldn't remember where she was, or why, but then the morning's events came back to her. *My children, where are they?* She made her usual waking tally: The boys hadn't yet returned from Disney World. Sarah was in Cape Canaveral.

The two women remained slightly shell-shocked from the morning's holdup. They also watched as the ever-present fire ants, plump and stupid, batted themselves against the twenty-sixth-floor windows. *What do they want?*

'How do you think it changed you?' Nickie asked.

'The robbery?'

'No – when you found out you had . . . *it*.'

'*It?* Oh – don't *you* pussyfoot around me, Nickie. Say HIV.' Janet touched the scar of the bullet hole on her rib cage. 'What was it like? There was the usual stuff: *It can't be true. There has to be a mistake. You're confusing me with somebody else*. And then I thought, *Wait! Science will save me!* And science did – sort of. And now I think science is how the disease started in the first place. Some geeks from UNESCO making vaccines out of mashed monkey brains in Africa. We'll never really know. I mean, AIDS just isn't a disease a sixtysomething Canadian housewife *gets*. In my head I don't even call it AIDS; I call it Congolese Monkey Brain Particles.'

The ants made sounds as they batted against the windows –

like kitten paws. 'And after I recovered from the initial shock, I began to think, *Ooh – maybe I'm one of those one-in-a-hundred people with a natural* HIV *antigen in their DNA* – if such people even exist.'

'Go on.'

'Oh *pish* – I don't know. I tried to be scientific. I learned about vaccine trails and cocktail therapies – on the Internet mostly.'

'My mother used to say "pish".'

'She's my vintage, I imagine.'

'Yeah.'

Janet smiled. 'I even went down to Mexico once – with a friend, Betty, from my book club. She had Hashimoto's disease and a form of throat cancer. We were trying to find Laetrile – this drug from the 1970s made from peach pits.'

'I remember that – sort of.'

'What a hoax. It killed Steve McQueen. Betty's gone. The only option I haven't tried yet is crystals. The moment you start plopping crystals on your sternum, the game's over.'

'But I don't think you answered my question. How did you change *inside*?'

Janet sighed. 'Let me think. Nobody's ever asked me that.' *How have I changed?* 'You know what? The biggest change is that I stopped believing in the future – which is to say, I stopped thinking of the future as being a place, like Paris or Australia – a place you can go *to*. I started believing that we're all going, going, going all the time, but there's no city or place at the end. We're just going. That's all.'

'Do you ever blame Wade? Or me?'

'Wade? He stood in front of me to protect me from Ted. How could I blame him? Do I blame you? No. Ted's the idiot. Lately I've started to think that blame is just a lazy person's way of making sense of chaos.'

'What do you mean?'

'Suppose a weird or random event happens to you, like a

falling cedar tree crushes your pet cat, or you get held as a hostage in the hold-up of some cut rate diner – or Mrs. Drummond gets AIDS from a bullet that passed through her son's liver – I could blame the tree trimmers for not recommending I top that cedar. I could blame the Florida legal system for – I don't know – something. Or I could say that the bullet was divine retribution for not trying hard enough to make my marriage work. Or – you see what I mean. It's nobody's fault. It's chaos. Just chaos. Random numbers popping up in a cosmic Lotto draw.'

'You really think so?'

'More and more. How about you? You're only on Day Four of having gotten the news. What's going on inside of *you*?'

'Me? I always figured I'd get it – that I deserved it – if not AIDS then syphilis or some kind of superherpes that turned my body into one big walking canker. It's a relief, actually. No more waiting. The jury is in.'

'You really think it was Wade?'

'I do. My reputation makes people think I'm some vacuous slut, but Wade was my first stray in years. It was something in his eyes, some kind of gaze he inherited from Ted, and it was the Ted inside of Wade that was so seductive. I could theorize all night.'

The two women dozed fitfully. Janet pictured a trillion particles of an African monkey brain virus blipping about in her veins like toxic soda water bubbles. *I once believed that people never change, that they only become more like themselves. Now I think that people do nothing but change.* Janet thought of her father the philanderer, and of her mother who *must* have known all those years. *Time erases both the best and the worst of us.* She thought it strange how memory is erased in little bits without regard to memory as a whole.

'What are you thinking about?' Nickie asked.

'About this time in London,' Janet replied. 'In Piccadilly. I didn't have a watch and I needed to know the time. There was a

Rolex store with hundreds of watches in the window. I assumed they'd be collectively precise to the second. But when I looked, each watch displayed a completely different time, and for a few seconds there I felt as if I'd passed into the other side of the mirror where there was no time at all.'

The door knocked and Nickie shouted out, 'What!'

It was turn down service, to which Nickie shouted, 'No, thank you.' She turned to Janet and asked, 'What was the angriest you've ever been with Ted?'

Janet smiled. 'You won't believe me.'

'Yes, I will.'

'We were out in the front garden talking about buying manure for the azaleas. Ted asked me if I had any Kleenex and I said no, so he grabbed one of my beautiful pink peonies – so soft, with skin like a baby's eyelids – and he plucked it from the shrub and honked away and then threw the used flower underneath the sequoia.'

Nickie horse-laughed at this.

'You laugh! I suppose I could have seen it as funny, but instead I didn't talk to him for a week. That simmering thing I used to do. I just . . . *couldn't* bring myself to speak to a man who'd done what he'd just done.'

The two stared at the ceiling some more. Janet said, 'Let's go visit Kevin in the hospital.'

Nickie thought this over. 'Yes, let's.'

Janet had never had much luck with friends. She had always hoped Ted would be her pal, like characters in the lyrics of a song, but Ted was more of the distanced boss in her life and got bored easily with any family matters save those involving Sarah. Of her children, Wade was the only one with whom she felt a camaraderie. Sarah was too cool a cucumber, and while she never gave Janet a moment of grief, neither did she give her any moments of bliss. And Bryan – Bryan was always a child. Even as an adult trying to kill himself, he remained in Janet's eyes a child.

When Ted left her and she had the house to herself, she thought she was going insane, in the medical sense, with boredom and loneliness. She could put a good face on it – she knew *that* – but her days became quests to find someone, *anyone*, to connect with: checkout clerks, auto repairmen, carpet cleaners or fellow course takers at the community center (Celtic calligraphy; 'Slim and Sixty'; 'The Eternal Essence of Feng Shui'; CPR; lacemaking). Ultimately it was on the Internet where she could meet with people and not have them instantly spooked away by the look of near-surrender in her eyes, or the taint of Probably Never Being Loved by Anyone New Ever Again. On the Internet people wouldn't know that she went for days eating only pimiento cream cheese with English water biscuits, or that she obsessively fondled her crow's feet.

At least when she'd been shot there had been a brief and shamefully gratifying burst of attention, but that went away quickly enough. But then, with her viral diagnosis came a deluge of people from a surprisingly broad and emotional slice of the culture. The accelerated perception of death quickly eroded many of the traditional barriers between her and others, and she found she had a talent for organizing group discussion dinners. About a year into her diagnosis, Sarah had phoned and asked her mother what she'd been up to lately. Janet found herself, for the first time in recent memory, with plenty to talk about. She described a seropositivity potluck dinner at the house the night previously. Sarah asked who'd been there, and Janet said, 'Well, there was Mahir. He's twenty and Persian and his family will no longer acknowledge his existence. He brought falafel. There was Max – he's seventy-one, and a cardiac transfusion case. He overheard his ex-friends talking about him at the Legion, and now he's having a crisis along the lines of "Oh-my-God-what-have-I-done-with-my-life?" He has a heart of pure butter, and he brought along two-day-old donuts. Sheila's my age, and she's a lesbian whose lover of eighteen years left her after her diagnosis. She shaved her hair off yesterday and was in a foul mood. She brought along those American laxative potato chips, and we all had a good laugh. Wally is our "official compassionate gay guy". He wanted us to go downtown afterwards to dispense condoms on street corners, but I don't think I'm evolved to that point yet.'

'What did you make?'

'Everything as usual – lasagna, salad and garlic bread.'

'Was it fun?'

'Fun? I never think of it that way, but yes, it was very intense. Our get-togethers always are. We have to pretend we're brave, but then one of us explodes, and another one gets weepy, and suddenly we're all on the same raft. It makes me feel alive. How's *that* for irony?'

But she was still lonely, and she wouldn't discuss this with her daughter or anybody else. To even speak the word would somehow finalize her situation, and she knew there had to be more than just this.

16

Wade first met Beth in the Las Vegas hospital's diabetes clinic during its off-hours, at his first visit to a Think Positive! seropositivity workshop. The first thing he noticed about Beth was that she was wearing a . . . *muumuu*? He wasn't sure what her garment was – some sort of floral schoolmarm dress fresh from a high-school production of *Oklahoma*! And yet the woman inside the dress was anything other than an apple-cheeked farm girl. She was bony and strangely used-up-looking, as if she'd done her share of time strung out on crystal meth. Beth's out-of-date dress seemed to Wade to be the outer veneer of an inner conversion. She'd been where Wade was, but she'd found a way out.

The first sight of Beth seemed to smash his heart, yet mend it at the same time. He was determined to meet this woman, but decided this might be too important to use his thousand-watt breed-with-me face or his standard come-on line ('I know what you're thinking, and there's only one way to find out.'). Instead he maneuvered himself into the chair beside her. Like a border collie he sat waiting, hoping, praying that she would drop a pen or paper so that he could pounce on it and retrieve it for her. This woman had reduced him to kindergarten devotion, and yet he knew nothing about her.

She dropped a pen. *Pounce*! He returned it to her desktop in a blink. She looked at him coolly: 'Thanks.' She wasn't playing hard to get; she simply wasn't playing at all.

The class was asked to share their experiences. Debbie, who ran the workshop, said, 'We have a new member, Wade. Wade – tell the group members here your story – as much as you want to.'

'I don't know if there's much to tell,' Wade said. 'I mean about me and my life and how I got this thing.'

'Please,' Debbie said. 'No euphemisms, Wade. It's HIV.'

'Okay then, HIV. I'm straight and I've never done it with a guy, or even a three-way.'

Many of the class's twenty or so members sniggered.

'Hey, screw you – why would I go so far as to come to a class like this and then lie? The thing is, I used to be a big sleeper-arounder. It was my life. Sleeping around always landed me what I wanted. I know these rich kids who never had to work a day in their lives because they always got what they wanted. Well, instead of money with me it was my – shit – how do I say this without sounding like a jerk – my way with women.'

More sniggers. Debbie asked the class to be quiet. 'Go on.'

'Anyway, I found out about the infection by accident. The world's flukiest fluke.' Wade told the story of the shooting, and he embellished a bit. The class was silent in the most interested way, rapt at the oddity of the tale. 'So there you go. I have this virus in my body. It's never going to go away. I can't work at the moment – I was going to play hockey at that B-list casino across the highway, but that's impossible now. The months are ticking by. I just don't have . . . any idea what to do.'

Silence.

'What about your mother?' asked Beth. 'What's she feeling? Have you two talked much?'

'Some. I feel like the biggest sack-of-shit son in the world. She pretends it's no big deal, but you know it is.'

The group continued, and discussed various medical problems on the wax and wane. New procedures and medications and regimens were hashed out, and then the group ended, over by the clinic's kitchen, where everybody ate oatmeal raisin cookies and drank dishwatery coffee. Wade maneuvered close to Beth and asked her how long she'd been living with HIV. 'Three years. I was a junkie, but I don't do that any more.'

'No?'

'No. I found the Lord. That sounds stuck-up, and I don't like that. But I did – find Him, I mean. He keeps me sane, a side effect I never would have expected.' Other group members flocked around Wade; Beth vanished.

The following week passed slowly as Wade waited for the group to meet again. Beth arrived the next Tuesday night looking shaken; something was obviously awry.

'Beth,' said Debbie. 'You look stressed. Having a tough day?'

'I'm not sure what to call my day.'

'How so?'

Beth hesitated. 'I've been having these tests done over the past two weeks. But the full results didn't arrive until this morning. It turns out— ' She bit her lip. 'I don't have AIDS. I've never even been exposed to HIV. Nobody ever checked up on what turns out was a false positive three years ago. I'm . . . negative.'

There was a long silence.

Debbie said, 'Well, congratulations, Beth.'

'No – you don't understand,' Beth said. 'This disease is my *life*. I got off smack because of it. I stopped drinking. I found the Lord because of it. And I have all of you people as my friends because of it – and *it* is gone now. And I don't know what to do. There's nothing else in my life. I work as a croupier at Harrah's, and that's all there is to my life. Suddenly it's so small and I feel invisible. Last week I was fifty-foot tall brave survivor, and now I'm . . . a mosquito.'

Debbie said, 'Well, we're hardly going to kick you out of the group, and I can't think of anybody better suited than you to be a counselor.' The group made supportive noises, but Wade saw Beth leaving his life, almost as soon as she'd entered. 'For starters,' Debbie continued, 'maybe you can meet with Wade here and give him the drill on what's available to him here in Clark County.'

Ting! Debbie could only have been an angel. Afterwards over by the coffee maker, fellow group members swamped Beth;

Wade waited. When at last she came over to him, she said, 'Let's go to a Denny's. I'm starved.'

At the restaurant Wade tried making small talk, but failed. Instead Beth asked him, 'What's the sickest you've ever been yet?'

'How do you mean?'

'You know – PCP pneumonia? Viral meningitis?'

Wade couldn't believe the unromantic route the meal was taking. 'I've been pretty much asymptomatic.' Wade was glad he was able to respond with a medical term.

'Sorry to jump into symptoms like that. It's rude, but it's a habit I got into. I might as well ask for your T-cell count.' She looked at the menu. 'The chicken fingers here are good.'

They ordered, and then the waitress put their chicken fingers on the table. Wade went to reach for one, but Beth snapped, 'Grace.'

She made him hold hands with her. Wade could feel the skeleton inside her flesh; holding hands with her was like holding hands with Casper the Friendly Ghost, smooth and dry and almost not even there.

She said, 'Dear Lord, who gave us this day and who will give us all our tomorrows and eternity after that, we thank you for giving us our trials so that You may test our will, and we thank You for the days in which to make our wills manifest. This meal is Your bounty. We are Your servants, for forever and a day. Amen.'

Wade felt holy. He felt he was at home with a person he would choose to be his family. He ate a bite of chicken finger and burnt his tongue.

Three weeks after the dinner at Denny's, Wade moved in with Beth, whose religiosity had a blank spot when it came to shacking up. After the move, Wade was embarrassed by how few things he had, and by their overall shabbiness. When his possessions merged with Beth's possessions, his were all but erased, and this suited him fine. Beth's taste ran towards the slightly girly, the slightly wacky: pink sunflowers and a cow-shaped footstool – it was a pleasure to be absorbed into a kinder, less desperate world.

Beth's apartment complex was a run-down 1960s quickie, its superintendent a vagrant keno addict. Consequently, Wade was asked by Beth to do a fair number of household repairs. In all his years of smuggling and roguery, he'd never had to deal with such drab tasks as rewiring a lamp.

'Rewire the lamp?'

'Rewire the lamp.'

It crept up on Wade that whenever he picked up a screw-driver or putty knife, he automatically tensed his shoulders, waiting for his father's voice to call him useless or hopeless or a waste. Once he realized that the voice wasn't going to happen, he surprised himself with his own handiness. Beth had a long list of repairs, which suited Wade well – *immediate and gratifying results: a freshly painted wall; a door that no longer jammed; a properly wired stereo.*

One night, after Wade had spent twelve hours stripping and refinishing a small writing desk Beth had found at a garage sale, he was energized as though he'd awakened from a long and delicious sleep. His energy was contagious, and in bed Beth became playful and whimsical; normally in bed she was at her most serious, if not downright sad.

'You're my Superman, Wade.'

'Tell me again.'

'You're my handsome, dedicated Superman.'

'What are my superpowers?'

'*You* tell *me*. If you could have only one superpower, what would you choose?'

This question made Wade think. *The strength of a thousand men? X-ray vision? Superimmunity that would allow him to crawl through all the raw sewage of Mexico with no ill effects?*

'Hey, take your time, why don't you, honey.'

'I'm thinking, Beth. This is serious. I want to give the right answer.'

A minute passed. 'Wade?'

'OK, I know – my superpower – I'd be able to shoot lightning bolts out from my finger tips – great big Knowledge Network documentary bolts – and when a person was zapped by one of these bolts, they'd fall down on their knees and once on their knees, they'd be underwater, in this place I saw once off the east coast of the Bahamas, a place where a billion electric blue fish swam up to me and made me a part of their school – and then they'd be up in the air, up in Manhattan, above the World Trade Center, with a flock of pigeons, flying amid the skyscrapers, and then – and then what? And then they'd go blind, and then they'd be taken away – they'd feel homesick – more homesick than they'd felt in their entire life – so homesick they were throwing up – and they'd be abandoned, I don't know . . . in the middle of a harvested corn field in Missouri. And then they'd be able to see again, and from the edges of the field people would appear – everybody they'd known – and they'd be carrying Black Forest cakes and burning tiki lamps and boom boxes playing the same song, and the sky would turn into a sunset, the way it does in Walt Disney World brochures, and the person I zapped would never be alone or isolated again.'

He and Beth made love that night, separated by latex membranes in all the right places, minimizing saliva, but with an intimacy new to their relationship. Afterwards, Wade couldn't sleep, because he kept thinking about the people who'd show up on the edge of his own Missouri wheat field, and he thought of his family – about how messed-up they were – mentally and physically and emotionally. And Wade thought about all the other families he'd known and how they'd been messed-up as well: autism, lupus, schizophrenia, arthritis, alcoholism, too many secrets, words unspoken, bad choices, money problems . . . the list was infinite. Nobody escaped.

With that thought, he realized that his fortieth birthday had passed, that he was no longer young, and that he didn't mind.

Wade stared at the cracks in the gas station's tarmac, soft and chewy, like a brownie, ants crawling in and out like in a crazy art film. *I'm not alert enough; I'm not paying close enough attention. Dammit, I spend my whole life looking and looking and looking at the world, but I guarantee it, the moment I move my head away from this patch of tar will be the exact moment the earth cracks open – and if I'd been watching, for just that one second, I'd have seen the core of the planet, molten and white—*

Ted booted Wade in the rump. 'Hey, Lord Byron, go be a poet some other time. We've gotta haul ourselves out of here.'

Wade vomited. Again. *Not much left to come up. What did I eat today? Yogurt, a banana, trail mix—*

'Aw, Jesus, Wade—' Ted hosed him off.

Wade turned over and looked at his father's bright red face; Bryan was rubbing his shoulders, sunburnt and chewed-up by fire ants, and just recently scraped by Shw's having bounced him against the concrete. Bryan asked, 'Wade, are you OK?'

Wade sucked air in. 'No. I'm not OK. I'm actually busy sitting here dying.'

'Don't be such a melodramatic pussy,' said Ted.

'I'm not being melodramatic, Dad. As it turns out, yes, I'm dying – a slow, painful, ugly and frankly quite boring kind of death.'

'Bullcrap. Stand up. Bryan's nutcase girlfriend just drove away with my chance at money.'

Wade rolled up his pants, revealing lesioned skin that resembled a tablecloth covered in spilled red wine. Ted saw this and his face puckered up. 'OK already. Roll your pants legs down. Jesus. People will see.'

Wade was too tired to battle further. 'Bryan, where would Shw be driving – any ideas?'

Bryan asked, 'Where are we right now?'

'Don't sweat it,' Ted replied. 'Women always leave a clue. Wait – "clue" is the wrong word. What's one notch more obvious than a clue?'

Bryan suggested, 'A *hint*?'

Ted sprayed him with the hose. 'A hint is *less* obvious than a clue, stupid.'

'Call a taxi,' said Wade.

'To go where?' asked Ted.

'I know where we can find a car,' Wade said.

A cab was phoned while Wade went to the men's room to wash up. He was shivering, white and pink-eyed. The cab arrived and the driver asked where to go. Ted was in the front, Wade and Bryan in the back. Wade gave him the Brunswicks' address.

'Why there?' Bryan asked.

'That's where Howie's staying,' said Wade. 'Over at the Space Family Robinson's.'

Ted became brittle. 'I want *Howie* in my life right now like I want a hole in the head. The little suckhole.'

Bryan added, 'He always acts like he's so perfect. In high school he'd have been one of those guys who always smiles at you because he can't imagine somebody not liking him, except people *did* hate him.'

Ted said, 'Bryan, Jesus, stop festering over high school. You left the gee-dee place almost two decades ago.'

Bryan proved fierce: 'You always sided with the principal whenever I got caught doing stuff. Just leave me alone, OK? My body feels like I've been barbecued and I thought for once we could just be nice to one another and be like a real family.'

Ted bit his lip and made eyes with Wade, who said, 'I don't think it works that way, Bryan.'

'Why can't it?'

Ted snapped, 'Because your knocked-up girlfriend has my future inside a Ziploc bag in her trunk is why.'

'Bryan, I don't think she's going to abort.'

Bryan turned on Wade. 'How would *you* know?'

Wade told him about the episode the day before, about Shw showering to remove all traces of thalidomide from her body. Bryan's face became a living, morphing before-and-after photo. The cabbie, Wade noticed, couldn't help but listen in.

Ted asked, 'So what's the deal with this Florian guy in the Bahamas?'

'Here's the deal,' said Wade, 'I used to work for him a few years ago. He's the heir to a Swiss pharmaceutical fortune. He makes half the painkillers and pesticides on earth, but he's a total "I worship England" freak – his gardener told me his nanny used to diddle him every Sunday after church – so he lives in the Bahamas now, which is very English and also the shadiest place on earth – like a theme park of shade. People become caught up in the scene, but when they try to rejoin the rest of the world, it always looks so boring that they end up staying in the Bahamas. The place is like a drug. That, and from the Bahamas he can fly anywhere in the States any time he wants. Oh – there's also no taxes in the Bahamas.'

'There's always the tax thing,' said Ted.

'Yeah, Dad, like you're a high-flyer,' Wade said.

'Lay off me.'

'Do you want to know about Florian or not?'

Ted was quiet.

'Anyway, he's big on science. He really gets turned on by all this stuff his company cranks out, so he's not piddling away the company. He's actually a wicked businessman. If I had money, I'd invest in him.'

'How do *you* know him?'

'I used to do deliveries for him.'

'Deliveries? What – drugs and shit?'

The cabbie lurched to a halt at the side of the road, before a gang of prisoners on labor duty stripping the roadway sides of crushed pop tins, dead socks and crumpled-up cardboard french-fry containers. The lurch caused Bryan's right side to rub against the door, and he wailed in pain. The cabbie turned around, livid. 'If you people talk about drugs even once in this car, you're out on your butts. Got it?'

'Christ – yeah, we've got it. No need to foam.'

'Stop taking the name of the Lord in vain.'

'My back's hurting really bad,' said Bryan.

'We'll find you some ointment at Howie's house,' said Wade. The cabbie pulled onto the road and Wade then turned to Ted. 'No, Dad, I wasn't shipping *drugs*. It was plant specimens. Endangered and semi-endangered things from all over the States. For molecular studies. Or so I was told.'

'So *that's* what you were doing,' said Ted.

'What do you mean?'

'Your mother and I always tried to guess what you were doing after you took off like that. It always boiled down to smuggling.'

'I did other things, too.'

'Like what?'

'Forget it.'

They drove on without speaking. Wade figured they were three minutes away from Howie and the Brunswick family home. 'By the way, Howie is having a fling with Alanna Brunswick, so he's going to be acting all funny around me. Around you, too, I guess. Just so you know what's up.'

'You're kidding me.'

'No. Why would I? I caught them being all kissie-poo yesterday morning.'

'That sonofabitch. He's screwing around on Sarah?'

'Dad, you can't kill him. At least not until the shuttle lands.'

The cab pulled up at the Brunswicks', where a picnic was going full-force on the lawn, a garish space-themed tribute to one of the abundant Brunswick children. Parents were seated in folding chairs around the yard, eating noisily with their spawn. Howie was manning the barbecue, and when he saw Wade and Ted hop out of the cab, his face went blank.

Ted, in his one shoe, walked up to Howie. 'Howie, pay the cab driver.'

'Ted – I don't have my wallet on me – I . . .'

Ted poured a pitcher of lemonade on the grill, making a steam mushroom. 'Pay the cab driver.'

Howie stood silent for a moment. 'Will do.' He went to pay.

All eyes were then riveted on Ted, who paid no heed, his own eyes squinting meanly on Howie.

Wade walked over to the grill, as did Alanna, now fully clicked into cheerleader mode. She approached Ted as one would approach a *grrr*ing dog. 'You're Ted – I'm Alanna.'

Ted grunted.

Alanna looked down at the last whispers of steam lapping up from the grill. 'I see you didn't like our little barbecue . . .'

'Don't push it, lady,' Ted said under his breath.

He turned around; Bryan was in the wading pool, with his body covered up with soaking towels to preclude more sunburn. One of the children started to cry. Howie came back from the taxi. 'Looks like we could use some fresh lemonade, Alanna.'

Ted said, 'Give me the keys to your van, Howie.'

'Hey, father-in-law, why don't you join our party?' Howie giggled nervously.

'I'd love to join your party, Howie, but if I did I'd probably have a drink, and if I had a drink I'd start talking in a loud, graphic way about how you and the missus here are humping each other like a pair of Dobermans.'

'You wouldn't do that,' said Howie.

'I wouldn't, would I?'

'No. You wouldn't. Because Sarah would find out, and she'd go up into outer space as if you'd taken a big staple gun and gone at her heart a hundred times. As far as I can see, she's the only thing in your life that's sacred. The one solitary single thing. Hey – that's pretty pathetic, when you think about it.' He smiled. 'Turkey burger?'

Ted obviously hadn't expected balls from Howie and was temporarily quiet. Alanna looked at Ted, then to Howie. 'So it seems things are hunk-dory here.'

'I think so,' said Howie. 'Ted here is about to help relight the barbecue.'

'I need Tylenol,' said Wade.

Howie said, 'Up in the bathroom. You know where it is.'

Wade went upstairs and showered. Drying off, as though some prankster in another dimension had flipped a switch, his energy suddenly surged – he felt great, like a teenager headed out to vandalize on a Friday night. *God, I love it when this happens. I used to be like this all the time – like a poseable action figure: GI Joe with Kung-Fu Grip – I am going to see my kid grow up!*

Wade's energy came in surges that could vary in length from hours to weeks, and these surges seemed unrelated to any known form of cause and effect. They simply came.

He looked at his soaked, dirty, oily clothes and decided he couldn't be bothered to pick them up – *wait a second . . . I'm too lazy to pick up the laundry – my energy really is back!*

Wade faced yet another messy wardrobe change at the Brunswicks'. He looked out of the bathroom and saw what was probably the guestroom. *Locked.* A piece of coat-hanger took care of that, and he entered what proved to be the room assigned to his brother-in-law for the weeks leading up to the launch. He rifled through Howie's personal effects, cozied inside a wicker duck that had once held gift soaps. *Hey, hey, my, my – Volkswagen keys!* He then sifted through Howie's cupboard and selected a nondescript shirt and pants – *should events ever reach the police ID lineup stage I don't want to be too memorable-looking.*

On Howie's bedside phone he then dialed directory assistance for the Bahamas and asked for the number of Buckingham Pest Control, Florian's shopfront in Nassau. He soon connected to a profoundly disinterested female Bahamian voice: 'Buckingham Pest Control.'

'Hi, I'd like to leave a message for Florian.'
'Uh-huh.'
'It's Wade Drummond. I used to mow his cricket field.'
'Mmmm.'
'A few years ago.'
'Mmmm.' The voice at the other end might just as well have been a patient on a respirator.
'Tell him I have a message from his *mother*. A letter.'
'Mmmm.'
'He'll be very interested to know about it.'
'Mmmm.'
'Make sure he gets the news.'
'Uh-huh.'
'I'll call back in a few hours with instructions.'
He hung up. Then he brushed his hair and loped down the stairs onto the front lawn, where Howie was all smiles; Ted stood glaring at the guests like a bulldog on a chain. 'Dad, let's go.'
'I'm going to kill Howie.'
'Wait until Sarah's in orbit. Besides—' He held up a key. 'I have a key.' He walked over to Bryan lying in the wading pool, face up. 'Bryan, get out of there. And bring a big towel to cover yourself.'
Bryan snatched a Tweety Bird in Space towel, and the three men walked over to Howie's van. Wade got into the driver's seat. Howie was frozen with indecision as Wade leaned out. 'Howie! Thanks for letting us use your van! I told Sarah we'd have it back to you in an hour. She's right, man – you're the nicest guy in Florida.'

The year was 1970-something, and Wade and Janet were in a pet store to buy white mice for Sarah's pet snake, Omar.
'Mom, was Dad always a prick?'
'Wade!'
'Well, was he?'

'Look for good mice, Wade.' Sarah was returning that evening from a school field trip to a Portland science Olympics; the mice were a surprise.

'Those ones there,' Janet said, 'They look . . .'

'Juicier?'

'I suppose.'

'Mom, I think snakes prefer "crunchy" over "juicy".'

'They do not.'

Wade watched his mother smile. He said, 'Juicy mice take too long to go through the length of the snake. Juiciness is constipating.'

'Wade!'

'You didn't answer my question about when Dad started being a jerk.'

'He used to be nice, you know. Fun. He was *fun*.'

'Har-de-har-har.'

A clerk walked over. 'Looking for feeder mice?'

'Yeah,' said Wade. 'A dozen.'

'Those ones there,' Janet said, pointing to the fat ones. 'Are they more expensive than the regular ones?'

'Yup. They're pregnant, so they're a buck more.'

Wade and Janet *ee-yoo*'ed in unison. The clerk said they could upgrade to nonpregnant hamsters for only $1.25.

'Just the mice,' said Wade. 'Unpregnant. A dozen.'

'How could anybody feed pregnant mice to a snake?' asked Janet, more to herself than to elicit any real answer.

'What I can't figure out is why don't they just eat hamburger?'

The clerk spoke up: 'No good without a kill. The kill releases enzymes to aid in digestion. You can't kill hamburger.'

'Oh dear,' said Janet. 'I never would have believed buying mice was so hard.'

As the clerk gathered mice, mother and son walked over to the bird section, shrill and hot, rife with the sharp phosphate zing of guano. Wade looked at the budgies and wondered how such a toy of a creature could ever have existed in the wild. *It's like the poodle of the bird world.* Wade tried to imagine small white poodles hunting alongside cavemen. He spoke up: 'You said Dad used to be fun once. When? Prove it.'

'When he was younger. When I met him in university. He was so unstuffy. He'd say *anything*, and I've always liked that in people, maybe because I'm such a wallflower myself.'

'What's a wallflower?'

'You know. Those girls who stand along the walls at school dances who never get asked to dance.'

'You?'

'Nobody ever told me how to pluck my eyebrows. Until university I looked like a female East German weight-lifter from the 1960s.'

'You did *not*. I've seen pictures.'

'I used to be so passive. I'd never think of asking a man to dance with me.'

A cage of budgies erupted into a bout of squabbling over what appeared to be territorial rights to the perch beside the tiny mirror. Janet said, 'Your father was sort of like Helena. She's so outrageous. Helena drove my parents batty. So did Ted, but not as much as Helena did.'

'Hmmm.' Wade found Helena disturbing; he'd caught her sizing him up in the kitchen a few weeks before. She was, even to his as-of-then presexual eye, dangerous. She'd looked at Wade, narrowed her eyes and said, 'You're *just* like your father. You try to pretend you're not, but you are. You little *faker*.'

Wade returned to the moment. 'But we were talking about Dad – do you have, like, *any* proof that he isn't a jerk?'

'I just don't understand why the two of you can't get along. You're both so much alike, you know.'

Wade froze. 'No. No *way* are we alike.' *Uh-oh.*

'Struck a nerve, did I?'

Had she? 'He drinks too much.'

'Drinks too much?' Janet looked puzzled. 'He drinks as much as any other man his age.'

'What does that prove?'

'I don't know what you're implying, Wade. Everybody drinks.'

The mice were ready at the counter. Janet paid. In the car driving home, Wade looked in on the mice, scampering about the bottom of a picnic cooler. 'Uh-oh—'

'What?' asked Janet.

'We've got a deadie.' He lifted a dead mouse up by the tail.

'Wade, get that thing out of the car immediately.'

Wade placed the dead mouse in the vest pocket of his down coat. 'I'm not going to just throw it out. It's not an apple core or litter. It was a living creature.'

'Stick it in the compost out back when we get home.'

Back at the house, Wade went to Sarah's bedroom. 'Hey, Omar, time for your delicious mousy treat.'

From behind him, Janet said, 'No. Let him build up his appetite so when Sarah feeds him, he jumps on it.'

'Mom, you have a twisted side.'

'Wade, any mother will give you the same answer. Why do you think we always eat so late in this house? I want the food I serve you to be *eaten*.'

An hour or so later, Ted came home from work just as Sarah was dropped off by her science teacher. Ted carried Sarah up to the house on his shoulders. She was beaming: 'Oh, *Daddy*!'

'You won, honey, you're my little winner. Look, Jan – three trophies!'

A small buzz of activity ensued as Sarah relayed tales of bridges built of macaroni holding fifteen-pound payloads; a lens that burned paper from across a room; frogs that were flash-frozen in baths of liquid nitrogen and then sprung back to life. Wade brought in the cooler containing the mice.

'Wade! You're my hero – Omar's going to love these mice. Have you been feeding him properly?'

'Oh, yeah.'

Ted opened the liquor cabinet door and removed his favorite brand of rye, which he then poured into a tumbler. He made puzzled sounding noises. 'What the—?' He slammed the bottle down on the counter. 'Come here, you little creep.'

'What's wrong, Ted?'

'There's a dead fucking mouse in the rye bottle.'

Wade looked at Sarah with conspiring eyes, and Sarah said, 'Dad, the alcohol in the rye will have sterilized the mouse. It's perfectly drinkable.'

Ted ignored this and grabbed Wade by the collar, busting his puka shell necklace and sending the small beads around the kitchen.

'Put me down, you alcoholic goon.'

Ted tossed him out the kitchen doorway into the hall.

'Oh,' said Wade, 'I guess that's supposed to prove you're not an alcoholic? Well, you *are* – you're a goddamn drunk and it's the worst-kept secret in Vancouver.'

Sarah stood up and barricaded the door with her arms. Nothing in the world would make Ted lay a finger on Sarah. 'Dad, the mouse is Wade's idea of a joke. Laugh, OK?'

'That little—'

'Stop.' Sarah turned around to Wade. 'Wade, the mouse is dead, so Omar's not going to eat it. You owe me a mouse.'

'But it died on the way home from the store,' said Janet.

'Oh,' said Sarah. 'Then we're even steven. C'mon. Let's go feed Omar.'

The three men headed down to Kissimmee in the orange van. Traffic was a mess and they lost nearly half an hour at the tollbooth scraping together $1.25 in change. Bryan's skin was flaring up in an ominous uniform bubble-gum pink color, and Ted stubbed his unshod toe on the van's running board just as they found their final nickel. When they arrived in Kissimmee, the shadows of the local cypress trees, cycads, grapefruit trees and Washingtonia palms were lengthening; the men were cranky and bored, and without a plan as to how to locate Shw. Wade looked at Ted's opulent borrowed lodgings and hooted, 'Viva Las Vegas!'

'Shut up. It's free.'

Inside the front hallway was a fountain. A shiny curlicued celebration of the brassmonger's craft. A peeing cupid supplied sound effects.

Bryan asked, 'When's Nickie back?'

'Hell if I know. She's out. Not spending money. I hope.'

Bryan went right upstairs to soak in a cool bath. Ted went to change into fresh clothes. Wade checked out the fridge: a family-pack of forty-eight hot dog wieners and a four-gallon tub of salsa. *I didn't even know salsa came in sizes that big*. In an instant he was ravenous. He stuck six hot dogs in the microwave and over by the sink dug into the salsa tub with an opened bag of tortilla chips. The microwave *ping*ed and Wade grabbed the hot dogs, sending them into his stomach only partially chewed. He missed being hungry and he loved the ability to slake the hunger so easily and pleasurably, like sex.

Wade heard water running upstairs and the taps rattling. Full, he sat on a kitchen chair. Ted walked into the kitchen. 'I need a rye. You want one?' He pulled a bottle out from a cupboard. 'I still inspect my bottles for dead mice, you asshole.'

'We have to go to the hotel. I need my pills.'

'Relax. We'll be there soon enough. I hope that mental case Shwoo or whatever her name is has left us a clue at the hotel. Or she doesn't dump the car in the Everglades.'

'Dad – if I don't take my pills, then my insides get twice as bad as they were before.'

Ted stared at Wade; Wade sensed that this was the first time Ted was acknowledging his disease on an adult level. 'OK. I'll get Bryan, we can stop by the hotel so you can load up on pills. And then we should go to the hospital and find him something to numb his skin. He's like a pig on a spit.' Ted was about to leave the room, but turned around. 'Shouldn't you call that kraut Florian guy again?'

Wade checked his watch. 'Good idea. He ought to be pretty hungry by now.' Wade dialed and once again got the bored woman, but the line died a few seconds into the call, and when he tried again, he couldn't reconnect. 'It's no big deal,' he said to Ted. 'The Bahamas are connected to the U.S. by a fishing line and a lot of wishful thinking.'

Bryan came downstairs, so pink that Wade wondered how white people ever got called white. They drove to the Peabody hotel and once up in the room Ted caught the scent of Nickie's perfume. 'What the hell?'

Bryan was prowling through Wade's shaving kit for Tylenol; Wade again dialed the Bahamas, but got the same useless connection that died after five seconds. The men then drove to the local hospital, where staff saw Bryan, recognized his condition immediately and plopped him onto a gurney, only to spend a half hour examining his insurance history before electing to treat him as a patient. In the end he received various injections, plus a prescription for painkillers and some ointment, which was paid for with the last hundred dollars remaining on Bryan's MasterCard.

Bryan was lying on the gurney, blissed out on painkillers, when Wade and Ted looked across the hotel's emergency room and saw Janet and Nickie.

What the hell? 'Mom?'

'Wade? Ted? What are you doing here?' She saw Bryan. 'Dear God!' She ran over to Bryan.

Ted said, 'Cool your jets. It's just a sunburn. He's in LaLa Land at the moment. More to the point, what are *you two* doing here? And was that your perfume I smelled up in the hotel room, Nix?'

'Yes, Ted, it was. Janet and I are having a lesbian romance. You can't deny us our forbidden love.'

'Very funny.'

Janet said, 'We were involved in a restaurant holdup this morning. We came here to see the waiter who was shot. We just arrived.'

'Holdup?' said Wade.

'We're fine. Shw was there, too.'

The men's ears perked up at the sound of Shw's name. 'Really now?'

'I honestly wonder if that woman is evil,' Janet said. 'She's selling the baby to some auto parts magnate in Daytona Beach. Selling the baby! Ted, we're going to have to put our differences aside and hire some lawyers on this one.'

'Daytona Beach . . .' said Wade.

'Did you get the guy's name?' Ted asked.

'No. Why?'

'Ted? Wade?'

'Is she headed there now, you think?' asked Wade.

'Who knows. Probably.'

Wade and Ted swapped looks. 'Mom,' said Wade, 'we have to go.'

'Go where?'

'Long story.' Already Wade was halfway to the automatic doors, as Ted dragged Bryan off the gurney.

'Ted . . .' called Nickie.

'Can't talk now, Nix – we have to go.'

And in a blink they were gone.

17

Janet and Nickie walked through the emergency room doors, a swoosh of hot night air blasting their faces. Across the lot the three men were barreling away in Howie's orange van – with no Howie inside. Wade burned some rubber as they left the lot, making Janet turn to Nickie: 'How do men *do* that? I've been driving for forty years and I've never once burned rubber.'

Back inside the hospital they learned that Kevin's condition was stable and that he was sleeping. The two women bought a stack of pinkish silver Mylar balloons and a sympathy card and placed them beside his bed. A nurse asked if Janet and Nickie were family. Janet said, 'No, but—'

The nurse zipped her finger up to her lips: '*Shhhhhh!* Don't tell me anything more. I don't know who you are in this guy's life, but this guy is taking some serious meds. We don't know who to contact, and someone has to go to his place and get his stuff. Could you do that?'

'Sure.'

The nurse handed Janet a Post-It with an address on the back copied from a driver's license. 'And here are keys that were in his pocket. One of them ought to do the trick.'

The two women elevatored downstairs. Janet said, 'You know, this was supposed to be a happy family week that drew us all closer – all that NASA hokum: prayer breakfasts, zodiac boat tours through swamps, a chance encounter with a Kennedy family member . . . And you wouldn't *believe* the other astronaut families. They're practically astronauts themselves – shoes buffed like mirrors; too many teeth; half of them are military and talk in barking Navy SEALs voices. They drive me nuts, they're so enthusiastic. Our own family is a disaster.'

Nickie said, 'I doubt it. People are pretty forgiving when it comes to other people's family. The only family that ever horrifies you is your own. Hey – do you get along with Sarah?'

'Sarah? I think so. Yes.'

'What do you mean you "think so".'

'The two of us have never actually had a fight, per se.'

'I don't believe you.'

'Then don't. But I'm serious. Not one in nearly forty years.'

'Then why do you say you *think* you get along?'

'Sarah's always been Ted's baby. I was so scared and frightened when she was born. Ted wasn't. He leapt in. He's stronger than me in some ways. He saw a spark in Sarah that I didn't. I feel ashamed of that.' Janet looked down into her lap and said, 'Sarah sees something in my eyes; I don't know what it is – but she's always held back with me. *Nicely*, mind you, but she's never truly opened up to me. Ever.'

Nickie was quiet.

After deliberating over a map, the two women drove to Kevin's neighborhood. The night air was dark and floral, oily and infected. Janet saw a flock of birds off to the right and realized what a rare thing it is to see birds after sundown. They passed a black Mercedes with an engine fire, and a pile of lemons sitting at the roadside for no apparent reason.

Florida.

Minutes later the women were in a trailer park in the northwest section of Orlando. 'Welcome to Kevin's house,' said Nickie, as they opened the door to the gently listing trailer. Janet sat at a kitchen table, one of its legs propped up by a pile of unopened bills stained with coffee and cigarette burns. She looked at photos inside $5.95 WalMart frames, mostly Kevin clowning with his friends amid bits and pieces of Disney characters in mid-mock copulation – a cast party? There was also a field of magnetized words on the fridge door.

'These magnet-word thingies drive me crazy,' said Nickie.

'How come?' Nickie was pouring herself a grapefruit juice; Janet was jealous because grapefruit juice was off limits – its acidity burned her gums.

'Nobody ever makes anything good with them. But people never throw them out, either.'

Both women's eyes landed on a beefcake calendar by the phone. 'It's so faggy in here,' said Nickie. 'What a riot.'

'Let's just retrieve the pills. I'm sleepy. I want to go to bed.'

They found two dozen bottles of Kevin's pills, which they placed in a supermarket bag. Nickie dropped off Janet at the Peabody then left to deliver the cache.

Janet yearned only for a quick shower and sleep, but upstairs she opened the room's door to find Beth wearing panties and a singlet, well into a series of cocktails, and quite snippy. The room smelled like a steakhouse.

'Where's Wade?' asked Janet. 'And what's that smell?' She saw two fully disemboweled room service trolleys.

'The crap I tolerate from your son – *Jesus*. He dumps me to go to DisneyfuckingWorld, and so I waste the day piddling around the tourist traps. When I get back there's a guy from Budget Car Rental on the phone and it turns out he wrecked my car – my credit's trashed for ever now, thank you – and then he takes off with that moron ex of yours, and Bryan.'

She is drunk. She is random. Play this carefully, Janet.

'I see.'

'Then he goes and leaves some lame message on the machine about having to do some work for *Norm*.'

'Norm?'

'One of Wade's old lowlife pals. Owns a baseball team or something. He radiates darkness as the sun radiates light.' Beth opened a minibar bottle of tequila. 'You know you're scraping the dregs of the minibar when you drink the tequila.' She poured it into half a glass of water, took a sip and then looked at the carpet. 'Wade is lost. It's hell for him.'

'Well, whatever. Who ate all the food?'

'I did – steak – not just one order, but *two*.'

The notion of steak being somehow . . . *swanky* struck Janet as dated and sad.

'Wait until he sees the room bill,' Beth said. 'He'll shit.'

'Yes, well, won't he, though?'

Janet had little patience for drunks, but saw this as an excellent opportunity to milk answers to a few lingering questions. 'Beth, you must be excited about the baby.'

'Yeah.' Beth looked stubborn.

'Maybe you could drink something other than alcohol. Can I get you a juice from the minibar?'

'No. My mother was pickled when I was a bun in the oven. A drink here tonight isn't going to make a whiff of difference.' Her grip on the glass tightened.

Janet said, 'You seem worried.'

'Wade's going be dead and in hell, and I'm going to be alone with another mouth to feed.'

'Why is Wade going to die?'

'You're cursed just like him. You have the same mark.'

'The same *mark?* Beth, Wade and I have a chronic but manageable condition, as did you until recently, I might add.'

Beth spat out some air, and her head sagged slightly as the alcohol slackened her muscles.

'OK, tell me, Beth, what does your family have to say about your pregnancy? Wade's told me nothing about them.'

'My family might as well be dead. Their brains are like moldy bread. Booze.'

'Beth, you're drunk and this conversation is going nowhere. Today's been too long and I just don't have the energy to suss it out of you. I'm going to bed.'

Janet went to her suitcase and removed her nightie, and was heading into the bathroom when Beth said, 'He has lesions on his shins. Big ones. Lots of them. And on his calves.'

Janet stopped and turned around. 'When?'

'Two months now. His legs look like Gorbachev's head.'

'I see.'

'It's the beginning of the end.'

'No, it isn't. There are medications for KS lesions now.'

'Janet—' Beth was suddenly clear. '—they're not working.'

Janet sat down on a chair by the bathroom door. 'I'm sorry I snapped at you.'

'I deserved a snapping.'

'Does he talk about being sick?'

'Wade? What do you think?'

'I guess not.'

Beth pleaded exhaustion and fell asleep in minutes with the TV on local news. Janet shrouded the two room service trolleys with their own white linen sheets, rolled them into the hallway, and then prepared her couch for sleeping. Beth snored like a garburator, and in spite of the day's frenzies Janet had insomnia. At 4:00 A.M. she saw the blinking red message light on the phone. As Wade had done the night before, she checked to see what the message might be.

> Wade? Are you there? What's going on? I'm on my coffee break again. Alanna says you, Dad and Bryan came and took Howie's van – naughty, naughty. And then a few hours later these two guys rang the doorbell and took Howie away with them, but NASA says it has no idea who would have picked him up, so . . .
>
> I also haven't heard from Mom today, and she's pretty good about calling, so maybe something's up there, too. All this Drummond drama. The Brunswick family probably played Scrabble until sunup, except they would have pulled a stunt to make it more challenging, like removing half the vowels.
>
> Well, big brother, you may well be asking how did I spend my day? Thank you for inquiring. Highlights in-

cluded checking agar emulsions used to bind skin cells for zero-G cloning, a test drill of a new depressurization protocol and a modification of the strap-on peeing device which was slightly embarrassing.

Wade! Call me! I'm sitting here – you're not going to believe this, but yes, I'm on my coffee break and I'm drinking coffee!

'Bye.

Sarah had left a number and Janet called it immediately. 'Sarah?'

'Mom – you're up so late.'

'I couldn't sleep.'

'Hey – what's going on over there?'

Where to begin? 'Do you have a few minutes? Sit down, honey.' Janet informed Sarah about the day's chain of dramas – about Nickie; the holdup (minimizing the graphic details); Shw and her blood-soaked fifties; the baby-buyer in Daytona Beach; the men at the hospital; the trip to Kevin's trailer; Beth's boozing and religious yo-yoing. 'So there you go.'

'I think I need a minute to digest this.'

'Take your time, dear.' Janet made herself more comfortable on the chair and had a sip of water.

'You sound a bit better tonight,' said Sarah.

'My cankers and ulcers have calmed down.'

'That's good news, Mom. I'm glad to hear it.'

'Sarah—?'

'Yeah, Mom?'

'It's about my ulcers in my mouth—'

'Uh-huh?'

'They didn't just go away on their own.'

'No? Are you taking a new medication?'

'As a matter of fact, yes.'

'Oh. What is it?'

Janet heard a bell go off somewhere in the background of

Sarah's phone. *I owe my daughter honesty:* 'I'm using thalidomide, Sarah.'

No response.

'Sarah?'

'I heard you.'

'Sarah, there was nothing else left to take. And I have to ferret out the entire Internet just to obtain it from countries like Brazil and Paraguay.'

'It's OK, Mom.'

'And . . .'

'Mom, stop it, OK?'

'I've been so worried these past few weeks . . .'

Sarah changed the subject: 'Did Wade and Howie have a fight yesterday? Or today or something?'

Janet had to think a second. 'I have no idea. Yesterday Howie picked Wade up at the jail, but that's all I know.'

'Alanna was sounding weird when I spoke on the phone with her earlier tonight. There were words going unsaid.'

'With Wade it could be anything, Sarah.'

'I think Howie and Alanna are having an affair.'

'What?'

'They are.'

'How can you say that?'

'Well, it's true.'

'You have no evidence.'

'Stop defending him!'

Janet thought she was slipping into dementia. She'd never heard Sarah speak to her like this. *Oh, geez Louise, that goddamn thalidomide went and busted the dam open.* 'You're imagining things, Sarah.'

'I'm not, and don't *you* go telling me what to feel or think.'

'But I'm *not* telling you—' *Suddenly at thirty-nine, Sarah's acting like a teenager.*

'I only ever married Howie because he was smart and good-looking.'

'What's wrong with—' *What on earth is going on here?* 'Why are you telling me this?'

'You think I don't know what a bore he is? Or how pompous? He's like a King Charles spaniel back from the groomers half the time. But I thought he was good breeding stock, and I guess he figured he'd rise faster through the ranks if he married me – which proved to be the case. So I guess we both got what we wanted.'

'You said breeding stock. Are you pregnant?' Janet wondered if the dismay she felt at having no grandchildren had leaked into her voice, possibly mocking Sarah.

Sarah quickly replied, 'No.' After a pause, she added, 'You know, I have to *live* with him. Imagine that – Funsville, huh? *Sarah, did you know the tire pressure is down on your Toyota? Sarah, I think they've changed paper stock on the* Journal – *I'm going to write them a letter to complain* – It never ends with him.'

'No marriage is perfect, Sarah.'

'Well, ours is – I don't know – freezer-burnt.'

'I thought you—'

'Think again.'

Janet tried to regroup her emotions. Stay calm. 'This is because I told you about the thalidomide. You'd never have spoken like this to me otherwise.'

'What if it is? I can't believe you actually sought the stuff out – hunted for it – the worst molecule in the universe. If—'

'Sarah, *stop* – stop right now.'

Sarah's voice went calm. 'Mom, if you'd known beforehand – excuse the pun, would you have had me?'

'Sarah, how can you—'

'Well?'

'It was a different era. We—'

'Stop right there, Mom. A simple "no" would have been sufficient.'

'Sarah, don't do this to me.'

'My coffee break's over. I have to suit up now. 'Bye.'

'Sarah?'

Janet cradled the empty telephone to her ear, which stung as though slapped; her head was a helium balloon, and she was unable even to hear her own thinking. She'd never meant to cause harm and yet she'd brought harm. This was the conversation she'd had in her mind for decades, and she'd botched it horribly.

Suddenly – *oh, God – my family. I have to be near my family.* The need to be with her two sons was so intense, so purely chemical, like a fast-acting pill.

Inside the hotel room, Beth snored away. Janet silently packed up her meds and cosmetics case, her few garments, tossed them into her suitcase and headed down to the parking lot. *I can't go to NASA but I can go to – Daytona Beach. My boys! My children! I'm alone – I can't bear this. Lift me up. Hold my weight. Don't leave me feeling like this*

Janet drove east, but mixed up her highways and got lost. At five A.M. she found herself in the parking lot of a pleasant little shopping plaza that wished nobody harm. It was a few miles south of Cape Canaveral, in the NASA bedroom community of Cocoa Beach; she'd had to park there when her insomnia hit the wall, and she lay down in the backseat to sleep, her hastily packed suitcase acting as pillow; a map of Flagler, Orange and Volusia Counties screening her eyes from early morning sunlight. She was awakened by a bleeping FTD delivery van reversing into a florist's delivery way.

Where are my children?

Wade and Bryan were probably headed to Daytona Beach, and Sarah was most likely asleep within the titanium bowels of the space shuttle gantry. *Sarah!* Janet sprang fully awake. *Oh, geez, we fought.* Her head stung. She had to go to the bathroom and she was hungry. Rumpled and feeling muzzy, she spotted a downmarket fast-food chain across the lot and walked there, used the bathroom, and took her medication. She then went out to the counter area, only to find . . . Wade and Bryan, *Good Lord!* The two men were bickering about the menu board. Wade looked gaunt, while Bryan looked like a pink sunburnt scarecrow.

'Boys?'

'Mom?'

Janet wrapped her arms around them both. Her eyes welled up.

'Mom – what's happened?' Wade and Bryan were sharpened with worry.

'It's Sarah—'

Her two sons froze. 'What about Sarah – Mom, what happened?'

'We had a fight.'

Wade said, 'You had a fight?'

Janet grabbed a napkin and blew her nose. 'I've never had a fight with her in my life and then, last night—'

Wade said, 'Wait a sec – she's OK, right? She's not dead or something? The mission's not canceled?'

'No.'

The two men slumped their shoulders with relief. Wade said, 'Mom, let's talk about this in a second. First, are you hungry?'

'I'm starving.'

'Let's buy you breakfast then.'

Bryan asked, 'What do you feel like?'

'Pancakes,' said Janet. 'Fifty pancakes.'

They placed an order and the cashier asked for money. 'Mom,' Wade asked, 'do you have any money?'

'Yes, of course I do.' She opened her purse and divvied out singles to the cashier. 'Don't you have any money, either of you?'

'Well, actually, no.'

Janet paused. 'Wait – how were you going to pay for your food?'

'We, um—' Wade fidgeted.

'We were going to eat and run,' Bryan said.

'You *what*?'

'We're broke.'

'Where's your father?'

'He's in the car around the side of the building.'

'Boys, how *could* you?' The food arrived, and Janet looked at her sons. 'You're both *men*, for God's sake.'

'We're starving,' said Bryan. 'We spent the night sleeping on the beach.'

Wade added, 'We could have slept in the van, except Bryan sloshed gasoline all over the inside.'

'I didn't *mean* to, Wade.'

'Hey, Mom,' Wade said, his radar for the unusual finely attuned, 'what about you? I mean, what are *you* doing in a dive like this in Cocoa Beach at 8:00 A.M. in the morning, for that matter?'

'I was looking for you two. You're on the way to Daytona, right? Right?'

Her sons looked guilty.

'So I was right. What matters is, all I wanted was to find the two of you, and I did.'

Their food was on the counter. 'Come on, guys, let's sit down.' Wade pointed them to a booth, the table top of which was sprinkled with dandruffy sugar particles and coffee rings. 'Let's eat.'

They unwrapped and deboxed their breakfasts as Ted came in. 'What the hell?'

'Hi, Dad,' said Bryan. 'Have a seat.'

He looked at Janet with surprise and curiosity. 'What are *you* doing here? When did you—?' He then looked down at the food. 'Christ, who cares. I'm starving.' He sat down. 'Which one of these things has the least fat in it?'

'Ted, this is fast food,' Janet said. 'Even the ice cubes contain fat.'

'Right.' He opened a box and inserted an entire English muffin into his gullet.

Wade said, 'Jesus, Dad, you aren't Omar the snake. Chew your food, why don't you?'

There was a quiet patch, after which Janet said, 'Well, fellas, I'm so glad to see you're all so interested in my nearly being shot yesterday in the restaurant holdup.'

The men erupted into apology. *It's not that they're unable to care – it's that it never crosses their minds to do so. They're so unlike women.*

Janet spent the next while telling the three men about the restaurant holdup. One she'd finished, Wade and Bryan leaned back and whistled. Ted was silent. This was more sympathy than she'd received from anybody in years. *Well, at least they all seem to be kind of happy I'm still here.*

Ted's cell phone had no juice, so he went to the pay phone to call Nickie, but he returned shortly. 'No one there. I left a message saying everything's fine.' He sat down and resumed eating his breakfast dregs.

Bryan had been buying fresh coffees. Sitting down at the table again, he said, 'Mom, what about the big fight you had with Sarah?'

On hearing this, Ted shot a semichewed English muffin onto the soiled laminate tabletop. 'You *what*?'

Janet said, 'We had a fight, Ted.'

'What do you *mean* you had a fight? You two don't fight.'

Janet rolled her eyes; Wade said, 'Dad, shut up and eat.' Wade then turned to his brother: 'Don't discuss this while *he's* around.'

Ted persevered: 'You and Sarah have never had a fight, *ever*.'

'There's a first time for everything, Ted.'

'What was the fight about?'

Janet refused to answer.

Ted said, 'Oh, the *silent treatment*. I see.'

'Yes, Ted,' said Janet. 'I'm going to sit here and simmer away. Simmer, simmer, simmer, simmer. Bryan, could you pass me a salt packet?' She nibbled at a cold hash brown patty. She said, 'I hear you had a lovely al fresco sleep on the beach.'

'Dumb-dumb slopped gasoline inside the van. Sand flies bit me all night.'

Bryan said, 'At least the sand was cool for my sunburn.'

Janet said, 'Won't Howie be thrilled to hear of the adventures you're having in his van.' This garnered conspiratory giggles. She lowered her coffee onto the table. 'You know, I was going to ask the three of you what you're doing with Howie's van and sleeping on a beach en route to Daytona Beach, but you know what? I've decided it's probably for the best that I don't know.'

Bryan said, 'Dad flipped Beth's rental car yesterday – totally wrote the thing off. Hey – guess what – Shw's going to keep the baby!'

'Lovely,' said Janet. She looked at Wade and raised her eyebrows: *Does Bryan know about the impending baby sale?* Wade shook his head: *No.*

Bryan continued recapping: '. . . and then we had to walk to the nearest gas station, but Shw saw us and picked us up and made us ride in the trunk of her car.'

'You don't say.'

'Numb-nuts got sunburned walking on the freeway,' Ted added, 'hence our brief visit in the hospital last night.'

'My, *my*.'

The men had stopped by the hotel to pick up Wade's pills, then drove towards Daytona Beach, but took the wrong exit somewhere along the way and then ran out of gas. With no money between them, they spent the night on the beach.

'Aren't you all so clever.' She was waiting for a lull in the discussion so she could ask a set of questions: *Why do you have Howie's van? Where did Howie go? Why is finding that grotesque little Shw creature so important to the three of you?* Cheerfully colored greasy litter lay strewn across their booth's counter. 'Mom,' said Wade, 'I need money.'

Janet's expression indicated not a whiff of surprise.

'If you could lend us a little, it'd be great,' said Wade. 'We need to do this road trip, and otherwise we'll probably keep on doing stupider and stupider things until one of us ends up in the U.S. jail system again, and won't that be a treat?'

'I want to hear about your fight with Sarah,' Ted said. 'What happened?'

Janet's guard was down: 'If you must know, I told her I was taking thalidomide for my mouth ulcers. I felt I owed that much truth to her.'

The flesh of Ted's face leapt away from his skull. 'You're taking *thalidomide?* Tell me I didn't hear you say that, oh, *Jesus.*'

'Ted, shut up. It's not like I'm going to get myself knocked up.'

'Putting that shit into your body is evil. They should take every last molecule of that vile crap and burn it.'

Ted's depth of feeling on the subject took Janet aback. 'Ted, I don't see why *you* have to be so rattled over this.'

'You wouldn't. Oh, Jesus.'

'I'm not going to tell you any more, then.'

'There's more?'

'Yes, there's more. She asked me if I would have . . . aborted her if I'd known about her hand. I didn't blast out the word "no" right away. I was obviously *going* to say "no", but I was just speaking the way I normally speak, but then she took offense and—'

'And *what?*'

'She hung up. That's all.'

'My little girl's about to go into space, and you tell her you never wanted her in the first place.'

'Don't be an idiot, Ted. You know that's not the case.'

'I do, do I? Since when are you a mind reader?'

Their voices were escalating. Wade grabbed Janet and said, 'Let's go, Mom.' They walked out the door, Bryan acting as a shield from Ted, who followed them outside, continuing to berate Janet.

'How could you do that to her?'

'I didn't do *anything* to her, Ted. It's in her mind.' They were now out in the parking lot beside the orange van.

'You were never close to her,' said Ted. 'You never opened up to her. You were cold.'

Janet stopped in her tracks and turned around. 'I beg your pardon?'

'You heard me,' said Ted. 'You felt guilty about her hand. You felt ashamed—'

'How dare you even *think* of accusing me of—'

Wade stepped in. 'Dad, you apologize to Mom. *Now.*'

'No. I won't. Because it's true. Look at her eyes. It's there. At least I saw Sarah as being marked for greatness. Your mother here only saw her as marked.'

'That's it,' Wade said. He dove into his father's midriff and yelled out, 'Bryan, get the rope.'

'What are you doing?' Janet asked.

'Get *off* me, you frigging chowderhead.'

Bryan quickly retrieved coils of rope from the van's emergency box while Wade straddled his father's shoulders, police-holding Ted's arms behind the small of his back. In a flash, Bryan's Boy Scout training kicked into gear and Ted's feet were neatly bound like a rodeo steer, while Ted swore like an army platoon.

'Grab his arms,' Wade said. 'Rope 'em up.'

With considerable finesse Bryan completed his father's trussing.

'That rope hurts, you cretin. Untie me.'

Bryan said, 'No. I don't think so.'

Ted said, 'Jan, call these goons off me. Jesus.'

Janet looked him over and said, 'You know what, Ted? I think not.'

Wade said, 'Bryan, grab his feet. Let's dump him in the van.' Swiftly the two men did a one–two–three – *heave!* and Ted was dumped on the van's floor like an old gym bag. 'There,' Wade said. 'You're our hostage.'

'Hostage from *what*?'

Mother and two sons paused to consider this. Janet spoke: 'From Sarah's launch. No lift-off for you, Ted.'

'You stupid fuckers, you insane little—' but his invective was brought to a muffled halt by Bryan, who'd rustled about inside Howie's plentifully stocked first-aid box, finding a thick coral-colored bandage and slapping it onto his father's mouth.

'Voilà.' Bryan beamed.

There then followed a brief quiet moment as Janet and her sons stood outside the van, looking at Ted. 'Mom,' said Wade, 'Hop in.'

Janet paused for just a beat and said, 'OK. But let me get my stuff from my rental car.' They did this, and Janet felt . . . *fabulous* as they pulled out onto the road. 'Hey, I thought you guys were out of gas—'

Wade and Bryan smiled.

Don't ask.

'Wade, could you be a darling and tell me a bit more about what exactly is going on here?'

Wade shrugged and he told his mother about Disney World, Norm's cardiac death, the letter, Shw's trunk, the race to Daytona Beach . . . At the end of it, Janet was silent and stared at the passing marsh grasses, condo development signs and squashed animals.

'So, Mom, what do you think?'

Janet thought of the letter – such a perfect crystal of all words left unspoken between mother and child. And then up in the sky she saw a mound of mashed-potato Columbia Pictures clouds. She had an idea – or the germ of an idea. 'I think we should stop at the next mall we come to.'

'Why?'

'We need to buy envelopes and make duplicate letters.'

'What are you talking about?'

'Wade, look in my eyes. Look at me and tell me that you would hand over a letter as precious as that to some monster who'd actually pay for it.' Janet waited a second. 'See? You can't. If you were able, then you wouldn't be my son.'

Wade absorbed this; Janet thought he seemed to take to the idea rather well. Wade said, 'OK. Sure. But why would we make duplicates, then?'

'What – and not make that easy money? I may be your mother, but I'm not nuts.'

Bryan said, 'Good. We don't have to bother finding the real one in Shw's trunk.'

'Over my dead body. That letter is going to be rescued.'

'But the royal stationery—' said Bryan.

'Nonsense. It's Hallmark or a similar brand. Norm just didn't want you taking the card yourselves. Did you take measurements?'

'I did,' Wade said. 'It's seven by five.'

'Did you use a ruler?' Janet felt like a Mafia kingpin.

'My fingers. The tip of my index finger to the tip of my thumb is exactly five inches. My pinky to my thumb is seven.'

'Pull into that mall.'

The next mall up the road was slightly more touristy. They parked and left Ted on the floor like a bag of groceries. The greeting card store opened for business just as they arrived. 'See?' said Janet. 'A good sign – the universe *wants* us to make duplicates.'

They went through the store and ended up with several boxes of wedding invitation envelopes that were a close match, dozens of assorted cards to go inside, and a variety of pens and scribbler pads.

'What next?' Bryan asked.

'Over there.' They went to a discount book mart, and quickly found books about Princess Diana, and one with a photo of the envelope on the coffin. They bought it and walked to a Starbucks clone, bought coffees and sat down with a selection of pens.

'OK, boys,' she said. 'Let's practice our penmanship here.

First thing is, we have to make the envelope just right. We can do the card inside afterwards.'

They began writing the word 'Mummy', over and over, trying to perfectly mimic the original. Bryan said, 'Wade, shouldn't you phone Beth? I mean, you pretty much abandoned her at the hotel.'

Wade's face flushed and he looked at Janet. 'Dad's cell phone died. For now I just want to do these envelopes.'

Mummy *Mummy*

Mummy *Mummy*

Mummy

Janet thought about her own mother, who had died of a stroke during a holiday on Lake Huron in the 1970s. Her death, in and of itself, didn't sadden Janet. What saddened her was that she had never really known who her mother was as a person. Janet was frightened that her mother might actually have been unknowable, and by extension, maybe all people were unknowable. So much of her mother's life had been colonized by her husband. Once, after Janet was three children into her marriage with Ted, she asked her mother if she missed her maiden name.

'Miss my maiden name? Good heavens, no. I threw it away the moment I said, "I do".'

Threw it away? Such self-erasure was beyond Janet. To her such a gesture evoked pictures of Quebec nuns allowing themselves to be bricked into walls in a backfired idea of devotion. But for all that, Janet's mother had, for a human being born without a penis in the year 1902, done quite well for herself, whereas Janet, given an infinitely larger array of options and freedoms, had blown it. *Blown it? By what standards? If I'd played my cards right I'd be what, now – a judge? Wearing shoulder pads while heading some electronics corporation?*

Owning a muffin shop? That's success? Success is failure; failure is success. We were given so many mixed signals at once that we ended up becoming nothings. But my daughter – she escaped.

Blink . . .

'Maybe we should let Dad go to the bathroom,' Bryan said.

'No,' said Wade.

Janet said, 'It was very naughty of the two of you to tie him up like that.'

'He deserved to be tied up.'

'I'm not saying he didn't.'

'Oh. OK.'

They continued writing out the word 'Mummy'. Bryan, to Janet's surprise, was the best of the three. 'You know, you're very good, Bryan.'

'Thanks. Playing the guitar makes my fingers more dexterous.'

'I can see.'

'What are you thinking about?' Wade asked his mother. 'You have that I've-got-a-secret look on your face.'

'Nothing really. Well, actually my mother. You never really knew her.'

'I did a little bit,' Wade said. 'Grandma Kaye. She never talked and she smelled like skin cream.'

'No, she didn't talk much,' Janet said. 'Did she?'

Wade went on: 'What were you thinking about her?'

'How her life wasn't much of a story – nothing wrong with that – look at *mine*. But I keep on thinking that if I look at my life long enough, there'll be a sort of grand logic to it – a scheme. But I don't think there is.'

'Does that scare you?' Wade asked.

'No. And I think the future is pretty pointless, too.'

'Mom,' said Bryan, 'You sound like the Sex Pistols.'

'Those dreadful punk rockers.' Janet's lips pursed.

'Mom,' Wade said, 'the thing I can't figure out about you is how can you be so moral and TV mom about life, but not believe in anything at the same time. I don't understand.'

'What made you think that those TV moms believed in anything, Wade?'

'Uhhh—'

'They didn't. Not really. We weren't robots but we weren't complete people, either.' Small birds flitted about Janet's feet. 'Anyway, that was so many eras ago. So long ago. I feel like a fraud living in the year 2001. I'm not supposed to be a part of all this.' She put down her pen and looked at her son's efforts at forgery. 'Bryan, you're going to be our official calligrapher.' She handed him a stack of envelopes. 'Write on these, please.'

Bryan, happy to be chosen for a task, penned away with scientific calm. Janet turned to Wade. 'Beth says you have lesions on your shins. Can I see them?'

'Why not?' Wade rolled his pants up and his mother looked at the purple lesions, shaped like the states and counties of the United States, scrambled together.

'Do they hurt?' Janet asked.

'Nah. Not at all. But it's hard to look at them. I feel like an apple that's been in the basket for a month too long and I'm rotting from the inside.'

'Can I touch them?'

'Be my guest.'

'Let me.' Janet bent down and touched her son's shins and she thought of Sunday School and Jesus washing the feet of his disciples and yet again became angry at the way the past was always inserting itself into her present. 'Can you do anything about them?'

'Yes. No. They're not going away, if that's what you mean.'

'I'm sorry, Wade.'

18

Wade and Beth's trip to Milan was a somber, penny-pinching experience – a charter flight cramped in tiny seats, which made Wade motion sick for much of the flight – He was almost hallucinatory when they got to the tiny *pensióne* in Milan – a city the color of graham crackers and soot that resembled Toronto more than Wade's preconceptions of rustic fishing villages where everybody drank Chianti and drove itty-bitty bumper cars. And the taxi ride to the fertility clinic was a sci-fi experience as they passed through Milan's industrial outskirts, devoid of color or plant life and feeling like the year 2525. Once there, Wade was told to cab back to the city, that Beth was 'going to be administered to' – a creepy choice of words – and would stay for the day. Wade could come back around five.

Wade walked around the streets all day and became crashingly homesick. And when he wasn't homesick, he was worried about money and about the procedure's success. He was a tangle of short-circuiting thoughts. *Could Europe be any bleaker-looking? Where's all this history I've been hearing so much about*? Instead Wade kept seeing only things that looked . . . *old*. The shops had been not merely closed, but barricaded in metal shutters laced with graffiti. *Graffiti? That's so 1992*. The streets felt drab in the extreme. Stores seemed to open and shut down again shortly thereafter for unexplainable whims of culture. *How long can it take to stick a sperm into an egg? And could this country be any more expensive if it tried?*

At five he retrieved Beth, who was pooped, and the two went to bed. Beth began playing with Wade's eyelids. 'Hey, Wade – what are you thinking about?'

'A little baby quail dancing on my eyelids.'

'Do you want a boy or a girl?'

'A girl. Boys are pricks – no, wait – maybe a boy so I can undo all the scary evil shit my dad did to me.'

'Like *what?*'

Wade thought about it. 'Nothing specific. I mean, he hit me *all* the time, but that's not even the thing that sticks in my craw.'

'None of that matters any more, Wade. Your parents are lost. They can't help you any more. They no longer dream or feel. The only valid viewpoint for any decision is eternity.'

'No, Beth, hang on—' Wade opened his eyes and sat up. He looked down into Beth's eyes. 'We've been through this before. If a parent ignores you for your first fifteen years – never even says hello, let alone holds you or teaches you to shave or go to a ball game – and he only acknowledges you with a fist – that's cruelty – it's like confining a kid in solitary.'

'I'd rather have had your kind of cruelty.'

Wade plopped down on to the mattress. 'Don't wish cruelty on to yourself. Not even theoretically.' He turned sideways and stroked Beth's cheeks. She'd had bad acne as a teenager and the scars made Wade sad. 'Don't.'

Beth said nothing.

'Our baby's never going to be afraid,' said Wade. 'Our baby's never going to be yelled at. Our baby's going to be loved for ever and always. We don't drink. We don't drug. We don't preach. We—'

'Stop.'

'Huh? Why stop?'

'We'll jinx what we have. We're not normal people any more, you and me, Wade. We're not doomed or anything but we're—'

'We're what?'

Beth sat up, lit an Italian cigarette with a pink Bic lighter and exhaled her first drag. 'Growing up we used to have this garden out back. Everybody did, I mean, it was South Carolina. My parents – my mom mostly – they were terrible gardeners, but the vegetables made it through each year OK: boring stuff like potatoes and cabbages – some lettuce, some tobacco plants and pumpkins my dad tried growing every year. No flowers.' She took another drag from the cigarette. 'But then one year the booze kicked in, and that's when they really started losing it and going in for the kill on each other. They just kind of stopped doing the garden work. They just ignored it, and I was only about twelve, and in my head gardening wasn't an activity for twelve-year-olds. I was into smoking and older guys with cars. But I always kept my eyes on the garden. Weeds came in real quick. And rabbits. The cabbage went wild, and when cabbage goes wild it looks kind of, I don't know – like a homeless person. Then the bugs ate it up. And the peas never did come back. I'd go out to the garden to smoke when the furniture started flying. I'd go watch what happened to the garden once it lost its protection. Only little bits survived here and there – a potato plant; some chives. Mint.'

'And?'

'That garden's you and me, Wade. We're a garden that's lost its gardeners. The garden still goes on but it's never a real garden ever again.'

'Beth, that is so totally not true.'

'Wade. You're already in God's house. Now it's just a matter of locating your room.' Three floors down, a police car honked past their *pensióne* window. Beth looked away. 'I hate Europe, too.'

'What's on your mind, Beth?'

'Shush, Wade. I know we've taken that Course in Miracles stuff in our seropositivity group, but it's what I believe. We're the untended garden.'

Wade's heart broke like an egg on the kitchen floor. His sense of time quickened. Here was the moment where the hammer strikes the anvil and the chain is forged and the love grows only stronger, more real, deeper and permanent. Wade saw the truth in what Beth said. He agreed in his heart and thought of his child, who would flourish and bloom long after the rabbits and weevils had taken him away.

'God saw me in that insemination room today, Wade. He did. He saw the test tubes and sheet metal and the ultrasound stuff and—'

'And what?' Wade propped himself up on his elbow and traced circles on Beth's forehead.

'He sees everything. I don't know how I feel about that. He saw me. He saw the test tubes. The sperm spinner. The *News at Six*. Icebergs in Antarctica. Inside my heart. Everything.'

'I want a girl,' Wade said.

'I want a boy,' said Beth. 'Girls never have good lives. God hates girls.'

Bryan and Janet continued writing Mummy cards, and Wade slunk off to a pay phone.

'Wade?'

'Beth, God, I'm sorry, sugar, I'm so sorry.'

'I know you are, honey.'

Wade was humbled. 'I'm weak. I'm a shit. I *am* shit. You're too good for me.'

'No, you're too good for me. I drank again last night. Four years, three months and two days of sobriety, all gone.'

'Beth, you drank because I left you alone. I stopped to get my pills, but you weren't back yet. You were out shopping or something.'

'What's going on, honey? Something's fishy. Did that Norm creep land you guys in trouble?'

'Norm? Uh, no, but we're going to help him on a business deal.'

'What kind of deal – drugs? Because if it's drugs, I'm leaving you, Wade. You know that's our agreement.'

'Drugs? God, no. Mom's even helping us out.'

'Mom? Your mother? *Janet*?'

'That's right.'

'Well, she's not here, so I guess she's with you. When are you returning?'

'Tonight I guess – I promise.'

Beth was unimpressed. 'Well, just so's you know, I thought I might go to Kennedy Space Center. I—'

Beth's voice vanished as Wade looked across the parking lot and saw the orange van's panel doors slide open and the trussed lump that was Ted drop out onto the pavement. 'I have to call you back, hon.' He ran over to the van, followed by Bryan and Janet. 'And what do you think *you're* doing, Dad?'

Ted mumbled into the bandage over his mouth. A clean-cut family walked past en route to a sporting goods outlet store.

'Nothing to look at,' said Wade, but this seemed not to appease the family. 'Move along.'

'It's OK,' Janet said in her 1965 hostess voice. 'He has Klemperer's palsy. It can overwhelm him.'

Once they were gone, Wade said, 'Klemperer's palsy?'

'After Colonel Klink on *Hogan's Heroes*. I made it up on the spot.'

Wade looked down at Ted. 'Come on, Bry – let's lock the Gimp back in his cage.' Ted writhed in a full lather. 'Dad, calm down, because your spazzing out like this isn't going to help you, and it only makes our job harder.'

'Our *job*?' Bryan asked.

'Yeah,' said Wade, as his father landed on the floor. 'We need to sell Florian his goddamn fake card.'

'But we don't need Dad to do that.'

'Bryan, we can't just throw him off on the side of the highw—' Wade stopped, and his eyes caught those of his brother and mother. Ted squealed as he foresaw a possible fate.

'How's he going to get home, then?' Bryan asked.

'He's a big boy,' said Janet.

'Yeah,' said Bryan. 'But he and Nickie are going to need their share of the money for all their medical bills.'

Wade instantly regretted having told Bryan about Nickie's HIV status.

Janet looked at Ted. 'Oh, God. Just when I was building up the nerve to become a callous soul.' Ted's eyes showed that he knew he was about to receive a humdinger of information. Janet sat down and removed the bandage from his mouth. Before she could say anything more, Wade said, 'If you say or do even one tiny mean thing to Mom I'm going to cover your whole body with duct tape, not just now, but the rest of your life. Got it?'

Ted was more interested in Janet's news.

'Ted, now's as good a time as any to find out. Nickie was going to tell you, but here goes.' She took in her breath. 'Nickie's HIV positive—'

No reaction.

'—and I have to say, Ted, she's one good egg and you're damn lucky to have found her, or rather, that she puts up with you. Or whatever your deal is.'

'He's going to go apeshit,' Bryan said to nobody in particular.

'I dunno, Bry—' said Wade.

Ted remained motionless.

Janet went on: 'It doesn't mean that you're HIV, Ted, but there's the poss—'

Ted broncoed about the van's interior, swearing with such force and thrashing with such violence that Janet, Wade and Bryan scattered like bits of broken glass.

'Jesus, Dad, calm down.'

Janet kept calm and said what soothing things she could. Wade said, 'Mom, could we continue this conversation as we drive up the coast?'

They became mobile, and a half hour later, Ted lay in stunned submission. Wade was at the wheel, and Janet sat in the passenger seat as the orange van hummed up Florida's Space Coast, the sun having resumed its daily role as a permanent flash cube popping over a world of vitamin huts, golf shops, strip joints, car washes and gas stations.

This landscape is from an amusement park. I'm on a ride – a ride shaped like an orange VW camper.

Bryan and Ted were in the rear seats, with Ted unbound. By no means was it love holding the three men together – rather, only the prospect of quick money.

Janet sipped from a bottle of Volvic water she kept in her purse and took a 3TC capsule, clasping her pill bottle shut with a defiant click.

'Are those 3TCs? Can I borrow one, Mom? Mine are in the back of the camper.'

'Sure.'

Ted said, 'I really don't see why we have to slip this kraut a fake letter. Thanks, Jan. Count on you to come in and screw up a good thing.'

'Thank *you*, Ted,' said Janet, 'and such a good plan of operation you were having this morning, too – stealing breakfasts and sleeping on beaches. I smell a winner.'

'Dad,' Wade said, 'I'm not calling Florian until we rescue the real letter. Love it or leave it. It's wrong that he should buy it.'

'*You*. Morals. Perfect.'

. . . police station . . . discount mattresses . . . a pain clinic . . . liquor . . . pet food.

Wade ignored the comment and kept steady at the wheel.

19

Janet sensed that her opinion of her life was changing. Two days ago, it had felt like merely a game of connect the dots – a few random dots, spaced widely apart and which produced a picture of a scribble. But now? Now her life was nothing *but* dots, dots that would connect in the end to create a magnificent picture – Noah's Ark? A field of cornflowers? A Maui sunset? She didn't know the exact image, but a picture was indeed happening – her life was now a story. *Farewell, random scribbles*.

She heard Bryan speaking to Ted: 'Geez, Dad, you've already finished that bottle?'

'I need another.' Ted had polished off a mickey of golden rum found in the van's fridge.

Wade said, 'Getting sloshed isn't going to fix anything.'

'*You* shut up. I've heard enough out of you.'

'No, Dad, I'm *not* going to shut up.' The car came to a red light and Ted bolted out the door to a nearby convenience mart. Wade was about to race after him, but Janet restrained him. 'Just let him have his little drink, dear.'

From the door of the liquor store, Ted shouted at Wade, 'I have *bugs* crawling underneath my skin because of you, you little prick.'

'Yeah? Well, cry me a river, you cruel shit.'

'Wade,' said Janet, 'your language. Please.'

'Sorry, Mom.' He stuck his head out the window: 'Buy yourself shoe polish and mouthwash and go suck it and *die* and then see if any of us care.'

'We're never going to find her,' Bryan croaked.

'Don't be such a gloomy Gus. It's a piece of cake.'

'How?'

Janet leaned out the window and asked a passing pedestrian for the location of the local library. Ted returned to the van with a bottle of gin: 'Bulk martinis.'

'How did you pay for that?' Janet asked.

'I didn't.'

'Oh, good Lord.' She got out and went into the store to pay for it and returned with the Yellow Pages.

Minutes later they were at the local library's Internet browser section. The library's insides were cool and normal-seeming, a place visited by people whose lives contained no randomness, whose families gave one another CD box sets and novelty sweaters for Christmas, and who never forged each others' signatures or had affairs with pool boys named Jamie or girls in payroll named Nicole. Outside the library, Ted was underneath an ancient live oak draped with Spanish moss.

As Janet keyboarded, she thought out loud: '. . . If this Mr. Baby Buyer is in the auto parts business, he's most likely a Republican. Car dealers and car people love Republicans – all those Rotary and Kiwanis lunches and handshake photos taken with vice presidents. So he probably donates heavily and lives in a fancy zip code.' She continued on her search.

Bryan said, 'I don't think I've ever been in a library.' His voice was empty of any ironic trace.

'I have,' Wade said. 'In Las Vegas, when I became sick. They're so weird, aren't they? I mean, all these . . . *books*.'

The two brothers went silent.

After a few minutes during which Wade thumbed through a copy of *Teen People* and Bryan looked at picture books of punk rock stars, Janet announced that she had narrowed the selection to three candidates, and they left the building. Outside they found Ted passed out; two young boys in private school uniforms were using his nose as a paper airplane target. Wade booted his father's bottom. 'Jesus, Dad, you're like the town wino. You're embarrassing us – get up.' Ted promptly vomited into the tinder-dry lawn.

'Plop him into the van,' Janet said. 'Lay him on top of that striped awning Howie hangs over the camper door at barbecues.'

Once they were in the van and moving, Ted rolled around on the floor like a log; Bryan stopped this by laying a foam cushion between his father and the door.

'I think we should rent a hotel room in Daytona Beach,' Janet said. 'Your father's in no shape to help us.'

'I think you're right,' said Wade.

Janet prowled inside the glove compartment and removed a black-corded item, which she then inserted into the cigarette lighter. 'Bryan, pass me your father's cell phone.' Bryan removed it from Ted's front right pocket, and Janet plugged it in. It bleeped like a cheerful sparrow, and Janet announced that they were once again linked to humanity.

'I didn't know Howie had a charger,' Wade said.

'You have to look for things, Wade.'

The phone began to recharge itself atop the dash. North coastal Florida rolled by. She smelled subdivisions burning to the west in Orange County. Janet's vision went black and white, and she was taken from the present into the past, and she hated the feeling of having traveled back in time. She looked at the cheap hotels smeared with joyless stucco mayonnaise, oceanside landscapes scraped clean by the endless Atlantic winds that left behind only palm stumps and stubby sea-grape. She felt she was looking at the third-best seaside resort in a place like Libya, where the prim ideas of middle-class leisure had been collectively abandoned ages ago. The world felt vulgar. Inside the hotels they passed she imagined *real live crack whores!* on trash TV, and she imagined elevators rusted to a stop somewhere on the upper floors. She saw images of doorless rooms inhabited by prophets stripped of their founding visions, images of teenagers fucking on towels designed by beer companies, wooden floors gone rotten, the strips of wood turned into dried-out slats – a world robbed of values and ideals and direction. And then Janet felt she was now officially in the future, one so far away from the dreams of her Toronto youth that she was reminded of Discovery Channel sermons on travel at the speed of light, of young men and women shot out into the universe, returning to Earth only to find everything they'd ever known dead or gone or forgotten or mocked, and this world was Janet's world.

'Wade, does this place make any sense to you?'

'Huh? Yeah, sure – US 1 goes right up the coast.'

'No. That's not what I meant. I mean – what's the reason behind a place like this?'

'Is it weirding you out?'

'It is. Explain it to me. Explain Daytona Beach to me.'

'Daytona's a fun kind of place – a place where—'

'Stop, Wade. Stop right there. You can do better than that. Pretend I'm not your mother. Pretend that I'm drunk and that you're drunk and that you know that if you have just one more drink you'll be too stupid to explain anything, but for now you possess the superpower of insight that comes just before that last drink.'

Wade took a few breaths. He was obviously taking the question seriously. 'I have this friend, Todd, who got cleaned out in a divorce, and so now he sells lottery tickets in a mall booth out in Richmond. He asked me once what day of the lottery cycle is the biggest day for sales. I said, *I dunno, when the jackpot's really big* – but he said, no way, it's the morning *after* the big jackpot. People come running to him the moment the door's open. They want to have that ticket in their hands for the maximum amount of time possible. Unless they have a ticket in their hand, then they don't have any hope, and they have to have hope.'

. . . nail clinic . . . wet T-shirt contest . . . foam beer coolers half price . . . vacancy . . . no vacancy . . . Citgo gas . . .

'So I think Daytona Beach is for all those people who run to the ticket booth first on the morning after a lottery. They know that the really *good* beaches were swiped by rich people at least a century ago. They know this is the only beach they're ever likely to get – but they also think that maybe for once they'll get a deep tropical tan instead of burning all pink, and maybe for once the margaritas'll make them witty instead of shrill and boring, and that maybe they'll meet the lay of a lifetime in the hotel lobby, hot and ready to go. If it's not Daytona Beach it's Lake Havasu, and if it's not Lake Havasu, it's, I dunno – somewhere on Long Island.'

. . . *all the shrimp you can eat . . . dead car dealerships . . . helicopter rides . . . Bikers Welcome!*

'Rich people – shit, they'll probably never set foot in Daytona Beach even if they reincarnate as a rich person a hundred times. They might fly over the place. Maybe their drugs'll pass through it. But that's it. So I guess Daytona Beach is also a way of crowd-controlling middle-class and poor people.'

. . . *Taco Bell . . . discount golf supplies . . . acupuncture*

They found a hotel, a peacock-blue twelve-story blank of a building chosen because it seemed like a place that would ask no questions if the desk staff were, say, to witness two men carrying another unconscious man into the elevator from the side lobby door – this assumption proved correct. They dumped Ted on the bed. The view outside the window was of ocean and sky and nothing else – one blue rectangle on top of another, not even a bird. Janet closed the sheers.

The cell phone, now partially charged, chirped; it was Nickie. With mock politeness, Nickie asked her, 'Hello, Jan, how are *you?*'

'How are we, Nickie? We're supercalifragilisticexpialidocious. And we're all together in a Daytona Beach hotel – it's a long story – and you wouldn't believe the half of it. Where are you?'

'I'm at Kevin's – with Beth.'

'Kevin's? With Beth?'

Janet took down Kevin's phone number and called on the land line while the cell recharged.

Wade said, 'What's going on? Mom, what's—?'

The time-share in Kissimmee had been ransacked while Nickie was window shopping at Dillard's. Around the same time, Beth had gone to Kennedy Space Center, but had forgotten her asthma inhaler, and when she went up to the room to fetch it, she saw the room had been ransacked. She'd phoned Nickie in tears. The odd thing was that nothing had been taken from either intrusion. In a panic they decided to hide at Kevin's.

Wade took the receiver, then held the receiver away from his ear: '—that moron Norm and his fucked-up scheme, and now you're into some deal so deep it scares the living shit out of me.'

'Beth, just stay there where you are. I'll come get you.'

'Come *get* us? You'll probably get us killed. Have you never heard of the invention called call display? You called one of Norm's ice-blooded thugs on our telephones? What were you *thinking*?'

'I wasn't thinking, Beth – no one's going to be killed,' said Wade, Janet thought, a touch unconvincingly.

'How could you *do* this to us, Wade?'

20

'Where are the boys?'

'They're downstairs, Ted.' Janet was lying beside her ex-husband on the hotel bed.

'D'you send them down?'

'Yes. I wanted quiet.'

'Good.' Ted turned his head to the curtained window. 'What time is it?'

'Early afternoon. Ish.'

'I feel awful.'

'I can imagine.'

'Why's the curtain closed?'

'Do you really want to know, Ted?'

'Yeah.'

Janet paused. 'Because I'm afraid of death. I looked out and there was this big blank sky and this big blank ocean, and it didn't even look like a real ocean, just this big pool of distilled water – clean but sterile . . . *dead*. So I closed the curtains.'

The two were silent and the room's cool air felt like baby powder on Janet's arms and face.

Ted said, 'I'm scared shitless of death, myself.'

'Yes, well, it always boils down to that in the end, doesn't it?'

'I'm going to die.'

'Ted, don't expect too many tears from me.'

'Huh? No, of course not.'

Janet asked, 'Are you still feeling woozy?'

'As long as I don't move my head too quickly, I'm OK. The sun made me sick more than the booze. I barely touched that gin.' He paused. 'Did you tell Nickie? I mean, does she know that I know?'

'No – why?'

'No reason. You think I'm going to be pissed off at her, don't you? That I'm going to abandon her or cast her away.'

'It crossed my mind.'

'I'm not. Pissed off, that is. And I won't be leaving her.'

'Now I *am* surprised.'

'It's not what you think it is,' Ted said.

'Nothing ever is.'

'I have liver cancer.'

'I see.' Janet rubbed her arms. A phone in the next room began to ring. 'It's not too warm in here, is it?'

'It's nice.'

'How far along are you?'

'I'm toast.'

'Can we stick a number on that?'

'Nine months maybe.'

The phone next door stopped ringing. 'You're a man of surprises, Ted Drummond.'

'I wish I weren't.' He closed his eyes. 'Don't tell Nickie.'

'I can't guarantee that, Ted. I know too many secrets already. Something's got to give.'

'Whatever. I don't care too much. I just wanted to have my bills paid before I go. This HIV thing, now that I think about it, is almost like a relief – it's like we're a part of a big death club.'

'There's a baby or two in the works, I might point out.'

'Oh yeah. Took the kids long enough.'

Down the hall, a vacuum hissed to life. Janet said, 'I feel so calm in here, Ted. Do you?'

'Yeah.'

'I feel like we're at the end of *Our Town*, where the people of Grover's Corner are talking to one another from inside their graves.'

'Huh.'

'That's what I always thought death would be like,' Janet said. 'Me – next to you – together – quietly talking. Maybe for ever.'

'That play always scared me crapless.'

'Oh, I know. Me, too. The play should come with a warning label. But the one thing it *did* do for me was to clarify in my mind what death would be like. And at the same time it made me not want to think about death.'

Ted said, 'I try not to think about death too much. But I can't stop. And I can't bring myself to tell Nickie about my liver.'

'Why on earth not?'

'She was supposed to be my proof that I was alive and invincible and young still. Once she thinks I'm checking out, then in my own head I really *will* be checking out.'

Janet giggled. Ted asked her, 'What's so funny.'

'Irony. Like an O. Henry short story. She thinks you'll drop *her*.'

'Oh, *geez*.' Ted smiled: *big American teeth*. He put out his hand and Janet accepted it, and they looked heavenward together. People walked past the door of their room; somewhere a door slammed. 'Wade and Bryan should have tied me up years ago, but you're a bad girl for not stopping them.'

'I am, aren't I?'

'Nah. Not really. I'm the shit around here.'

'I won't contradict you.'

'When did I turn bad, Jan? Tell me, because I wasn't always such a bad guy. I was an OK kind of guy when you and I started out. Jan? You listening?'

'Yes. No. I'm in shock. That's one question I never thought I'd hear from *your* mouth.'

'Pretend we're dead. We can say anything we want. We can ask each other anything we want. Wouldn't that be the best thing of all? If life were like that?'

Janet thought about this: 'The two of us – dead – I like that.'

'Yeah.'

A flock of Harleys gunned down the main strip twelve storeys below them. Janet said, 'I think you started going bad when you started cheating on me. My guess is that it was a few years after Sarah was born – shortly after we moved West – with Violet – that receptionist of yours who was always too nice to me.'

'You're *good*,' Ted said. 'One, two, three, *bang!*'

'Didn't have to be a genius to figure out that one. Was she the first?'

'Yeah. But it didn't go on long. I cooled on her, she started blackmailing me, so I told her I'd mail her father nudie snapshots I'd taken of her with an Instamatic. Never heard from her again.'

'Instamatic?'

'Yeah – talk about ancient history – but that was how I turned on to porn. You never knew that about me, did you? At my office – *wow* – a huge locked credenza full of the weirdest shit going.'

'You should check the Internet, Ted.'

'Yeah. Well, I burned out on the stuff and chucked it out in, maybe, 1975. I remember staying late at the office and carefully shunting boxloads of it down into the alley Dumpster, back when the office was on Dunsmuir Street. But then once it was gone I felt dirtier and more burnt out than I ever did when I had it locked up in my office. I guess that's when I knew there was no going back. When I started getting mean.'

'1975. That's about right. I didn't realize how sexual your life was. I thought it was your work stressing you out – I mean, you left aerospace to go into oil pipelines. I though maybe you felt as if your wings had been clipped. Like you'd lost your reason for being.'

'Did you ever cheat on me?'

'No. But I would have. With Bob Laine, your old tax guy, the night of the party and your brouhaha with Wade on the lawn. I was that close.'

'What a disaster *that* night was.'

'I cried the whole next day – on the tennis court bench.'

'Geez, I'm sorry. You should have gone for it.'

'You *can't* be serious.'

'I am. A fling would have been fun for you.'

'You're right, it *would* have been.'

'Hey – did you know about my drug problem?'

'Your drug problem?'

'In the early eighties, coke. By the shovel.'

Janet sighed. 'I'm such a dumb bunny at figuring out that kind of thing, Ted. That's probably why you got away with so much.'

'Pretty much.'

Janet added two and two: '*That's* where our stock money went – it wasn't the 1987 market crash at all.'

'Bingo. Sorry.'

Janet sighed. 'Ancient history.'

'The reason I'm not so much of a shit right now is because I'm not doing drugs. For one thing, I couldn't afford it, and second, I want to die clean. How's that for sappy?'

Pieces were falling into place for Janet. 'You're bankrupt because you blew all your money on drugs – didn't you?'

'Yeah, well, thar she blows.'

'Huh.'

In the hallway the housekeeping staff were having a squabble over who did or did not forget towels that were, or were not, of the right type.

'Let me hold you,' said Ted.

'Really now?' said Janet.

'Yeah, really now.'

Janet weighed the ups and downs of the offer. 'I used to love you dearly, Ted Drummond.'

'I used to love you dearly, too, my dear.'

'You want to hold me?'

'Yes. I want to hold you.'
'Our little girl's going into space, Ted.'
'Our little girl.'
Shortly, like twins in utero, arm in arm, they fell asleep.

21

At a pay phone down on Daytona Beach's main drag, Wade dialed Sarah at her private number. Bryan was browsing in a nearby shop that sold NASCAR baubles.

'Sarah?'

'Oh. It's *you.*'

'Huh? What do you mean "Oh, it's *you*"?'

'Just what I said.'

'Are you OK?'

'Yes. I'm *OK.*'

Something's going wrong. 'What's up, little sister?'

'Wade, you're really pushing things by phoning me like this.'

'What – is it your training time right now? Should I have called at four A.M.?'

'That's not what I mean.'

'Sarah, what's happening?'

Sarah mimicked him: '*Sarah, what's happening . . .*'

Wade felt dizzy, as if he'd just gotten off a Tilt-a-Whirl. 'Sarah, come on – this isn't fair. I have no idea what's happening.'

'I found out once and for all about Howie and Alanna.'

'Oh.'

'Yeah, *oh.*'

'How? Who told you?'

'Does it matter?'

'Yes, it *matters.*'

Sarah went quiet on the other end. She sniffled once and was on the cusp of tears.

Wade said, 'Oh, geez, Sarah. I'm sorry. I'm so goddamn sorry

I feel sick, and I really do feel sick. Oh, geez. Oh, *geez.*' Sarah sniffled again. There were loudspeaker sounds in the background. Wade asked, 'Who told you?'

'Gordon.'

'Gordon Brunswick?'

'Yes – Commander Gordon Brunswick, husband of Alanna.'

Don't be defensive. 'Why? How?' Wade sensed Sarah collecting her wits.

'Alanna blabbed. Because you caught her – *them*. Because she felt guilty. Because she's a meddlesome cow.'

'I see.' More background noises – a drill of some sort: a PA system. Wade tried imagining what he'd feel like if Beth cheated on him. He said, 'Christ, I'm sorry, Sarah.'

'You don't understand, do you?'

'Understand? Understand what?'

'It's not Howie I care about.'

'You're losing me, Sarah. You don't care about Howie?'

Sarah sighed; whatever tears there'd been were gone. 'Wade, you think I'm perfect, don't you?'

'Well – yes. I always have.'

'I can't take it any more.'

'Well, I mean nobody's per—'

'Shut up, Wade.'

'Sarah?'

'Gordon and I were having an affair. It's been the most liberating thing that's ever happened to me.'

Kaboom. What was blurred becomes focused. 'Like I'm someone to judge anything, Sarah.'

'We were going to make love up in zero-G.'

'Oh, *man* . . .'

'Now Gordon's called things off and shut himself off to me. He might as well be my tenth-grade chem teacher.'

'Oh, Sarah.'

'I was in love with him, Wade. Shit, I still *am*. What I have with Gordon is *totally* different than anything I remember feeling for Howie. Howie was OK, but I don't worship him. Never have. Do you worship Beth?'

'I haven't thought of it that way. I suppose I do.'

'I don't care about this mission any more. I don't.'

'Sarah – don't say stuff like that. You *have* to care.'

'Do I?'

This is all my fault. This is all my fault. I had to go wear clean clothes to the hotel. 'Sarah, you've been working towards this your whole *life*.'

'Correction: Everyone *else* has been pushing me towards this my whole life. Dad especially.'

'You can't just drop out. It's not like NASA has understudies. This isn't a high school production of *Bye, Bye Birdie*.'

'Oh, I'll go up there into orbit. And OK, I'll do my job. And that's *all* I'll do. I might as well be running a diagnostic test on an Audi. It's just a job.'

'Sarah, let me come see you. Can they give you an hour off at this point? Can we just talk?'

Sarah sighed. 'Wade – this is all kind of new to me. I don't know.'

'Is this why you were so pissy with Mom last night? Pardon my French.'

'Yeah. I shouldn't have yelled at her. It's the last thing she needs.'

Good. She still cares about other people's feelings.

In the background a bell went off. 'I have to go, Wade.'

'When can I call you next?'

'I'll call you. I promise. Doesn't anyone there have a cell phone?'

Wade gave her Ted's number. 'Recharging the damn things is like sorting out Mideast politics. I'll call tonight.' Wade then remembered Howie. 'What about Howie – didn't two NASA guys take him away yesterday?'

'Yeah. I guess so. Whatever. He's probably planning a

surprise clambake or organizing a happy-wappy balloon-o-gram or something dorky.'

'I love you, little sister.'

'Thanks, Wade. G'bye.'

Click

Geez.

Bryan had emerged from the shop and stood beside Wade at the phone booth. 'Let's get Mom and Dad and go find Shw.' Bryan was slathered in zinc cream; a T-shirt was draped over his head, clamped in place by a Miami Dolphins baseball cap. The rest of his tender pink body was draped in discounted *après* beachwear, purchased with money donated by Janet. He looked like a bin of Salvation Army remnants.

'Not so fast,' said Wade. His mind was reeling.

'How's Sarah?' Bryan asked.

'Good. Good. Fine.'

'You OK, Wade?'

'Yeah.'

'Call that German guy.'

Diversion! 'Right. I'll call Florian.' Cars roared past, mostly down the main drag of Daytona's tourist district. *It's like Reno – no – it's like Laughlin – Laughlin by the sea.* Wade clanked a mound of quarters on top of the pay phone and dialed the number of Buckingham Pest Control in the Bahamas. The deeply bored Bahamian woman's voice answered once more: 'Buckingham Pest Control.'

'Hi. This is Wade calling Florian about the letter from his . . . *mother*. I spoke with you yesterday.'

This seemed to cause the slightest twitch of enthusiasm in her voice. 'I'll patch you through. One moment.'

Wade was glad to have passed the gatekeeper.

A sarcastic German accent, filtered through umpteen cell towers, satellites, optical fibers and copper cables, came on: 'Well, hel*lo*, is this really young Wade?'

'Hi, Florian.'

'Oof! This is *too* rich. How on earth did a little piss-ant *comme toi* end up with *my* delivery?'

'More to the point, what's a bag of Eurotrash like you doing ransacking my family's goddamn hotel room?'

'Temper, *temper*, Wade. You'll notice I waited until nobody was there. Was anybody hurt? No. Was anything stolen? No.'

'Only because you couldn't find it.'

'Why pay for something I can have for free?'

'You immoral scum—'

'Oh, shut up. I'm not immoral, I'm merely very, very rich, and because I'm very, very rich I live by different rules. It's the way things work.'

I will keep my cool. I will keep my cool.

'Wade, do speak to me, because I can practically hear your therapist's voice coming through the receiver telling you to contain yourself.'

He is a European shitbag. He is not worth my time.

Florian went on: 'You're still keeping silent, so I must be correct. What are you enrolled in – an 'anger management' workshop? Lots of winners there, I imagine. By the way, the Bahamas misses you. I heard via the tom-toms that you ended up in Kansas City. Excuse me while I gag. Dear boy, you should have phoned me – *whoops* – sent me an *e-mail* – and told me of your plight. I could have sent a packet of culture your way – tickets for regional dinner theater, paintings of weeping clowns painted by celebrated funny man Mr. Red Skelton.'

'Florian, shut up. Do you want the bloody letter or not?'

'*So butch.*'

'Well?'

Florian changed direction. 'It was brought to my attention that there was a prescription bottle for ddI in your hotel's bathroom, Wade. Hardly a recreational drug.'

I forgot my ddI. Shit, shit, shit. 'Does your nanny still spank you to sleep at night?'

'Gee whillikers, Wade, hit where it hurts. So what's with the ddI, huh?'

'What do you think?'

'Mumps? The croup? Tonsillitis?'

'You're a real wit, Florian.'

A tractor-trailer belched by. Florian asked, 'Was that a truck I just heard?'

'Yeah, it was.'

'Wade! You're in Zimbabwe, aren't you? Having hot, steamy unprotected sex with central African truckers.'

'Florian, talk business.'

'So manly!'

Best not to tell him Norm's dead – best not to mention Norm at all. 'Before you start razzing on me too much here, Florian, I'm just the courier on this deal, OK? I'm just the messenger.'

'You mean to say Donald Duck brought our friend Stormin' Norman back from the dead?'

Shit.

'You know, *Wade*, all those dancers prancing about Small Town USA – young gypsies with a song in their heart and a cell phone in the changing rooms – of *course* I found out. Your shit could come out sideways while sitting on a Disney latrine, and every freshman inside their Minnie Mouse costume would know before you've even flushed. And tell me this, Wade, did Norman tell you there were other people who wanted this letter badly?'

Wade said nothing.

Florian continued: 'I'm assuming that's a "yes". And did Norman also hand you a line about royal stationery being made out of titanium and the Queen's recycled panties?'

'Well—'

'You are *such* a chump, Wadie-kins.'

'There was a blackout at Disney World and suddenly he was . . . *dead*.'

'Wade, I've done some iffy things in my life, but I have yet to either infiltrate the Disney World power system or shoot poison darts at morons who own a bunch of money-hemorrhaging sports franchises. And the only reason poor Norman couldn't come to the Bahamas himself was because last year he got caught fencing stolen Cézanne sketches, which, granted, in the Bahamas is as common as jaywalking, but not when the buyer is one of the governor's best cricket buddies.'

'It's a cash deal, Florian.'

'Wade, you're starting to bore me.'

'I've gotta go, Florian.' Bye.

Click

'Well?' Bryan was trying to stand inside the thin lazy shade cast by a telephone pole. 'Can we go?'

'Yeah, let's go.' Wade realized he'd forgotten to ask about Howie.

'We've gotta buy Mom some pads for her heels. She said her heels are hurting'

'I know, I know.'

'That German guy really pissed you off. Sounds to me like you know each other really well. What's the deal? Did you work for him?'

. . . *applying defibrillators to the dolphins being smuggled into North Carolina* . . .

'Wade?'

. . . *Wade, the only thing heavy enough on the boat to make a body sink is the anchor* . . .

'I'm right – you *do* know him.'

. . . *Yes, she's sixty, Wade. So close your eyes and think of Fort Knox* . . .

'Yeah, OK, I've worked with the guy before. No big deal.'

'Doing what?'

. . . *Keith just poured liquid nitrogen onto his goddam hand. Throw him out of the truck before the Dukes of Hazzard find our trail* . . .

'Doing nothing. What's it to you, Bryan?'

. . . *It was either eat the packets or spend the next thirty years in a Montego Bay correctional facility. So we ate the packets . . .*

'It's pretty bad stuff, otherwise you'd have told me what you'd done.'

'Bryan, I oughta—'

'No, you *don't* oughta *any*thing, Wade. Let's just find Mom's heel pads and I'll forget we had this conversation. *Zheesh*.'

The two men found a drug store a further walk away than they'd anticipated. Wade was preoccupied with Sarah, interspersed with worries about his forgetting his ddI, wondering whether its absence would speed up his body's slow, sure unraveling. He remembered as a child removing the smooth white skins of golf balls, watching the neurotic disintegration of the little rubber bands inside them. *Stupid, stupid, stupid to forget it.*

On the hotel's twelfth floor, they entered the room, Wade saying, 'We bought you your—' and there were his parents, asleep together like two ageing sheepdogs.

Janet opened her eyes. 'Oh hello, dears.'

Wade found himself unable to muster up the words to meet the situation, and his mother said, 'What were you expecting, Wade, that we'd be in here bashing each other over the head with a door ripped off the bathroom cupboard? We're people, not cartoons.'

Ted was still asleep, snorting intermittently as moist folds of skin within him relaxed and convulsed.

'But—'

'After the life you've led, you find *this* surprising?'

Bryan said, 'Wade called that German guy – the Flower dude – and Wade used to do all sorts of nasty shit for him.'

'I rest my case,' said Janet. 'Decades' worth of sinful doings, but Mom and Dad in bed retains the power to shock.'

Ted bolted awake: 'Is he giving you a hard time?' His demeanor suggested to Wade that a beating might be imminent.

'Everybody get off my case. Geez, it's like I'm suddenly on trial.'

Bryan asked, 'What was the baddest thing you ever did?'

'Bryan, shut up.'

Janet said, 'No, why not answer, dear? I mean, face it, we've been a bit curious these past two decades.'

'I am a married man! I have a wife and soon a child – my past is no longer the issue it once was!'

Ted said, 'Ha!' and Janet giggled.

'What? What's so funny?'

'Dear,' said Janet, 'your past isn't something you escape from. Your past is what you *are*.' His parents propped themselves up on pillows.

Bryan was comfy on a side chair. He asked Wade, 'Did you ever, like, actually *kill* somebody?'

'I can't believe this is happening.'

Janet said, 'Well?'

'OK. Fair enough. Yes, but not intentionally. It was an accident, and it occurred in international waters, so I'm innocent and blameless.'

'What happened?' Janet asked.

'This moron, Ron, got beaned on the head with a jib pole during a run into Cuba.'

Janet asked, 'A run into *Cuba?*'

'Yeah. We had about five thousand Wonder Bras we were trading for cigars. This was before the Wall came down, and the Soviets were extra prickly about smuggling ladies' products because they're so much harder to fence. This neighbor of Florian's bought a Da Vinci sketch with the profits from a Greek sardine trawler loaded with Kotex. And this other guy, Rainer, retired after delivering a boatload of canola into a private facility south of Havana. He bought a 1936 Cord with that one.' Wade didn't want to go any further into his past. 'Shouldn't we go find Shw?'

'I suppose yes,' Janet said. 'Up you go, Ted, upsy-daisy.'

Ted lugged his body upright then lumbered off to the bathroom to vomit again.

Janet put on her shoes and massaged her wrists. 'I want to phone Sarah.'

'I don't think so,' Wade blurted. 'Now's not a good time.'

'No? Why not?'

'I was just talking to her – downstairs, on the pay phone. She's, uh, uh' – *think, think, think* – 'loading tadpoles into a special tank, I think.' *Hey, that sounded good.*

Janet didn't press the issue. 'Oh. OK. Ted, come on, let's go find the mother of your grandchild.'

Once in the orange van, the Drummonds seemed almost half asleep, drugged by the flattening afternoon sun. All birds had vanished, and traffic was approaching zero. The hotels seemed beyond dead – hotel mummies. Wade wondered how a place like Florida was settled in the first place – the thorny, insect-infested scrub and swamps; rancid waters; predators – the lack of air-conditioning and freeways – with machetes and Bibles. In Wade's mind, Florida wasn't so much a place where one went to reinvent oneself as it was a place where one went if one no longer wished to be found.

'Turn left there.' Janet pointed at a street up ahead. 'It should be on the left, in the middle. Yes – there it is – 1650.'

'That's Shw's car!' Bryan slipped out the moving car's side door.

'Bryan, you frigging idiot—' Ted snapped fully to life.

Wade hopped out of the car, ran Bryan down and tackled him on the driveway.

22

Life is just so much easier if we simply wing it. Maybe if we wing it properly, we can trick ourselves into winging death, too. Or is that too simple a strategy?

Janet was looking out the van's window at Wade, tackling Bryan on the terra cotta brick driveway of a Floridian muffler king. Janet thought a bit more about the muffler king and what she'd read about him on the Internet back at the library: *Well, he isn't really a muffler king, per se. He's really more of an in-dash cigarette lighter king, or an injection-molded-vinyl-insert-that-fits-into-the-window-rolling-up-knobby-available-in-any-color king – or the king of standardized automotive snippets that can be made in one of those itty-bitty equatorial countries with no human rights or distinct regional cuisine.* Mufflers? *But to manufacture nothing* but *mufflers – an undiversified product line? How archaic. How sentimental. A formula for failure.*

Ted, meanwhile, seemed to be kicking both his offspring with equal vim. *Isn't this just peachy – whatever next?*

Next was a German shepherd seemingly shot from a cannon on to Bryan's leg, its fangs and jaws like a wood-chipper. Behind the dog appeared Shw, clad in a white terry-cloth robe, her hair in a white towel, at the top of a set of palm-kissed stairs. 'Kimba! *Stop*!' Kimba unclamped from Bryan's tibia and sat down and made a relaxed happy-dog face, while Bryan was transformed into a concentrated, twitching clot of pain. This pain, however, garnered him no sympathy from Shw. She skittered down the stairs, threw Kimba a Milk-Bone, and said, 'Christ, Bryan, count on you to bring your family along. Look at you all – you look like a bunch of carnies.' She stuck an emery board in her right front robe pocket. 'Scram. Now. Before I give Kimba the attack signal. *Now*.'

'Shw – you can't sell our baby – it's sacred. The baby's my love for you made into a person—'

'Bryan, put a gag in it.' Shw noticed Wade and Ted eyeing the rental car. 'What are you two looking at the car for?'

'I left my prescription list in the trunk when you gave us a ride yesterday.'

'A prescription list? What's that?'

'It's a printout of all the medications I have to take.'

'Big deal. Get a new one.'

'I can't. That one is—' Wade was obviously fumbling for a lie.

'That one is *what*? Look at me – you're shitting me, aren't you? You're lying. What did you leave in there, money?'

'No.'

Shw was evidently X-times more shrewd than Wade, and immune to his charms. 'No, you're not the money type, are you? Well, whatever it was, Gayle probably hucked it in the trash. She cleaned the car for me.'

'Gayle?' Bryan asked.

'Yeah. The mom-to-be. They worship me, and they wait on me hand and foot. I have a good gig going here, and you losers are going to screw it up, so scram.' She turned to the dog: '*Kimba*!' The dog stood erect, awaiting her command.

Bryan cried, 'Oh, God, I love you, Shw, I love you. Don't you remember we set fire to the Gap together? We destroyed a field of Frankenstein beans together – it was *real*. Did all that mean *nothing* to you?'

'Bryan, we had a moment, but it's over.'

'Okay, sic the dog on me, do what you want, but don't sell the baby.'

Kimba's bloodbath was forestalled by the sound of a jolly 'Ahoy, mateys!' in the darkness-free vocal tones of a cruise director.

'Shit—' said Shw. 'It's Lloyd. Act normal. If that's possible.'

Janet happily watched the show.

'Emily!' shouted Lloyd, 'I can't believe you brought the Drummond family along. I'm' – he placed his hand over his heart – 'deeply, *deeply* touched.'

In unison, Bryan, Wade, Ted and Janet said, '*Emily?*'

'Emily is the most thoughtful womb donor I could ever hope to meet, and you' – with his arms he took in the whole of the Drummond family – 'as the genetic forebears, are the embodiment of kindness. Come! Come into the house. Oh my! What a feast we'll have tonight.' He turned around. 'Gayle! Gayle! Little Emily has brought us the entire Drummond family!'

Gayle, a pretty fortysomething, poked her head out the window. 'God bless you, Drummond family! Come in! Come in! But ignore the mess. The place is a disaster.'

It was all Shw could do not to spontaneously combust, as the group entered Lloyd's house, a spanking new showcase of software modernism: 'I designed the place from a kit I bought at Office Depot,' Lloyd said. 'Something else, huh?'

The room's contents all seemed to be . . . *shiny*. Or pink. Or fuzzy. Or brass. Not a right angle was to be seen anywhere. '*Lovely*,' Janet said.

Gayle appeared in the room and spread out her arms and curtsied as if in a children's ballet: 'The grandmother of my Chosen Child!' She hugged Janet with animal force. 'Oh my, the child is going to be so smart – and so pretty.' She turned to Ted. 'Or handsome. Lloyd! Lloyd! Let's have drinks for everybody – open the bottle from France.' She turned to the Drummonds: 'It's *French*.' Then she turned to Shw: 'Emily, come help me pour.'

The family could only crow at Shw's humiliation, as Gayle hovered over her. 'Careful now, you'll topple the fluted glasses. And don't shake the bottle or else you'll make that lovely expensive Champagne spew, and it'll be wasted. And apple juice *only* for you, mother-to-be.' Shw looked at the Drummonds and gave a martyred smile. Janet assumed that the loving daughter act was a sham, and that more money was still to come Shw's way. *Thank God Bryan has the presence of mind to keep his mouth shut.*

'I want to use your phone to call my wife,' said Ted.

Gayle turned to him with a brief but unmistakable icicle of a stare.

'It's a local call,' he continued, turning to Janet for confirmation. 'Right?'

'Nickie's long distance, Ted.'

'You have a calling card?' Gayle asked.

Janet said, 'Ted, I've got your phone, but the phone number's in the van. Nickie and Beth are just fine in Kevin's trailer.'

'When did Nickie say she'd call again?'

'I don't know, Ted.'

Bryan, who was swooning from the pain of the dog bites and sunburn, caught Lloyd's eye. 'Looks like you have one major ouchy-doodle there, Bryan – *son* – I don't know what to call you. I feel so close to you.'

'Codeine. Vicodins. Percocets. *Now*,' Bryan wheezed.

'I'll see what I can rustle up.' Lloyd left the room.

Wade said, 'Hey, Gayle, Emily's been saying so many kind things about you.'

Shw's body visibly clenched, but Gayle beamed with delight as she passed the Champagne flutes around. 'Oh, now really, she didn't have to . . .'

'No,' Wade went on, 'she couldn't say enough good things about you, right, Mom?'

'Oh, yes. She even said she felt guilty accepting so much money for being a Chosen Mother. She said that all that money didn't feel *right* – that she'd become too close to you, that it'd feel wrong – *un-Christian*.'

'Did she now!' Gayle's bargaining radar was in full operation.

Shw cut in, 'Oh, Janet, joking like always.' She turned to Gayle. 'Janet is always such a caution.'

Janet said, 'Oh, no, Shw . . . *Emily* – don't hide your light under a bushel.' Janet turned to Gayle. 'She actually said that if she could, she'd donate her womb services for free, but then she has to cover her expenses.'

Gayle said, 'Oh yes, you do have to cover your overhead. *That* much I can understand.'

Lloyd came into the room with a prescription bottle of Tylenol 3.

Gayle, almost squeaking with glee at the chance of a price break, burst out, 'A toast! To my loving and generous Emily, and to the whole Drummond clan.'

Everybody drained their flutes in one gulp. Gayle and Lloyd then bombarded Ted with NASA-related questions, which were answered with pamphlet-like accuracy. Janet, left out of this conversation, asked to use the bathroom. Down the hall, her arm was painfully yanked behind her by a furious Shw. 'OK, what's it going to cost to make you people shut up?'

'Shw – *Emily* – truly ask me if I care here. Because I don't think I do.'

From behind, Wade clamped his hand over Shw's mouth. 'I think Bryan's the one to worry about, you little witch. He's stunned right now, but in a few minutes he'll be in the pulpit. And good for him.'

Shw bit him but quickly unclamped.

'Ow, *shit*.' Wade nearly yelped. 'Why'd you do *that*?'

'I didn't break your skin, did I?'

Wade checked. 'No, you're uninfected, thank you.'

'Be quiet,' said Shw. 'They'll hear us.'

Wade looked at a steel door beside the vanity. 'A steel door? Why would anyone have a steel door in their house?'

Shw said, 'I dunno. A bomb shelter, I think.'

'A bomb shelter?'

Wade opened the door; it revealed a deep, fungal-smelling staircase. 'This is Florida. People don't have basements here.'

'NASA's twenty miles south, bozo. This place was a primary nuclear target for forty years. It probably still is.'

Janet followed along. *Fascinating. All of this, just fascinating.* They walked down the dimly lit stairway that smelled of concrete blocks. At the end there was another steel door.

Wade said, 'If this isn't curious, I don't know what is. We're going in.'

'It's locked. I tried already,' said Shw.

'Some Nancy Drew *you* are.' Wade pulled out his key-chain and used one of its keys to fiddle with the lock; in moments the door was open. He flicked on a light switch just inside the door, and the three entered. Inside was an obstetrical chair, isolated and cold, like a Mississippi prison's lethal injection facility – it appeared to be a home delivery ward. On the wall behind the chair was an array of stainless steel medical instruments, handcuffs and leather straps. To the right, the three saw a perfect, pink and dainty bedroom for one person set behind a set of steel zoo bars.

None of them spoke. After the most cursory of inspections they fled up to the main hallway. Gayle shouted, 'Did you find the little girls' room OK, Janet?'

'Yes, and such a lovely home you have here. A clear sense of taste and vision. And very thorough, too. Did you or Lloyd do the interior?'

'I won't let Lloyd even go near a color chip. He'd choose school-bus yellow or mental-ward green, and then we might as well be living in a trailer park roasting Spam with pineapple rings tacked on to it with toothpicks.'

'Such a colorful word picture.'

'Forty-two hundred square feet of Gayle is what you see here.' She turned to Shw. 'Emily, come into the living room. I found your letter for me in the car's trunk – such a thoughtful gesture. I thought we could open it now as a sort of bonding ceremony.'

'A letter?'

She's quick. And she knows she needs us here. Janet took Shw's arm. 'Yes, dear, the one you were telling me about. Truly a generous gesture.'

'Oh yeah, that one. Of course.'

They walked into the living room. Janet said, 'Ted . . . Bryan . . . Gayle is going to read us a letter from Emily.'

'Letter?' They sat bolt upright.

Gayle prattled on. 'Emily, you sly fox. You even inserted it between plastic sheets to keep it clean. And you labeled it "Mummy" – that's what I used to call my own mother.'

'The letter meant a lot to me,' Shw said, whereupon a crash of cinematic proportions came from beside Ted across the room; he'd dropped a solid brass gazelle statue through a glass side table. The crash had its intended effect. Gayle dropped the letter, and Janet dove for it. Gayle stormed over to Ted, palpably on the brink of shouting a blue streak. 'I paid *retail* for that table.'

'Can't be much of a table if it can't hold a small piece of brass.'

'It's *ruined*.'

Ted looked at the shards and said, 'I think the gazelle's leg looks bent, too,' which sent Gayle into a further fit; Lloyd came over to comfort her, and the others were ignored.

Wade grabbed a dummy letter from Janet's purse and flicked it to her, but by mistake he threw two letters stuck together; she caught both.

Janet then removed the real letter from between the sheets, used her pen to make a blue dot on its top right corner, tossed it to Wade and put a fake letter inside the plastic sheets. It was a lightning-fast procedure. The extra dummy letter she slid under the couch seat.

Gayle clucked about with a Dustbuster, paper bags and a broom, while Bryan, caught up in this family activity, knocked over his Champagne flute to buy an extra minute or so for Janet and Wade.

Janet said, 'Gayle, don't worry, it'll be just fine.' Things settled down, although Gayle's initial friendliness had worn measurably thin.

Janet said, 'You were going to read a letter?'

'Yes.' Gayle picked up the duplicate, brushed a wisp of hair from her face and turned on her smile. 'From little Emily.' She opened the letter with less finesse than she might have before Ted broke the table. Inside was a card saying *To the Finest of Sons on the Occasion of His Bar Mitzvah*. Inside the card was a coffee cup ring. 'Emily?'

Shw looked at her and said, 'So, what's with the downstairs pink dungeon, huh?'

Gayle and Lloyd's faces at first looked as if they might project a sort of chipper *Who, me*? innocence, but they quickly morphed into blank business-like stares.

'Dungeon?' asked Bryan.

Janet said, 'Yes, we just took a tour – obstetrical chair, handcuffs, leather straps and the cutest little pink bedroom inside a gorilla cage.'

Wade said, 'Hey, Lloyd, hey, Gayle – aren't *you two* the sick fucks?' Lloyd and Gayle had nothing to say.

Janet knew that this was the point at which weapons, if they were to be used, would appear. She said, 'Wade . . . Ted . . . Bryan . . . Emily . . . could you please capture Lloyd and Gayle. Perhaps we should lock them inside their own jail. Kimba, I believe, is in the backyard kennel.' There was a moment of silence, then a bark, as though Janet were addressing Kimba: '*Now*!'

. . . a blur . . . some cussing . . . some thrashing . . . some shiny broken furniture, and Lloyd and Gayle were downstairs inside the pink room, locked behind bars. Lloyd became vocal: 'You people are fucking *nuts*. I'm going to have every cop between here and Atlanta carving you into fucking steak tartare before you have a chance to even blink. I don't care if your daughter won the Nobel Prize – any child in your family has to be fucking *crazy*.'

Janet, surveying the dungeon at leisure, said, 'Watch your language, Lloyd. Oh, look – my, my, a cattle prod. Obstetrics have come a long way since my own children were born. Handcuffs, too. How smart. Who'd have thought?'

Shw pulled a chair up to the bars and glowered at Lloyd and Gayle. 'What was your plan, huh? When was I going to end up in your little Barbie's First Lockup Facility?' Bryan stood beside her, spitting at the two.

'You were never going to be in *here*,' Gayle said.

'You saving the space for someone else perhaps?'

'I can see how this must look . . .'

Shw waved the cattle prod through the bars, causing Lloyd and Gayle to shimmy up against the wall.

Wade said, 'Shw, give it a rest. We have bigger fish to fry.'

Shw spun around. 'So what's the deal with that letter, huh? You people probably don't even read the Sunday comics, so what's in a letter that's so important to you? Huh? Huh? *Huh?*'

Janet said, 'OK. Fair enough. We'll tell you, but you have to promise not to abort your baby or go selling it to the highest bidders.'

Bryan's face lit up.

Shw asked, 'Is there money in it for me?'

'I suppose.'

'Deal.'

23

Janet said, 'I think it's best we find evidence to build a solid blackmail case. Don't you think?' And with this, her family began sifting through drawers and cupboards ferreting out more information about Lloyd and Gayle's baby factory cum dungeon.

Wade was aware of the fact that his family was immersed in a world of cheese, cruddiness and illegalities from which they might never emerge. Was there any going back? Was there anything to go back *to?* Wade had slogged in the crud for over two decades and that was his life, his father maybe just as long. Bryan? Fifteen years. Sarah? As the past week had revealed, maybe a year or so. But *Mom*? So pure and crud-proof, now seemingly born to the role of navigator through the warm, farty waters of sleaze – upstairs, scooping out the potpourris and emptying vases looking for dirt. She called to Wade, down in the kitchen going through the cupboards.

'Yeah, Mom?'

'There's a beautiful shirt up here, and it looks like it'd fit you perfectly.'

'Mom, this isn't Abercrombie and Fitch. I don't need a new shirt.'

'But you do, and this one is so soft, and a tattersall check, which is always so flattering.'

'I don't want Lloyd's shirt, Mom. The karma alone . . .'

'You wouldn't be so Mr. Karma if you'd gone through the Depression and the war, buster. This is a good shirt. Well-made. And I only want you to try it on.'

'I am *not* trying it.'

'Then *don't*, but don't come crying to *me* when the soup kitchens reopen.'

Ted, in the den, called out, 'Take the effing shirt, ferchrissake. A good deal is a good deal.'

'Dad, that's stealing. I can't believe *you'd* be so casual about swiping other people's stuff.'

'How can *you* of all people say that?'

'What are you calling me?' Wade charged off to the den.

'I'm calling you someone who can't spot a good deal when he sees one.' Ted was going through a drawer full of ball bearings.

Wade said, 'Oh, I see – that coming from Mr. Chapter Eleven. It's because you're in such deep financial shit that we're even pursuing this stupid mess further.'

'Oh, like you're not getting cash out of this? Well, if *you* hadn't gone and shat away your life doing God only knows what garbage, we wouldn't have hooked up with that lousy kraut who gets spanked by his nanny on Sundays.'

Ted seemed to be anticipating a reply that, historically, would only escalate the situation into a brawl. But instead Wade went quiet. 'Uh-oh.'

'Uh-oh *what*?'

'Howie.'

'What about *him*?'

'I, uh . . . just that Florian probably kidnapped him.' Wade recalled Florian's penchant for Danish-built radar and data monitoring systems. 'I used his phone at the Brunswicks'.'

'Serves him right.'

Wade sat down in a green leather captain's chair, and Ted across from him on a stool. Janet came into the room. 'Did I just hear you say that this German fellow's kidnapped Howie?'

'You did.'

'Oh.' Nobody seemed overly troubled by this news. 'You don't think they'd *hurt* him, do you?'

'Florian? Eventually.'

Ted said, 'This could solve problems for us, couldn't it? We can simply tell Sarah he was there for the launch. She'll be up in the shuttle, so how's she going to know?'

Janet seemed to mull this over.

Wade said, 'I can't believe I'm hearing this. What if launch time comes, and instead of Howie standing with us in the VIP bleachers, we only have Howie's pancreas inside a picnic cooler?'

Ted, with a rich lack of self-awareness, said, 'Wade, don't be such a bore. He's a philandering putz.'

Janet added, 'I don't even think Sarah likes Howie much.'

'Yeah,' said Ted, 'Good riddance. Where's Shw?'

Bryan walked into the room, eating cold ravioli out of a can. 'She's in the garage. What's Dad so razzed about?'

'Howie and Alanna's affair.'

'Gee. Tell me something new.'

Janet looked at Bryan's snack. 'Bryan, how can you eat that stuff? They put *cat food* inside those raviolis.'

'Thanks, Mom.' He stopped eating.

The Drummond family sat around Lloyd's den, posed as if modeling for a Burda knitting catalogue. The office was an oak fantasia filled with electric doodads purchased in the wacky electrical doodad shop at the mall. Ted said, 'I say let the kraut turn him into ravioli filling.'

Janet said, 'We'd all like that, but I think for Sarah's long-term happiness we'd better rescue him alive.'

Bryan said, 'Maybe we can let Florian torture him just a little.'

'That makes sense,' said Ted.

'Yeah, I like that,' added Wade.

'Does Florian use physical or psychological torture?' Janet asked Wade.

'How should I know?' *If she knew, she'd freak.*

'Call him on the speakerphone.'

'He'll know we're here at this phone number.'

'Phone him *now*, Wade.'

Mother knows best, and it does get me off the hook. Inside a minute Florian was on the line, and Wade put him on the speakerphone with Janet. She asked, 'Is this Florian?'

'It is. And who might this be?'

'I'm Janet, Wade's mother.'

A Teutonic cackle burst from the other end. 'Oh, this is too rich, *far* too rich. Wade, whoever this actress is, please spare her having to play an impossible role.'

Wade said, 'That's my mother, Florian, you be nice to her.'

'Oh *gawd, Wade* – you're serious, aren't you? Very well, I shall indeed mind my manners. Hello' – Florian adopted the manner of one addressing a child's imaginary friend – '*Janet.*'

'Yes, well, we might as well do our business. How much will you pay for the letter, and how much do we pay to get' – a freighted pause – '*Howie* back.'

'Yes, your son-in-law. A charmer.'

'You can imagine how thrilled we are to have to actually pay to retrieve him. You should see him at Christmas. He has to have the floor to himself to sing Christmas carols. Here's an impersonation—' Janet burst into a mock soprano: ' "*Frawwwwwwwww*sty the *snnnnnnnnnnowwwwwwww*man . . ." And on. And on.'

Ted burst in, 'He's a goddamn pain in the butt.'

Florian was genuinely curious. 'And who might this new speaker be?'

'It's my dad, Florian. Be nice.'

Florian seemed insulted. 'My manners are always good, Wade. Who else is there in the room with you?'

'My brother, Bryan.'

'Are you playing Scrabble? Pick-up Stix?'

Janet said to everybody in the room, 'Please be quiet.' She turned to the speakerphone's grille. 'Florian, let's play "garage sale". Whatever you're charging for Howie, we want a hundred thousand more for the letter.'

Florian said, 'I want a billion dollars for Howie.'

Janet said, 'I want a billion dollars plus a hundred grand for the letter.'

'I've already tracked you down via call display, you know.'

'We'll be gone in five minutes. And then what? Big deal. We'll shred the letter. A hundred thousand, Florian. That's one one-hundredth of the original asking price.'

'Fifty thousand.'

Janet said breezily, 'You know what, Florian? No. A hundred, firm. I'm an old lady dying of AIDS, my ex-husband's an old man dying of liver cancer—'

Wade and Bryan froze and stared at their unconcerned father. Janet continued on: '—and Wade's not looking too hot, either.'

'So I hear. Are you in pain?'

'Yes. A bit. Mouth ulcers, but I can take medications for that. But these pills, Florian, good God, they swallow up my entire life, thinking about them. It's making me more crazy than anything.'

'My mother had breast cancer. She lived on pills, too.'

'Oh, you poor thing. When?'

'When I was younger.'

'Did it go on for long?'

Florian sounded thoughtful: 'With what she had to go through, a single day was too long.'

'You poor lamb. How did your family take it?'

'Daddy dearest was embarrassed, and you know why?'

'Why?'

'Because here he is, the world's leading maker of pills, pills, pills, and he can't find a single pill to save my mother. He took this failure as a personal disgrace, and the disgrace overshadowed my mother's death.'

'People respond to dying in unpredictable ways. That was his.'

'But Janet, you must understand that after the funeral services were over, did he bother to throw money into research? No. He drank himself into the gutters of Nassau. Disgusting. *Cochon.* And then he got Alzheimer's.'

'My father had Alzheimer's. Four years of hell.'

'How do you deal with it?'

'I don't know if I did. Did he recognize you at the end?'

'No.'

'Mine neither. It's so cruel. It robs you of everything. Do you have any brothers or sisters?'

'My brother was killed in an avalanche in Klosters in 1974. So I'm the end of the line.'

'So do *you* put more money into research to make up for what your dad lacked?'

'Research is my passion.'

'Then your mother would be proud of you.'

'You think so?'

'Oh yes. I'm sure she's listening in on this phone call right now and thinking what a good boy you are. And have you discovered anything that might help people with liver cancer now? My ex-husband, Ted, has liver cancer.'

Ted said, 'Do we need to dig in for a long, cozy chat?'

Janet shushed the group of them, and the men settled in to listen to the call as if it were yet another CBC radio documentary about New Brunswick barrel-making.

Florian continued, 'You know, Janet, there are a number of ways of treating cancer that the *New York Times* hasn't heard about yet, and might well not for a while.'

'How so?'

'You see, fixing cancer is one thing, but fixing society is another. Curing a huge disease like cancer would effectively wipe out the insurance industry and consequently the banking system. For each year we increase the average life span, we generate a massive financial crisis. That's what the twentieth century was about – absorbing, year by year, our increased life spans.'

'Florian, surely—'

'Oh no, Janet, I assure you. I run one of the world's biggest pharmaceutical firms. Glaxo Wellcome or Bayer – or Citibank, for that matter – will chop out my tongue for what I've just told you.'

'Do you ever have a chance to talk about this? Is there someone in your life?'

A pause: 'No.'

'Oh, you poor dear! It must be awful for you.'

'Oh, it *is*.'

I don't believe it – Mom is bonding with Florian.

'You must be in knots inside. I have colitis from worrying. What do you get?'

'Shingles.'

'Ooh – shingles is bad.'

'And a rosacea rash. All over my nose and forehead.'

'Have you found anything that works for it? Rashes are so iffy.'

'A few things, but nothing that's a magic bullet.'

'My friend Bev has rosacea. I found her this cream sold out of Arizona that's done wonders for her.'

'Really?'

'You should try some.'

This is not happening. This is not happening.

'At this point I'll try anything.'

Ted cut in, 'Sorry to bust into your sewing circle here, gang, but, uh – are we going to talk about moolah?'

'Ted, how can you be so vulgar at a time like this? Florian, I'm sorry.'

'You are a *dear*, Janet.'

Janet said, 'Florian, come have dinner with me.'

Florian sounded taken aback, almost teary. 'Me? Really?'

Wade, Ted and Bryan mouthed, *What*?

Janet continued: 'Yes, and it can be just the two of us. I'll send the others out to Shakey's for pizza.'

Florian was touched. 'I – don't know what to say, Janet.'

'Say yes. And I'll give you this ridiculous letter, too. Good riddance. We're in Daytona Beach. Is it driveable for you? I assume your computers have already located our address. How does six o'clock sound?'

'Perfect.'

'Very well, then. Six o'clock.'

Janet hung up. 'The poor boy misses his mother.'

Shw walked into the room, grimy with automotive oil and carrying a thick stack of snapshot folders. 'I think we're finally having fun.' She dropped the folders on the desk.

'Excellent,' Janet said. 'Now, could all of you make sure those two dreadful people are safely locked up, and then could you all get out of my hair? Go meet Nickie and Beth at Kevin's trailer. *I* have a date.'

'Ooh, look at her – isn't *she* a plump one.'

A few hours later around dinner time, Shw, Beth and Bryan were sitting in Kevin's trailer ogling the photo album of womb donor applicants Shw had found under a steel plate beneath Lloyd's Buick LeSabre. Shw was in a good mood – her brush with captivity had made her uncharacteristically pleasant to be around. Watching from across the room, Wade caught a flash or two in which he could see the attraction she might hold for Bryan. Meanwhile Wade tried to pretend he wasn't roasting, but failed. The trailer's interior, while punishing, was nothing compared to outside, where even with the sun below the horizon anything alive was being turned into a festering variant of beef jerky.

In the trailer's tiny kitchen, Ted and Nickie were sitting on the floor, backs against the sink cupboard, holding hands and not saying much of anything. Nickie now knew about Ted's liver cancer; their shared medical sagas bound them more closely together than might have any joyful experience. On the fridge opposite them was a snapshot of Kevin attending what appeared to be a bash for Disney mascots. He was defiantly smoking a Virginia Slim, and the lower part of his torso was clad in the body of Scrooge McDuck, while he bandied about Scrooge's head as though it were a bracelet given to him by an unwelcome suitor. Beside this photo was a letter from Disney management, giving Kevin notice of his dismissal for mascot protocol violation.

When Wade had first imagined this week in Florida leading up to the shuttle launch, this trailer was *not* part of the scenario. He'd envisioned – what? – noble dinners inside jet hangars, food served on aluminum plates, with sixteen-millimeter films of past launches played for him and his fellow diners, after which silver-headed astronauts of yore would emerge from behind a curtain and swap tales of close calls and post-flight dinners along with starlets wearing skimpy dresses with spaghetti strap shoulders. Young sexless children in jumpsuits would take him on tours of complex underground facilities in which he'd be exposed to blinding white lights that made him smarter and stronger and kinder. Afterwards, up on the tarmac, Bruce Springsteen and Pamela Anderson would be waiting inside a Hummer, and they'd go out for a smart French dinner, at which Wade would understand French and his tales would amuse and delight the assembled crowd.

Ted called from the floor: 'Is this thing a cockroach? What the fuck is it?'

'It's a palmetto bug,' Wade said.

'You can't even see it from where you are. How can you tell?'

'Everyone asks the same thing when they see them.'

'Aren't *you* Mr. Florida-the-Sunshine-State? Nickie, smash the bastard with your pump.'

'Righty-oh, dear.'

Thunk

Was this a new low? Was it a new high? Yet again Wade could only wonder at this new place he and his family had entered.

'So, how long do we stay here?' Shw asked.

'A little while,' said Wade.

'How much is a little while?'

'Until my mother phones.'

Wade said he was going out for a walk and took the cell phone with him. On impulse he called Sarah, and, luck of luck, reached her. 'Baby sister?'

'Wade.'

'Hey.'

'Hey to you. You feeling any better?'

'A bit. I'm preparing for a sleep cycle. Gordon patted me on the butt a few minutes ago, but then a camera crew came in, and so that was the end of that. Our zero-G biological experiment might still be on, but frankly, I'm sick of myself at this point. Tell me some news that'll temporarily transport me out of this metal dump. Where *are* you? What's going on, huh? I *know* you, Wade. Something's stewing. Confess to me now. You are powerless against my will.'

Why not? 'Fair enough. I'm standing outside a trailer in Orlando's shittiest neighborhood. It belongs to a guy named Kevin whose arm was shot up in the restaurant holdup yesterday. By the way, Mom and Nickie are best friends now. What else . . .' *Probably best not to tell her that we're hiding out here from the thugs who kidnapped her husband. Should I go on? Why not.* 'And then a few hours ago, me, Mom, Dad and Bryan rescued Shw from these freaky rich people in Daytona Beach who were going to lock Shw in their basement prison, steal her baby, and then probably kill her – so suddenly Shw's all nicey-nicey, and Bryan's like a pig in clover. Oh, by the way, Shw's real name is Emily.'

Silence – and faint mechanical sounds on Sarah's end of the phone.

'There's more. Right now Mom's having dinner with this whacked-out German-Bahamian pharmaceutical billionaire I used to work for. She's going to sell him this, uh, historically important document I inherited from my pal Norm, who had a heart attack yesterday in Disney World. Splat, right onto the pavement.'

More faint mechanical sounds on Sarah's end.

Why not tell her about Dad? Go for it . . . No – don't. 'Sarah?'

'I'm listening, Wade. I'm digesting, actually.'

'I figured you might be. Where's Howie?' *Good – no sign of hesitation in the voice.*

'I don't know. If you were Howie, what would you be doing right now?'

'Groveling to you like a truffle pig.'

'That's what I thought. But he's being out of character on this one. And I *still* don't know what NASA was doing picking him up at the Brunswicks'. Usually I can read his actions like subtitles. This is infuriating.'

'Don't lose sleep over it.'

'Why not?'

'Howie's not built for mystery. He'll come to you soon enough.'

'I can't give the matter too much thought, Wade. Anyway, I have to have a full sleep cycle if I'm going to use lasers tomorrow. Say hi to the gang for me.'

She was ringing off a bit too quickly. Wade asked, 'Hey – *whoa!* Are you pissed off at us? Are you pissed of because we're not there on the sidelines 24/7 holding balloons and sheets of twenty-four-by-thirty-six cardboards with Bible quotes? Is that what the other families are doing?'

'Good *God*, no. It's the pressure here. People can't even pee in this place without Tom Hanks coming in and making a documentary, or IMAX capturing the moment. This phone probably isn't secure – we're probably going out on live webcast. The only thing I don't like about this whole astronaut thing is the lack of privacy. But then I was chosen for my compatibility with groups as well as for my low body mass and varied skill sets.'

'Romantic.'

'I'm practical, Wade. Always have been.'

'Are you going to be up at four A.M. again?'

'I will. Let me call you.'

Wade gave her Ted's cell number and they hung up.

A few minutes later back inside, Shw looked behind a panel and said, 'Have you seen the A/C in this rig? It's like a hamster on a running wheel. Couldn't we at least go to a restaurant and kill time that way?'

'No,' said Wade. 'We're all broke, and besides, this way Mom knows where we are.'

The others were too listless to comment.

Ted said, 'Was it really safe to leave your mother with that carnivore Hun?'

'He's Swiss, Dad. And since when did you start caring about Mom?'

Ted ignored Wade's baiting. 'German-Swiss. These days it's the same thing. We might just as well have tossed her into a wood chipper. And God only knows what he's done to Howie. Made into ravioli filling, probably. Bryan probably ate him.'

'And so now you care about Howie? Hypocrite.'

'Wade, use the brains God gave you. You know damn well Howie has to be in the bleachers for lift-off, even though he is a grating little shit.'

How can I tell Dad that the lives of Sarah, Howie, Alanna and Gordon Brunswick had devolved into a low-budget 1970s sex comedy with an aerospace theme.

Beth said, 'Mr. Drummond—'

'Ted. Call me Ted.'

'Ted – have you always told Wade he was useless?'

'Yeah, sure.'

'Why?'

'Why?' He paused. 'Because the little shit kept on landing in trouble – BB guns and rifles – neighbors showing up with half of their cats in each hand . . .'

'That was an *accident*, Dad.'

'Wade, let me finish here: cops arriving in the driveway every other day; setting fire to the neighbor's house—'

'Accident!'

'I could go on. A discipline nightmare. Wait until your centrifugal zygote turns into a teenager. You'll be coming to my grave and asking for advice from the Beyond.'

Nickie threw down her hand. 'Ted, stop talking like that. Liver's the one cancer they have under control.'

Ted hummed the funeral dirge; Nickie stormed out of the trailer.

Beth said, 'You spread love and sunshine wherever you go, don't you?'

'Skip the Sunbeam routine. Nickie's a survivor.'

Beth asked, 'Did you tell Bryan he was useless, too?'

'I didn't have to. With him, it was always self-evident.'

'And Janet?'

'Well, yeah. I suppose.'

'And Sarah?'

Ted clenched his body. 'I see what you're doing. You're trying to pin the results of their lives on me. Don't bother.' Ted shuffled a deck of cards, with rather too much noise and flourish.

Beth said, 'I barely know your entire family, but they strike me as textbook evidence of prophecy fulfilled.'

'Is this religious?'

'No. It's reality.'

Ted turned to Wade. 'Wadey-poo, if I'd hugged you back when you were eight, or pretended to give a damn about your scale model of the Pyramids at Giza, do you think you'd have been any different as a person now?'

'Let me think.' Wade sipped his drink. 'In essence, yes, but in circumstance, no. I think my life would be much more traditional-looking. I'd have a house and a wife and two kids and a dog. Maybe a—'

Beth shot a glass of lemonade in his face.

'What was *that* for?'

'Because I'm not a wife and two kids, Wade. Screw you.' She flew out, on the tail of Nickie.

'Thanks, Dad.'

The phone rang; Kevin's machine answered: *Kevin's gone out to play, but he'll be back soon.*

Beep

'Kevin, it's Mickey. I mended your slacks for you. Slacks – what a *scream* of a word. 'Bye, dear.'

Click

Almost as soon as that call ended, the phone rang again, Janet this time. '*Wade? Ted? Anybody there?*'

Wade grabbed the phone. 'Mom. Hey.'

'Hello, dear.'

'Are you OK?'

'Fit as a fiddle.'

To judge from the background noise, she was on the road. 'Where are you?'

'Flor, dear, where are we?'

She's calling him 'Flor, dear'?

Florian replied, 'We're in Kansas, dear.'

'Flor, don't be such a silly Billy. Where are we really?'

'Interstate 95 headed up to Daytona Beach.'

'We're headed up to Daytona Beach, dear.'

'Is Howie there?'

'Yes, Howie is here.'

'Did they do anything to him?'

'Howie is fine, dear. Come meet us.'

'Where?'

'Chez Lloyd and Gayle.'

'All of us?'

'No. Just you, Ted and Nickie. No need for the others. Please. I mean it. Please confirm to me that you heard me say that.'

'I heard you. Did you sell the letter?'

'We'll see you shortly, dear.'

24

Janet had always maintained her primness in the face of the modern world's countless assaults against it – but her primness had gently snapped just a month before Florida. She'd been in a downtown Vancouver Internet café (*must get out of the house; must get out of the house; must get out of the . . .*) having a pleasant enough time of it tracking down old university friends and reigniting contacts dormant for forty-five years:

> Dear Dorothy,
>
> It's me, Janet – Janet (Truro) Drummond. Can you believe it (!!!). Forty-five years later, living in Vancouver, three kids grown up [Sarah's in the news a lot, you probably see her every so often] and no more Ted. Yes, the Big 'D', he's off with some young thing. A surprise, but . . .

Too intimate too quickly. How about:

> Dear Dorothy,
>
> Janet Truro (Drummond) here. Surprise! This Internet is changing things so much. How are you? I don't think we've seen each other since – when? I bumped into you at the Loblaws' in Toronto in 1963 – has it really been that long?

No. Too boring. Janet then remembered Dorothy peeking into Sarah's stroller, seeing her handless arm, and beating a hasty retreat. *Forget Dorothy. Who needs her?*

It was at this point the man beside her, whom Janet had

noticed only in passing as a business type, gave an exasperated sigh. To judge from his puckered forehead, scrunched up lips and clumsy mousing, he was a neophyte. A dark burly man, he seemed friendly, and was of Janet's own vintage. He was also evidently deep inside a search but having no luck; Janet couldn't resist taking a peek at his screen. She was fully expecting an English-language Cambodian site along the lines of 'Me So Horny,' but instead saw a site for a propane firm in Missouri. The man's monitor made feeble *blink blink blink* noises, indicating mistake after mistake, and he was losing patience.

'Maybe I can help you,' said Janet.

The man looked as if he'd been caught thinking out loud. 'I just can't make this *thing* work. All I find is irrelevant crap.'

Janet gently asked, 'You were searching for specific information?'

'Yeah. My kids bought me this new CD player and I can't find any CDs I like in stores – so I thought I'd go onto the Internet.'

'What CDs are you looking for?'

'The Kingston Trio. Four Lads.'

'Oh! I don't believe it, those were my favorites.' Janet's enthusiasm was like a spaniel tugging at its leash.

'Yeah?'

'Oh, the fun I used to have with them in the background. They were so cute, and I was at university. Sweaters and ponytails. I was Little Betty Coed.'

'Where'd you go?'

'U of T.'

'My brother went there. I went to McGill. I'm Ernie.'

'Janet.'

Janet decided that she wanted Kingston Trio CDs, too. The hunt was on. Along the way the two bantered like old pals. Janet couldn't remember the last time she'd clicked so well with a man right off the bat, and soon they'd located dozens of CDs, five of which Ernie bought as a gift for Janet.

'Ernie – you shouldn't—'

'No. Consider it a finder's fee. You were great.'

'The Web's just common sense, you know.'

'No, it isn't. It's a mess, and you rescued me.' He squinted at the time in the screen's corner. 'I have to go and pick up my granddaughter at skating. What are you doing for dinner tonight? Call me forthright, but I don't see a wedding ring.'

'I didn't have any—' The wedding ring came off the day the divorce decree had been signed.

'So then let me take you out.'

'Ernie! You're so—'

'The guy who fixes my brakes recommended a place to me. I went and had a look – pretty nice. "Sir Steak".'

Janet suppressed a laugh.

Ernie said, 'I know, I know – what a dumb name, but I really like steak. See you there at 7:00?'

'OK.'

And then he was gone and Janet realized she was having her first date in forty-three years.

The weather that night was warm and un-Vancouver-like. The wind felt like hot breath against Janet's skin. She was early at the restaurant and waited outside; the heat reminded her of her summer youth, long before the era of air-conditioning.

Ernie showed up in a blobby late 1990s red Impala. This was the first car model Janet had noticed since the 1965 Mustang; Impala was the make her father had driven. *So something else from back then has made it this far, too.* She scanned the car to see if it had mutated as much as she had. Ernie said, 'So you're a car buff, then?'

'Me? No. My dad used to drive an Impala. I haven't thought of that car in years.'

'Good car. Reliable, affordable and comfy. Are you hungry?'

'Me? Hungry? Lord, no. Two Jell-O cubes and a grape would suit me just fine.'

Sir Steak was a carnival of rayon heraldic buntings fluttering amid air-conditioning gone mad. Delinquent-looking teens in ill-fitted period costumes carried about electronic clipboards and gave the illusion of service.

'This place is so gee-dee weird,' said Janet, 'it makes my head spin.'

' "Gee-dee"? I haven't heard that expression since . . . since—'

'The 1950s?'

'Well – *yeah*.'

'We're museum pieces, Ernie.'

Once seated, a waitress took their drink orders. 'I think I'd like a screwdriver,' Ernie said. He looked at Janet.

Best not to tell him about my mouth ulcers. 'Decaf coffee, please.'

Blip, blip, blip

Their orders were input into an electronic slate and their child waitress strayed from their table. Tinny generic-sounding Spanish music squeaked out of wall panels, as though mice were partying inside. Dinner menus arrived with drinks.

'Great-looking salad bar,' Ernie said. 'Did you see it?'

'I certainly did. Salad bars are like a restaurant's lungs, Ernie. They soak up the impurities and bacteria in the environment, leaving us with much cleaner air to enjoy.'

'Maybe I'll pass.'

'Ernie, I'm going to go wax my skis. I'll be back in two shakes of a lamb's tail.' Janet went off to the ladies' room and took a dronabidol tablet to boost her appetite. *Why is it still so shameful to be seen taking a pill in public?* She looked in the mirror. *I'm hanging together well today*. She returned to the table, where Ernie had removed his jacket.

'Ernie, you're relaxing, I see.'

'It's a nice place here. Fun.'

'Ernie, do you ever wonder why, of all animals, it was turtles and parrots who live for centuries? Why not, say, jaguars or mallard ducks? It's as if parakeets and turtles won the animal kingdom lottery draw.'

'People don't do too bad. Seventy-two-point-five is okay.'

'You mentioned your granddaughter, Ernie. Where's your family?'

'I'm a widower. Two years now – Lucy. Hodgkin's lymphoma. One, two, three, gone.'

'Sorry.'

Ernie sighed. 'We move on.' He sipped his drink. Another delinquent teen arrived and took their dinner order.

'So what's your story, Janet? What's a woman like you doing in a cybercafé? You seem to be more the SPCA and yoga type.'

'Today I was downloading NASA information. I have a daughter who's an astronaut. Sarah.'

'So you *are* . . . you're Sarah Drummond's mother. I wasn't sure. I didn't want to bring it up. *Caramba!* I'm dining with a celebrity. Wow.'

Janet wondered how Ernie would be different, now that he was connecting with fame in a once-removed way.

Salads arrived. They went on to discuss their teeth, the muggy weather, bees and the schools they'd attended – they had an acquaintance in common, a childhood friend of Janet who'd worked in Ernie's office in Manitoba. They talked about Ernie's two married sons, one far away in Strasbourg, France, the other in town and in the midst of a messy divorce with custody issues.

Their meals arrived, and they discussed the impending shuttle flight. *It's so nice to chew the fat with someone of my own vintage – no need to explain anything.*

Janet managed a few bites of her chicken; the plates were removed. Ernie asked if she would like anything more.

'How about a mudpie?' Janet asked. 'I used to make mudpies in the back alley in Toronto. They were wonderful. My mother would have died had she known we ate them.'

'Mudpies are pretty rich,' Ernie said. 'Why don't we share one?'

Janet agreed and they ordered one. In the meantime, two decaf coffees arrived. Ernie drew a deep breath and asked, 'Janet, you know, you still haven't explained to me how it is that *you* know so much about the Internet.'

'I used to be afraid of the thing, but if you know my story, you'll see why.'

'What's your story?'

'You'll think differently about me after I tell you.'

'Oh no, how could I?'

What am I going to do here – lie? Of course not. 'Here goes: My ex-husband, Ted, he dumped me for a trophy wife about four years ago. I'm an idiot for not having spotted it sooner, but I'm spotting that kind of thing these days. So now I'm in this big suburban house by myself, with the three kids gone. I adjust. I reignite a few old friendships, take night courses on the Internet. Then one day my first-born, Wade, makes a surprise visit from Las Vegas, where he's been living for I don't know how long. Wade's the family tumbleweed. Con man. Lovable. My favorite child, but I'll deny it if you ever bring it up in public. So Wade comes into town, meets a bimbette named Nickie at a local bar and they have a tumble. Afterwards he goes to visit my ex-husband, Ted, in this ridiculous new house he had then, and who should walk in the door but Nickie – turns out the bimbette is also Ted's trophy wife. It's a farce, I know. So Wade scrams. He comes over to my place, where we have a lovely little dinner until Ted shows up and pops Wade in the gut with a handgun. The bullet passes through Wade and enters my sternum.'

Janet pointed to her wound.

'Good God,' said Ernie.

Janet had told the story many times. She knew how to pace it. 'So fine, then. Ted's an asshole and no charges were filed. Wade returns to Las Vegas. A year later I come down with pneumonia. They run a check and . . . you guessed it' – *the moment of truth* – 'HIV. From my kid. So I call Wade and tell him, and it turns out he's been sick for a year but they thought it was his liver, which after the reconstruction is about the size of a dinner mint. He gets tested, and lo and behold, it's HIV. I don't know where he got it, and it doesn't matter. Both of us now live on pills.' Janet stared down into her cooling coffee. 'There's more, but that's the gist. The story of me.'

The mudpie arrived with two forks. Ernie was silent. Janet picked up a fork and took a bite of the pie. 'Ernie, you going to have some mudpie?'

Ernie looked at his hands.

'It's a good mudpie, Ernie.'

Ernie moved his hands in the pie's direction, but quickly stopped.

Janet put down her spoon. 'I think now's the time I leave, Ernie.'

Ernie's head appeared to be vibrating slightly.

'It's OK, Ernie. But I think I ought to be going.'

'I'd eat some of the mudpie with you, Janet, but I'm—'

'Shush!'

'But—'

'*Shush.*' She looked at his face. She walked out of the restaurant and got in her car.

Our leaders are dead.

History has abandoned us.

The past is a joke.

She drove west towards the sunset; the news had said that a forest fire on Vancouver Island was going to transform the sky into spectacular colors, and it was right. There in her car, Janet felt that she was for the first time driving away from the people in her life, their needs, their lovers, their flaws, their lists of unmendable wounds, their never-spoken-of unslakeable thirsts, their catalogues of wrongs.

She passed an overturned Camaro, surrounded by the RCMP and a cluster of dazed-looking teenagers, then drove on.

I'm diseased. My soul is diseased. She felt a lifetime of

chemicals washing through her body's fibers and bones: vaccines, the Pill, pesticides, Malathion, sweeteners, antibiotics, sulfa drugs . . . *God only knows what else.*

Maple trees, condos, seagulls and flatbeds loaded with SUVs slid past Janet's vision. *So this is the future – it's not the future I expected but I'll be damned if I'll be ignored by it.*

Janet felt her entire brain-load of personal snapshot memories fluttering out the window – all those sad little 1956 notions of propriety – gone like mosquitoes in August – six and a half decades of kindnesses gone unthanked, passionless sex, crippling guilt that went nowhere, abandonment, weekends spent trimming azaleas, darning holes in Sarah's stockings – all gone.

The sun made its final dive behind Vancouver Island.

25

Florian appeared at the front door promptly at six, a bland, slightly puffy gone-to-seed blond. The whites of his eyes were yellow, and one of his front teeth was ochre with nicotine, and snaggled. He could easily be the guy who sold Janet a set of snow tires the previous winter. *What was I expecting – a halo? Cary Grant? Yeah, I was.* Janet was pure hostess: 'You must be' – a pause – '*Florian.* Come in – please – it's so hot out.'

'But first I must kiss your hand.' Florian kissed her hand. Janet sensed the tip of his tongue – *or did I?*

'Ooh my – how continental.'

'*Enchanté.*' He stood up and peeked inside. 'This is your house?'

Janet looked around as if being charged with a crime she hadn't committed. 'Good *God*, no.'

'I'm so relieved to hear you say that.' Florian took a moment to fully absorb Gayle's interior design statement. 'The overall look really *does* leave one aching for a nice empty Japanese room with only a vase and a cleverly twisted branch.' He quickly peeked into the living room. '*Gott im Himmel!*'

'It's a scream, I know. What do you think of this place – Tara, eh?'

'And you, such a lovely magnolia.'

'Give me two shakes of a lamb's tail and I'll fetch my things.'

'Such as . . . your pills?'

Janet smiled. 'Like you wouldn't believe.'

'Oh, but I would. The family business, you know.'

'Why yes, of course.' Janet retrieved her pill caddy, and the two stepped out the front door, which Janet left unlocked. She asked, 'Where should we go for dinner?'

'I've selected a place a few miles down the coast. To be frank, I've never set foot in Daytona Beach or its environs before.'

'Well, around here it's either steak or a seafood-bacteria filet. What I'd *really* like is a French restaurant, but dream on, Janet Drummond. All that delicious butter, and the French *never* chintz on the salt.'

'Oh!' said Florian. 'You're a salt nut, too.'

'Oh *my*, yes. If you can locate a salt lick in a cow pasture, I'd happily have dinner with you there.'

'Janet, I simply *must* send you a bottle of this Maltese sea salt, Fleurs de Sel Sardaignain – little specks of anchovy built into each grain – so subtle.'

'I think I saw that on *Martha Stewart*.'

'Oh.' Florian briefly entered a sulk. 'Why must that woman popularize *everything*?'

'They've taken the salt out of all the food these days. Food has gotten so wimpy. Have you noticed?'

'Hasn't it, though? Please, hop in.' Florian held open the rear door of a Lincoln Town Car, the driver separated from the rear compartment by a slab of smoked glass. Janet got in, and Florian said to the smoked glass, 'Tio, to that seafood place we selected in New Smyrna Beach.'

'Yes, sir.'

'Is the rig set to go?'

'Yes, sir.'

'The rig?' Janet asked.

Florian turned to her, and pointed to a mobile home of Texan dimensions, pulling out into the street behind them, and said, 'I'm the opposite of a light packer. But enough about boring, boring me – what about you?'

'Me? Dull, dull, dull.'

'That's not strictly true, Janet. For starters, how did you contract HIV?'

'Oh. *That.*' The story took them the entire way to the restaurant, thirty minutes south, and with its telling Florian learned a great deal about the Drummond family and couldn't have been more sympathetic. He held her hand: 'You poor, *poor* woman. You deserve kindness, and what do you get? *This.*' Florian nodded toward a bar they were passing with a large BIKERS WELCOME sign out front, as if it summed up the entire aura of the culture.

'It's not so bad, you know,' Janet said.

'Janet, you lie like the rug. Tell me, how often do you take your pills?'

'Every four hours.'

'I rest my case.' The car entered a large mall parking lot and slowed down outside a place called The Shanty. The RV lumbered in behind them. 'Shall we dine?'

They entered the restaurant; the walls were mint green, and the air carried the odor of cigarettes, janitorial cleaning solution and a dock. Florian was obviously horrified, 'This is a gaffe on my part, Janet. My apologies.'

'No, let's stay, Flor. We'll smoke – I just decided that I'm going to start smoking again tonight, after a ten-year hiatus.' *Why did I decide that? Well, why not?*

'I love smoking,' Florian said. 'And you called me "Flor". So cheeky. So insouciant.'

Janet was surprised. 'You mean you didn't smoke in the car because of me? You're so sweet.'

A young and yawning woman with processed crimped hair of deepest mall showed them to a booth, or rather marooned them in a booth to the restaurant's east edge, where streaky sunlight limped through the window. Janet said, 'Thank you,' to which the young woman said, 'Like I have any choice in the matter.'

Once she was gone, Janet said, 'It really does make you wonder if management could drain the dining process of any more joy.'

Florian cracked open a pack of Dunhill cigarettes. 'Please.'

Janet accepted and lit up, a roil of nicotine licking her tonsils and transporting her to the world of 1950s sophomore mixer parties. 'This is so lovely,' she said to Florian. 'Why ever did I quit?'

'I bet you I can have our hostess fired in two phone calls,' Florian said.

'Bet me what?'

'If I win, you buy dessert.'

'You're on.'

Florian placed a call on his cell phone and barked sentences of German into the receiver, then hung up. He made one more phone call, put his cell phone away and said, 'Watch this.' The phone at the front desk rang, the hostess answered, listened, shouted, 'Same to you. I hated this shit-hole anyway,' hung up and stomped – noisy *stomping* – out the door.

Janet's cigarette wasn't even halfway smoked. 'Dessert's on me.'

'I love being petty,' said Florian.

'I wish I could be petty,' Janet said.

'No, you don't.'

'But I *do*. Because if I were petty, it'd mean I didn't care so much about things.'

The few staff members who remained ran about like rabbits, and took turns going out to the parking lot to commiserate with the axed hostess. Amid the service vacuum, Florian went to the bar and poured two gin martinis. As he sat down at the table and handed one to Janet, he nodded out the window and said, 'Look how even the sacking of one employee cripples an entire economy – in this case, The Shanty's economy. My father always said that the fastest way to cripple any economy is to manipulate the key labor unions into striking. This invariably makes the middle classes flip out, and before you know it, *boom*, there's a tyrant running the show. Anything to keep the lettuce arriving in the supermarkets on time. *Cheers*.'

'*Cheers.*' They clinked glasses. Janet said, 'But you know, Flor, that's nothing I haven't already figured out on my own.'

'Really now?'

'You wouldn't *believe* the things I find on the Internet.'

'You like trolling the Web, do you?'

'Oh, God, yes.'

'Your friends troll, too?'

'*Pffft.* No. I'm actually quite disgusted with my own generation. They've lost their curiosity, but not me – I love the Internet. All these facts that were once forbidden are all so easily available.'

'Such as?'

'Medical stuff first. And second, government files and documents – I'll never trust any government anywhere again.'

'A smart decision. Any naughty chat ever?'

'Yes, but I'd be mortified if my family knew.'

'What's your secret Web name?'

Janet blushed.

'Oh come on now, tell me, Janet.'

'Promise you won't laugh?'

'I'll try.'

'HotAsianTeen.'

Florian's laugh was like a dog's bark. Janet blushed.

'Any hot dates?' he asked.

'No, but I *could* have if I'd wanted to.'

'Why bail out?'

'Florian, I could have been talking to my kids even – oh, God, I shiver at the thought.'

'Did you always log on as HotAsianTeen?'

'No. I only created that persona because I wanted to see how men behave when the wife's in the kitchen and the den door is locked.'

'What did you learn, then?'

'Men are ruled entirely by their crotches.'

'That's all?'

'That's not enough? I was raised to believe men were ruled by political and social ideals. I *believed* that.'

'It's time for another martini. Another for you?'

'Please.'

A birthday party of eight seniors on the other side of the restaurant was preparing to mutiny; Florian's second stint at the bar went as unnoticed as the first. He returned to the table and passed Janet her drink. 'Cocktail for your thoughts,' Florian said.

'Well, there *was* one date, but we didn't meet over the Internet. We *did* meet at an Internet café.' Janet was dizzy from the cigarette.

Florian was interested. 'Oh?'

'But when he found out about my HIV, he bolted. End of story.'

'He did, did he?'

'Yeah. Ernie – Ernie Farmingham.'

'In Vancouver?'

'Yeah.'

A brief flash of preoccupation passed over Florian's face; Janet looked him in the eye. 'To be completely accurate, he lives in North Vancouver. You're going to destroy his life, aren't you?'

'Absolutely, Janet.'

Janet felt as if she were having dinner with God.

Menus were hurled onto their table. Janet said, 'We'd better order, but I don't know – I mean, I'm immunosuppressed, and this place is such a dive. Food here might be dodgy in an E. coli 157 kind of way.'

'Not if you order in the Florian style.'

'What style is that?'

'Watch.' He walked across the room, tapped a waiter on the shoulder and handed him a hundred-dollar bill. In a blink the waiter was at Janet's side.

'Well, I suppose a green house salad – vinaigrette on the side – and Fetuccine Alfredo would be fine.'

The waiter, name-tagged Steve, turned to Florian and returned the hundred-dollar bill. 'No need. The restaurant's going nuts tonight because Shawna got fired.'

'Why's that?' Janet asked.

'Karma. She acted like she owned the place because she's dating the weekend manager. *Ooh* – we're *so* impressed. Anyway, sir – your order?'

'Yes – a green salad with your undoubtedly captivating house dressing, tomato soup with double croutons, chicken fingers – *yummy, yummy!* – with mustard sauce, no less. Then, howzabout – yes, deep fried zucchini sticks, and then a lamb *entrée* substituting rice pilaf for potatoes, and then—'

'Sir?'

'Yes, Steve?'

'I'm not sure I understand you. Will anyone else be joining you?'

'No. Just myself and the lovely Janet here.'

'Well, then you already have more than enough food for the two of you – if I may be so bold as to say so.'

'Steve, thank you, but I would like to order more. There's no by-law in New Smyrna Beach regulating the amount of food one can order, is there?'

'No, sir.'

'Good.' Florian ordered ten entrées, each with meticulous attention to substitutions and the doneness of meats.

Steve was thoughtfully amused. 'Boy, the chef is going to freak.'

'Life is for enjoying, right, Steve?'

'Yes, it is, sir.'

'You have to live every moment and capture the joy. Have fun, fun, fun. Now off to the kitchen, Steve. We're nearly insane with hunger.'

Janet said, 'Feeling a bit peckish tonight?'

'Yes, and I shall tip the lad with my Piaget watch. Now, you were telling me on the phone about a new cream for rosacea—'

'Indeed I was.'

The two talked about legal and illegal skin care products for ten minutes, until staff members began to sneak peeks at the two of them. Shortly the chef came out. 'Are you making fun of my food?'

'On the contrary, I'm honoring your food.'

'You're a smartass?'

'No, I'm a *customer*. I'm sure your meals are excellent, and I look forward to the bunch of them. The Shanty is well-known throughout the entire 904 area code for its fine dining and convivial atmosphere. Everybody knows that. Now go cook, my good man!'

The chef, puzzled, left. Steve lingered.

Florian said, 'Steven, my boy, having lots of fat people eating a lot of fattening food is a good, *good* thing for America.'

'You've lost me, sir. And Steve is fine.'

'Like anything in life, Steve, it's numbers, numbers, numbers. Lots of fat people means lots of happy farmers, happy agro-chemical makers, happy teamsters, happy fast-food staffs – happiness and joy for all. Fatness ripples through the entire economy in a tsunami of prosperity.'

'Fat people have more medical problems, though. Common sense.'

'But that's the beauty of it, Steve. At present we're at the perfect equilibrium point between an obese society and a prosperous society. If all Americans were to gain even *one more ounce*, the medical system would be overtaxed and the economy would suffer. Were these same Americans all to *lose* even one single ounce, Steve, the economy would nose-dive.'

'I've never thought of obesity that way.'

'Well, now you have.'

'Right, sir.' Steve was off. Florian turned to Janet. 'What I was saying – before – about life being about good times – a facetious lie of the first order.'

'I'm glad to hear you say that.'

'As far as I can see, Janet, life is just an endless banquet of loss, and each time a new loss is doled out, you have to move your mental furniture around, throw things out, and by then there's more loss, and the cycle goes on and on.'

'You've been reading my mind. Life is a bowl of chainsaws.'

'It's not hard. I see it in your eyes.' Florian finished his drink. 'When did the notion first dawn on you?'

'I was a dumb bunny. I believed the script I was handed. And then one day in the early 1980s I hit a red light in North Vancouver and *ding!* I understood that I was now for ever in life's minus column and the plus column was over. Funny how you only realize how deeply events have affected you years and years after they've occurred. What about you?'

'It's been my whole life – loss – the sensation of things slipping away. Not money – I shit money – money *likes* me – but everything else: going, going, gone.'

'You're not going to get much sympathy in this world for that, Flor.'

'Ah, but you see, I don't ask for sympathy.' Florian looked toward the kitchen. 'Our food is on the way.' He stood up. 'Excuse me while I go pick up a friend. I'll be back shortly – as you say, in two shakes of a lamb's tail.'

Steven began to deliver plate after plate of food, and once the booth's surface was covered, he brought over another table as an annex. Most of the meals seemed repulsive to Janet – a Caesar salad with eczema; gray disintegrating mahi-mahi; blackened lumps of . . . *pig*; rubber bands and shoelaces mixed together and relabeled as pasta. Steve, having deposited all the meals, made a mock blow of his forelock. 'I'm forgetting something – wait, yes—' He picked up a pepper mill. 'Pepper?'

'No, thank you, dear.'

'Why don't I leave the mill here. Just in case.'

Janet surveyed the ludicrous foodscape before her, then looked up to see Florian walking in the door with an extremely tall, ink-black woman in tow, clad in brilliantly colored, shamelessly expensive designer wear – Pucci? Hermès? Her fingers and neck and ears were dappled with light bouncing off chunks of gold jewelry. Janet had never seen a woman clad in so many costly items at once. The showiness of it seemed almost illegal. Janet was mesmerized as the two approached the table, as were The Shanty's other diners.

'Janet, I'd like you to meet Cissy Ntombe.'

Janet stood up, spellbound. 'Hello.'

Cissy said, 'Charmed, I'm sure.' She sat down in the banquette opposite Janet and asked, 'What brings you to this part of the world, my dear?'

Janet felt like a yokel. 'Family business, you might say.'

'How delightful.' Cissy unfolded a napkin on her lap.

Janet asked, 'And you?'

'I, too, am here on business,' Cissy said. 'But not family business. My family are all dead, I'm afraid, my dear.'

'Good Lord – how awful.'

'Your sympathy is too generous, but I have grieved all I shall.' She looked at the food before her. Florian looked eager to hear her response, which was: 'Florian, we shall be needing lemon wedges, and I see none here.'

She looked at Janet. 'There is no such thing as a fish without lemon. Wouldn't you agree?'

'Absolutely.'

'This restaurant is not nearly so grand as last night's restaurant in Atlanta, but I suppose that is what happens when one ventures through the provinces.'

Florian was savoring Janet's bafflement over this exotic and slightly antique-sounding new guest. Janet shot him a pair of *Who-is-this-person?* eyes, but all he did was gesture towards the food and say, 'It's all for you, Cissy, dear – you dive right in.'

'As I said, I shall require lemon wedges first, my dear.'

Florian went off in pursuit of lemon wedges. Cissy asked Janet, 'Do you speak French perchance?'

'Me? A bit. I'm from Canada, which is a bilingu—'

'Oh dear – *Canadian* French, which one hears is a puzzling variety of its Parisian counterpart.'

'I suppose my French is a bit rusty.' Janet looted her brain for conversation topics but found none. In addition, Janet's not knowing Cissy's role in Florian's life was irksome indeed. 'Does Florian always order too much food like this?'

'I cannot say, Janet. I have only known him for two days.'

This is crazy. 'Your outfit is amazing. Hermès?'

'It is Versace, my dear.'

Silence.

More silence.

Cissy asked Janet, 'Have you read any good books lately?'

'Books?' The topic caught Janet off guard. 'Let me think – mostly I read newspapers and magazines. And the books I read are about health and nutrition mostly. Sorry I can't do better than that. What about you, Cissy?'

'I have recently reread my favorite book of all time.'

'Which one is that?' Janet asked.

'*Protocol and Deportment in Polite Society*, by Miss Lydia Millrod.'

'Is that a new book?'

'No! Heavens no, my dear. It was published in 1913, just before the Great War. But its classical nature rescues it from the fate of being dated.'

'I see.'

Florian returned with a plate-load of lemon wedges. 'Let us begin.' He and Cissy promptly scanned the meals as though it were a buffet for fifty. Both parties took only the most minuscule portions of food, further confusing Janet. She asked Florian, 'So how did you two meet?'

'Friends of mine told me about Cissy, and I simply had to meet her.'

'What did your friends say?'

'They told me that Cissy is from the city of Mubende, fifty miles west of Kampala, Uganda. She's been a prostitute for nearly twenty years and has had unprotected sex at a very minimum of 35,000 times. She's been directly exposed to HIV perhaps 15,000 times and yet her blood levels show no trace of either the virus or its antibodies.'

Cissy looked quite cross at hearing this. She said, 'Florian, it is improper to discuss business matters at the dinner table.'

'Cissy, Janet is almost family to me. No business will come of this. I merely want to keep her properly informed about you, my good woman.'

'Very well, then. But no mention of money. That is absolutely forbidden.'

Florian turned to Janet. 'As I was saying, Cissy was discovered in her roadside hut a few months ago by researchers from Atlanta's Center for Disease Control. They were conducting routine epidemiological surveys and happened upon her. She was brought to Atlanta two weeks ago and was given a large, utilitarian cinder block motel room that resembled a dorm room in an Ohio college circa 1967. Fortunately I have tom-toms beating all through the jungle and was informed of Cissy's plight. Two days ago I visited Atlanta armed with two garment dollies I had brought down directly from Seventh Avenue – the most exotic and expensive clothes available in all of Manhattan – as well as strips of silk on which a dazzling array of Harry Winston gems had been pinned. Cissy had a choice – cinder block dorm room or Versace. And thus I secured her rescue.'

'You *stole* Cissy from the Center for Disease Control?'

'"Stole?" Goodness no,' Florian said, 'And Janet, please, stop being so middle-class. It's unbecoming. If Cissy wants to leave, she's free to do so. Right, Cissy?'

Cissy said, 'My room in Atlanta was no better than a broom closet. So insulting.' She turned to Florian: 'I shall require a finger bowl presently.'

Florian turned to Cissy: 'Cissy, give me your hand.' He took Cissy's barbecue-sauce-stained right hand. 'Janet, give me your right hand – across the table – there.'

'I—'

'Trust me, Janet.'

Janet gave her hand to Florian.

'Good.' He picked up a steak knife, looked at Janet, lifted his eyebrow and made a small cut on her hand.

'Ouch. Florian, what are you—?'

'Shhhhhhh.' Florian then took Cissy's hand and cut a small slit in her palm, too. He looked back and forth between the two women, then held their bleeding hands together in a clasp.

Cissy's hand was so warm and dry, *so hard to imagine buckets of warm, potent blood flowing within*, but Cissy's blood did flow, dripping onto the tablecloth. Janet watched as blood seeped out through cracks in the bonds of the two hands.

Florian said, 'I'm going to count to sixty-two, Janet. Sixty-two seconds is the time required for blood to clot on an open cut.

'. . . one Mississippi . . . two Mississippi . . . three Mississippi . . . four Mississippi . . .'

Is this what I think it is?

'. . . thirty-four Mississippi . . . thirty-five Mississippi . . . thirty-six Mississippi . . .'

It couldn't be.

'. . . fifty-nine Mississippi . . . sixty Mississippi . . . sixty-one Mississippi . . . sixty-two Mississippi.'

But it is. It's true.

'Unclasp your hands.'

Cissy looked at Janet. 'You'll need a fresh napkin, my dear.'

Janet was stunned. Her hand remained hovering above the food.

Florian said, 'Look at me, Janet.'

Janet looked at Florian, but the colors and shapes in the room were shifting like TV channels.

'It's gone now, Janet.'

'Gone?'

'Yes. No more pills. No more virus. Nothing. All gone.'
'It can't be that simple.'
'Almost. I'll have to give you one or two shots using Cissy's plasma as a base. But for all intents and purposes, yes. It is that simple and yes, it's all gone.'
'I—'
'Yes, Janet?'
'I don't . . .'
'What are you feeling, Janet?'
'Light. I feel light.'
'Floating on air?'
'No – the other kind of light.'
'What do you mean?'
'White light. I feel like . . . the *sun*.'

26

The table was covered in fifteen desserts, and Janet was bloated from having gorged on two of them. On top of this, she was still heady from the blood swap with Cissy. She said, 'Florian, I won't lie to you. The letter I was going to give you is fake.'

Florian froze for a second. 'I'm glad you told me that, Janet, because then we couldn't have remained pals.'

'Why do you want the letter so badly, Flor? Just tell me – *why*?'

'Why do *you* think?'

'Because – because you lost your mother early in life. Because you seem to love everything English, and I guess buying this letter is how a rich Anglophile would funnel those energies and emotions.'

'Very good, Janet. I *do* miss my dear *Maman*, but that's not why I want the letter – or the card inside it – or whatever's in there.'

'You're not making sense.'

'Janet, what I really want is the *envelope*.'

'Excuse me?'

'Oh, I'm sure the card inside is sweetness and light itself, but the envelope is what I want.'

'Florian, what are you saying?'

'Janet, think for a second about the simple mechanics of card writing. Someone would have had to *lick* that envelope, wouldn't they? And I hardly think licking is the sort of job one entrusts to anyone, let alone one's butler, or even to Daddy.'

'So?'

'Embedded in the envelope's glue, Janet, are a good number of stable and intact somatic cells.'

'Somatic cells?'

'Non-sexual cells – neither sperm, nor egg. In a few years – not right now, mind you, but in a few years – as inexorably as CDs replaced vinyl records, it's going to be almost pathetically simple to clone mammals – *any* mammals – from somatic cells. Give these cells the correct goo on which to grow, and then deliver the correct stimulus, and *whaam!* Instant prince. Your daughter is, I believe, running tests on board the shuttle aiming towards this future procedure. The world is truly small.'

'I . . . you've got me, Flor.'

'It's a fair amount to swallow in one gulp. By the way, the launch is still on for 7:40 A.M. day after tomorrow?'

'Yes.'

'Bravo.' Florian looked at Cissy. 'Are you full, dear?'

'I have had enough.' Cissy was content just to sit and touch the palm of her hand so recently cut.

Janet dipped her tongue deep into the martini glass bottom dimple to retrieve the final drop of gin. She looked up. 'It can't be *that* hard to buy royal dandruff, Florian.'

'Actually, Janet, it is – and good for you for thinking like a business person. But availability of cells is only half the problem.'

'What's the other half?'

'The other half is the problem of telomeres.'

'Huh?'

'Human DNA is like a shoelace, Janet, and at each end are little caplets called telomeres. Depending on your family's gene pool – or depending on whether or not you're a one-hundred-fourteen-year-old Frenchwoman who drinks a glass of red wine each day – the telomeres fray after about seventysomething years. Your DNA unravels, you age and you die.'

'So?'

'The problem with cloning is that if I were to clone, say, *you*,

Janet – and trust me, Janet, cloning is going on like crazy in labs across the planet right now – the resulting baby would have used up sixty years' worth of telomeres.'

'Sixty-five.'

'So technically, we'd have a sixty-five-year-old baby. Therefore, the younger I can nab some cells, then the much, much more pricey they become. *Capisce?*'

'Yes, I *capisce.*'

'As an added bonus, these cells give me a benchmark against which I can verify future princely cells.'

'Of course.'

As a footnote, Florian added, '*And* there's also this cell material called chromatin, but that's a bit complex for our festive little dinner.'

Janet closed her eyes.

'Janet? Are you OK?'

'I'm overwhelmed.'

'We need to get smashed is what we need, Janet. You no longer need to worry about drug interactions with alcohol. Cissy has saved you.' Florian went to the bar and simply took a bottle of gin. He brought it back and poured three glasses. 'Cheers.'

'Flor, just so you know, the real letter is beneath a sofa cushion in the living room of the house you picked me up at.'

'How on *earth* did you end up beached inside that dreadful heap?'

'This particular tale begins with my son, Bryan, impregnating a little spitfire by the name of Shw.'

'Shw?'

'Yes.'

'Spell that.'

The usual Shw nonsense ensued. Janet then recounted the sequence of calamities ending up with Lloyd and Gayle imprisoned in their own pink dungeon.

'This is too, too much, Janet. I simply *must* meet these people. Are they still in jail?'

'As far as I know. The plan was just to scare them a smidge.'

'Let's go now.'

'Why not. Bring the bottle.'

'I *shall.*' Florian stood up and held Cissy's chair. 'Cissy's foster parents were English, you know, and she was raised inside Uganda's diplomatic community. Hence her perfect Mayfair patois. Right, dear?'

Cissy look slighted. 'Florian, it is impolite to discuss people in their presence as if they were not there.'

'Sorry about that, Cissy. You are correct.'

Florian left several hundreds on the table, and as the trio headed to the door, the staff burst into spontaneous applause. Florian threw his wristwatch to Steve. In the parking lot, Florian said, 'Jan, why don't you take a quickie house tour of the rig. I'm sure you'll find the decor most enchanting.'

Janet followed Cissy into a vehicle as big as a high school portable classroom, which on the inside proved to be a funhouse of shining nickel, beveled glass, hidden light sources and a wealth of mirrors. Designer outfits were strewn in layers about the minimal charcoal gray furniture. The sight of so much cash frozen in the form of clothing gave Janet an illicit tingle.

Cissy said, 'It is small, I concede you that, but it is a gracious home. The fridge is stainless steel and the countertop is made of travertine marble, just like the kitchens of the British embassy before Idi Amin and his reign of bloody terror forced me out on the street.' She opened the bathroom door; its interior was of marble and mirrors. 'Elegant simplicity. Florian is really too kind, my dear. He has spared no expense to ensure that my needs as a lady are adequately met.'

'He is a nice fellow, isn't he?' Janet said.

'Indeed. He even made accommodation for my other womanly desires. Come see—' She opened a door to the bedroom, which Janet entered, only to find Howie buck naked and asleep atop a chinchilla bedspread, snoring like a lawnmower. A half-empty J&B bottle rested on the side table.

'I've been with so many men, but never one as beautiful as this. He is my angel. He is my reward.'

Oh my – I'm not even shocked or embarrassed here. I'm amused. It must be the gin. 'You are lucky indeed,' Janet said.

'It's been enchanting meeting you, Janet. *Au revoir.*'

'*Au revoir.*'

Outside the car, Florian said to Janet, 'You Americans just love your house tours, don't you?'

'I'm Canadian, you're Swiss and Cissy's Ugandan.'

They hopped into the car. On the rear seat was a plastic Medevac cooler.

'What's in there, Flor?'

'Goodies and treats.'

'What *kind* of goodies?'

'Let's look and see.' He removed the lid and meddled about with the cooler's contents. 'I just love my trips to Atlanta. Such a hotel-loving kind of town. That's how I obtain most of my specimens, you know. Chambermaids are the content providers of the next human epoch. Just look at *this*—' He held up a Ziploc baggie. 'Bill Gates's hairbrush. Five hundred dollars cash. This hairbrush alone is going to put thousands of little Florians through beauty school. What else have we in here?'

Janet said, 'You're joking, right?' Florian's blank return glance confirmed otherwise. 'Sorry, Flor.'

Inside another vacuum-sealed clear plastic bag was a white towel. 'Ashley Judd was here – imagine billions of little Juddlings, just waiting to entertain the dickens out of us. Now Celine Dion, though – *she* remains my Holy Grail. Lordy, that woman has a scorched-earth policy when it comes to hotel rooms. *Ooh* – what have we here?' He removed a vacuum-packed black T-shirt. 'Garth Brooks, manly sweat and all. *Ka-ching, ka-ching*. And here—' Florian's tone indicated the pièce de résistance. He removed an aluminum canister, and his voice became borderline awestruck: '—a Tiger Woods used condom, nestled inside a bath of liquid nitrogen.'

'Stop!'

'*Janet*—!'

'Stop right there. This is becoming too much of a muchness.'

Florian closed the cooler. 'I can see how this might overwhelm a novice.'

'Just put the cooler away for a while.'

'Of course. Another drink?'

'Please.'

Florian poured drinks. Janet asked him if he didn't worry about being so rich and not having much security, but he smiled and curled back his right ear. 'A chip embedded right here. If I touch this chip firmly five times in two seconds, my, how shall we say, *wrestling team* will be with me inside of two minutes.'

'You have security people always within two minutes of you?'

'Always.'

'Impressive.'

'Necessity. But a part of their job description is that I don't have to actually *see* them. That's how the best security is always done.' Florian changed gears: 'So tell me, Janet, how many of your family members down here are sick?'

'Four: me, Wade, Nickie and Ted.'

'Ted?'

'Liver cancer.'

'Hmmm. Don't forget, you're not sick any more.'

Oh, God, he's right. 'Three.'

Florian went on: 'I suppose we'd better take care of them all. Call them—' He gave Janet a phone.

'You can fix liver cancer?'

'Oh, *please.*'

Janet paused a second, then began to dial the number of Kevin's trailer. Florian said, 'Have them come to Daytona Beach and meet us. But *only* the sick ones. I don't enjoy mob scenes.'

Janet called and gave Wade the message, and shortly, at

Lloyd and Gayle's, they parked in the driveway. The house was dark inside, so they turned on some lights. In the living room, Janet reached under a cushion and pulled out a *Mummy* envelope. 'Here you go.'

'Thank you, Janet. What *is* that whining sound I hear?'

'Kimba the dog, locked in the den. The Munsters are downstairs. Let's go look.' They walked down the cold – not even cool, but *cold* – stairs. Janet opened the door. She half expected monsters to grab her and rip out her bowels, or a sawed-off shotgun to be stuck in her face followed by being duct-taped to a stacking chair. But instead she found Lloyd and Gayle inside the pink jail cell looking very cross indeed.

'It's about time you shitheads came back. Do you have any idea the amount of trouble you're in now? *Any*?'

'Be quiet,' Janet said. 'We found your goodies hidden under the metal plate in the garage.'

'Oh.'

'Yeah, "Oh" is right,' said Janet.

Gayle asked, 'Who's *this* guy, then?'

'This is my friend Florian, and he's a thousand times richer than you small-timers, so be humble in his presence.'

Florian turned to Lloyd and Gayle. 'A million times richer, in fact.' He then turned his body and lectured them severely. 'You silly twits. You went and paid for the Full Meal Deal, I hear. Stupid, stupid, *stupid*. Donor mothers *always* turn on you in the end. How much were you going to pay for Janet's grandchild?'

Lloyd shrugged. 'Fifty K.'

'And what were you going to sell it for?'

Lloyd was about to speak, but Gayle cut him off with bravado: 'A half million.'

'Who buys them?'

'You should see the list.'

Janet said, 'We have.'

Florian turned to Janet. 'Janet, the pink color in this room is making my nipples turn tender. Let's go back upstairs.'

Heading upstairs from the dungeon and the undignified cries of Lloyd and Gayle, Florian said, 'Well, Janet, you can see how much cleaner my own business model is. The Lloyds and Gayles of this world will be out of business in no time.' They looked up in time to see Wade, Nickie and Ted walk in the front door.

27

The sky had been darkening as Wade, Ted and Nickie drove to Daytona Beach with the windows rolled up. Wade had felt as if he were in a mobile sarcophagus, and that death really was the fourth passenger. The A/C was on, the air-recycling button switched on, too. Wade had felt the air becoming increasingly full of death particles – from their lungs and their scalps and their skin. He rolled down a window a crack. His father's skin was pale and waxy; Nickie's veins were bulging, pulsing with kryptonite.

None of them had spoken. They arrived at the house, parked and walked up to the door, which was slightly ajar.

It was all Wade could do to keep his cool when he found Florian and his mother in the dimly lit living room. He switched the lights up briefly, but Florian gestured for him to lower them again. 'The decor, Wade. Look for yourself.'

'Hey, Florian. Good eye job.'

'Yes, hello, Wade, old chap.'

Ted and Nickie, drained and tarnished, trailed in behind Wade.

'. . . and this must be Ted and Nickie.'

A stiffly formal round of introductions followed. Wade plopped himself onto a living room sofa. 'I'm riding a burnout wave. They come and go.' His pill buzzer buzzed, and he leaned his head back, sucked in air, and said, 'I have no idea what I'm supposed to take right now.'

'*You're* pooped?' Ted sank into a piece of furniture, as did the others.

'Guess what, Florian,' said Wade. 'All of us are terminal.' As his father had done earlier, Wade hummed the funeral dirge.

'You're no such thing,' said Florian. 'And how vulgar of you to try and shock me merely for effect. Your mother brought you up better than that – didn't you, Janet?'

Janet was rubbing her temples and didn't reply.

Ted asked Florian, 'Did you get your letter?'

'I did,' said Florian.

Ted asked Janet, 'How much did he pay?'

Janet said, 'He didn't pay anything, Ted. Charging him money didn't seem right.'

'It didn't seem *right*?'

'Ted, Florian is my friend, and I didn't want to muck up our friendship with money.'

'Janet,' said Florian, 'you are too, *too* valiant, but don't fret. I'll pay a hundred thousand for it – but Canadian dollars, not U.S.'

'Gee, thanks,' said Ted.

'Take it or leave it.'

'Yeah, OK, we'll take it.'

'Good,' said Florian. 'I'll have my minions deliver it to you tomorrow morning.'

'Yeah. Sure. Whatever.'

Wade had expected a gloriously messy drama, but instead he felt as if he'd just sold an '89 Trans Am through the want ads. 'Are those two vampires still locked up downstairs?'

'They're bored and cranky,' Janet said. She looked as though she had news to tell but was thinking better of it. She changed the subject. 'Florian, Wade once worked for you. What did he actually *do*? Whenever we've brought up the subject he goes mute.'

'Wade's velvety bum used to transport me to the Milky Way every night.'

'Florian! That's not true and you know it.'

'Testy young lad. Compose yourself.' Florian looked at the others in the room. 'Mostly young Wade smuggled in samples for my lab – endangered or threatened species. The biggest load he brought in was a shipping container full of Pacific yew trees.' He looked pointedly at Wade. 'You little lumberjack you.' He resumed speaking to the room. 'I needed the bark for tamoxifen, a breast cancer drug. He also smuggled in dolphins for use in cancer trials.'

'They use dolphins in cancer trials?' Nickie was jolted.

'Of course, dear. Nasty, *nasty* little beasts. They'd mug you, and rape you, and take your handbag inside of three seconds if they thought they could. The tuna industry is doing us a large favor.'

'You're joking.'

'Wade, by the way, is actually a very good employee. Sometimes his jobs were, of necessity, messy, but he never once complained. On the other hand, I did pay him well, but what did he do in the end? He left me for a . . . *baseball wife*.'

Wade said, 'Remember the time Eddy's Chris-Craft full of codeine scraped out its bottom on the coral bordering Wilhelmina's lagoon. Her whole dolphin pod went into catatonic euphoria.'

'*That* mad cow. She still tortures me about that every time we play backgammon in that living room of hers – so many museum-grade Jasper Johns paintings turning to cheesecloth on the walls. All that salt air.' He sighed.

'Is Eddy still around?'

'Eddy's gone to a better place, Wade. Courtesy of a band of pirates out of Santo Domingo who wanted his boatload of Samsung electronics products. Take consolation in knowing that his skeleton will be just the ticket to start a spiffy little coral reef.'

Wade and Florian settled into reminiscences; Janet went over to speak with Ted and Nickie. After some minutes, out of the corner of his eyes, Wade saw his father and stepmother suddenly glow from within – a simple peaceful wave of light passing through them. Meanwhile Florian yammered away: '. . . but of course the old frog never spoke to me again after we accidentally dropped the Trinitron out of the Cessna and onto that old private runway – the Bahamian government bulldozed it just after you left, you know – and I *do* stress the word "accident". Apparently his brother-in-law made a night landing and his tire hit the TV, and he lost four thousand Monte Cristo cigars all over the runway. *He* should have his stomach stapled and lose fifty pounds, if you ask me.'

Ted and Nickie interrupted them, holding hands and smiling like teen sweethearts. 'We're going to go out for a walk and suck in some fresh air,' said Ted.

They both winked at Florian. Nickie said, 'Thank you,' and so did Ted.

'Oh,' said Wade. 'OK.' *They have a secret.*

'We'll be back in an hour or so.' And with that, they were gone.

Florian looked at Janet, who nodded. Wade began to feel excluded from the inner circle. 'Oh yeah – what about Howie, then?'

'He's fine,' Janet said.

'Where is he?'

'He's busy right now.'

'Doing what?'

Florian said, 'Howie is enjoying hot passionate sex with Cissy Ntombe, lately of Mubende, Uganda. They're in the trailer out front of the house if you want to go have a peek.'

'I believe you.' Wade paused for a second. 'So he's cheating on Sarah *and* Alanna.'

'Very much so, but forget about that. Wade,' said his mother. 'I have unusual news.'

'You do?' To Wade, unusual news equaled bad news.

'Yes, but it's *good* news.'

But Janet didn't have a chance to relay any sort of news. The front door shot open like a reality-based TV crime program. *Home invasion? Good Lord* – it was Bryan and Shw, guns in hand. Shw shrieked out, 'OK, gang, I'm in charge here.'

Wade said, 'Bryan, what the hell is this? Drop those guns. You'll hurt someone.'

Shw turned to Wade. 'I said *I'm* the one in charge, you sleazy vagabond.'

'Bryan, tell her to—'

Crack!

Shw shot the ceiling, taking out a globe lamp. Wade, admiring her marksmanship, hopped back. Shw shrieked again, '*Quiet!*'

Janet said, 'Bryan, this is utter nonsense.'

Shw was still furious that nobody was addressing her.

'Don't you people *learn*?' She shot out the central bulb in the chandelier.

'Ooh. We're so scared,' said Florian.

'No sarcasm from you, you shit-for-brains corporate gene pimp.'

Janet said, 'Mind your language, young lady.'

Florian said, 'So this little intrusion is about my day job, I see.'

Shw said, 'Yeah, it *is*. I just about freaked when Bryan told me who you were. You sell half the pills on earth, and God only knows what genetic nightmares you're brewing in Switzerland or whatever circle of hell you come from.'

Wade said, 'Where do you get off, coming in and treating us like cattle, you vicious little witch.'

'Don't call the mother of my child a vicious little witch,' Bryan said. Janet looked at Wade and made a small nod indicating to him not to press the matter.

Shw said, 'Right, Grandma – all of you – down we go – everybody downstairs.'

Wade said, 'Drop the guns, Bryan.'

'Do what Shw says,' Bryan ordered, refusing to make eye contact.

Shw shouted, 'Stop dawdling. Go downstairs *now!*' With humbling precision, she took out the first two of seven spun-glass unicorns prancing across the mantelpiece.

As though enduring a tedious game with children, Wade, Janet and Florian tramped downstairs. Janet said, 'Bryan, we were going there anyway.'

'Be quiet, Janet,' shouted Shw. 'Your fucking serenity is driving me crazy.' Wade was first at the door. '*In*!' commanded Shw, motioning them into the room with its sterile obstetrical workstation and pink dungeon. Florian giggled; Shw went berserk. 'I said shut the fuck up,' and she blasted out a light bulb on a standing lamp over in a corner. She received the silence she wanted. She pointed to Florian: 'You, Lord Krautwell – get into jail with Mr. and Mrs. Comparison Shopper.' Shw saw the cell key on the obstetrical chair's vinyl. She grabbed it and threw it to Bryan.

'Stuff them all inside.'

Bryan opened the door, looked at Florian and nodded. 'Inside. Get in.'

'This is silly beyond words,' said Florian. 'Wade, please have a little chat with your kin, will you?'

Wade was furious. 'Bryan, what exactly is the point of this?'

Shw preempted Bryan's reply: 'Krautwell here is going to suffer for a while. I'm going to extract some passwords and file names from him.'

Florian said, 'You *are*, are you?'

Shw looked at him. 'My family's been on to your company for a decade. You're a peril to the planet.'

'A *peril to the planet*?' asked Wade. 'That's so corny.'

'He's a nightmare.'

'*Ooh* – so you're going to hurt me,' said Florian. 'I'd think long and hard before you do that, you little brats.'

'Maybe I'll *kill* you. But first I want you in the jail.' She motioned Florian into the pink cell.

'Come on in, sugar,' said Gayle. 'You'll be safer being locked away from that family of idiots.'

Wade and Ted said, 'We're *not* idiots.'

'*Que será, será* . . .' Florian was inside the jail when Janet, seemingly from nowhere, plunged an epidural syringe the size of a straw deep into Shw's neck, viscerally, deeply into pale white neck tissue. She shouted, 'Florian, call your secret service!' The stunned look on Shw's face – as well as the looks on other faces in the room – indicated that nobody considered Janet the sort of woman to plunge syringes into the necks of others. Shw was busy trying to bat the syringe away, as if it were a spider that had jumped her jugular.

Bryan said, 'Mom? What are you—?' but Wade jumped on Bryan's back.

'My sunburn – ow!'

Wade knocked away Bryan's gun, sending it clattering into a corner. Wade scrambled to catch it, but Bryan said, 'It's empty. Don't bother.'

'Empty?'

Shw screamed, 'Bryan, get this goddamn thing out of my neck.' She was shaking.

A choreographic blur followed during which . . .

. . . Gayle reached between the cell's bars and grabbed Shw's gun, shooting Shw's foot in the process, making her flare like a smoke alarm detector.

. . . Lloyd and Gayle escaped the cell, grabbing Shw and tossing her inside.

. . . Bryan ran inside the cell to tend to Shw, as did Florian, who pulled the door shut after him.

The net result was that Shw, Bryan and Florian were locked inside. Wade and Janet were outside.

Florian was tending to Shw's foot, saying, 'Look what you inexperienced pinheads have gone and done. Where's the first-aid box?' There was one beneath the bunk.

Janet nodded to Wade, indicating where the cell key had fallen onto the concrete. Wade and Lloyd dive-bombed it at the same moment; it bounced across the floor, *plink*, then into a drain. The room fell silent.

'Shit, shit, *shit*,' said Lloyd.

Gayle said, 'Don't tell me you didn't have the dupes made—'

'I—'

'You doofus. One stupid little job I ask you to do, but no, you're too lazy to do it. You just have to go and waste your days at the greyhound races while I keep this place together.'

Shw was swooning; Bryan was in tears. Florian was applying antiseptic while rapidly tapping behind his ears.

Gayle said, 'Right then, you two—' She indicated Wade and Janet. 'If we can't lock you with the others, you'll come with us. Upstairs. We're going for a car ride.'

'What?' Wade began. 'You're going to kill us and dump our bodies? Good luck. We've stockpiled a dossier on you that's so thick and full of scary shit that once you die in prison you'll reincarnate as a prisoner. Don't even think of giving us a wedgie, let alone a bullet in our reptile cortexes. Harm us and you two are *toast*.'

Gayle said, 'Right then. But there's no law says we can't make you endure a little discomfort.'

Lloyd said, 'Discomfort?'

'The *swamp*,' said Gayle.

Lloyd beamed. 'Perfect! I'll go start the car.' He left the room. Gayle motioned toward two pairs of handcuffs by the obstetrical chair. 'I want you two to cuff yourselves together – hand to hand, foot to foot.'

Janet said, 'Is this really necessary?'

Gayle said, 'Yes, it is.'

'What if we don't?'

Without looking, Gayle pointed the gun toward the cell and fired, missing the trio inside, but making a very firm point. Wade handcuffed his mother's left foot to his right foot, her left hand to his right hand.

'Why are your legs purple?' Gayle asked.

'AIDS.'

'I should have known. Both of you, up into the car.'

Janet looked at the pink cell. 'Florian, call your security people, for God's sake.'

'Done.'

'Don't let Bryan or Emily be killed or beaten – they're not evil – they're merely idiots.'

'I promise, Janet.'

'You'll attend the launch with me?'

'Oh, yes!'

Lloyd's car was a walloping Floridian senior's cruiser, a plush leather casket. Lloyd drove, and Gayle sat in the passenger seat with the gun aimed at mother and son, blinded with Qantas eyeshades. 'Things were going just great until you monsters showed up.'

'Yeah. Well. Whatever.'

'Lloyd, play some music,' said Gayle. A wash of 1981 music – Van Halen? – filled the vehicle. 'Lloyd, this is a car, not a suntanning bed. Change it to classical.' Lloyd did so. 'There,' said Gayle, 'peaceful lovely *peace*.'

They drove into the country; the landscape became markedly wilder the further they strayed inland. The car hit gravel and then drove unmistakably over a wooden bridge – a surprisingly long wooden bridge that made the car go *thoomp-a-doomp-a-doomp-a-doomp*. Wade calculated five minutes at forty miles an hour.

Lloyd stopped the car. Gayle hopped out and opened the rear doors and told Janet and Wade to get out, and once they had, she said, 'Good riddance,' and booted Wade behind his knees, sending him toppling into a swamp, his mother with him. She looked over the edge: 'You might survive, so technically this isn't murder. But I hope you rot down there.'

28

As Janet fell with Wade into the swamp, she had the feeling that she was traveling back in time. She went back to the week before – to when she was flying from Vancouver to Orlando for the shuttle launch. The sight of so many purposeful and busy-seeming people, all of whom shared a focused destination, had inspired her. When the flight hubbed in Dallas, it was late afternoon and the temperature outside the terminal hit 120 degrees. Passengers inside the glass structure were looking at the sky as if it had just been diagnosed with a terminal disease. Crowds of strangers huddled around the air vents, sharing stray whiffs of coolness. A woman from Beaumont told Janet that after 118 degrees, the ignitions of many cars would refuse to turn over; parking lots melted like chocolate; water tables vanished and the planet began to cave in onto itself.

Janet then decided to flow with the airport's tide – in the inter-terminal shuttle train, in the newsstands and in the bathrooms. Her connection to Orlando was delayed; her daughter was on TV; her own mother had been dead thirty years; her father, fifteen. Her eyes and ears were tickled and molested by screens and speakers, all of them heralding the birth or death of something sacred or important.

She found herself in a cafeteria lineup with a tray, waiting to buy a bruised apple, greasy pizza and a warm pretzel along with dozens of fellow passengers. Suddenly Janet fell further back into time, to another era, to the Eaton's cafeteria, not the Toronto Eaton's cafeteria of her youth, but the downtown Vancouver cafeteria of her middle age. It was six weeks after the doomed party and Wade and Ted's fight on the lawn. Janet had still believed Wade might move back home, and she'd chosen the fifth-floor cafeteria at the downtown Eaton's store as neutral territory. Eaton's, by then, bore no resemblance to her father's Depression-era workplace, but simply seeing the name made her feel rooted. In the lineup, Wade had been making fun of Janet's choices: mashed potatoes, pork slices and a custard pudding.

'Mom, your food is beige.'

'It's good food, Wade.'

'But it's all the same color.'

'I suppose so. And what exactly have *you* chosen to eat, Leonardo?'

Janet looked down at Wade's tray – tinned fruit cocktail swimming in Jell-O, tomato juice and a starburst of chef's salad. His tray looked like Christmas tree ornaments laid out, ready for hanging. 'It's pretty,' Janet said.

'It is, kinda, isn't it?'

They sat down in a window seat that overlooked the courthouse below, and heard the timeless sounds of people – elderly people mainly – their Saturday department store lunch, the fanciest meal of the week for many of them. The sound evoked in Janet childhood memories she was powerless to halt.

'*. . . Houston to Mom . . . Houston to Mom.*'

'Sorry, dear. Memories. You'll understand one day.'

'I'm never going to grow old. I want *experiences*, not memories.'

Janet smiled. 'You're being silly, Wade. Besides, you're the sort of person who sticks around for a long time.'

'I am, am I?'

'Eat your lunch.'

They talked happily about goings on – mostly in Wade's life. He'd moved in with Colin, a friend who had a job at Radio Shack. 'It's a sleeping bag on the floor, but before you know it, I'll be on Easy Street.' For the time being, he was delivering carpets for a living, and his plans for locating Easy Street were vague.

Janet fished around inside her purse for cigarettes, but she'd run out. '*Drat . . .*'

'Take one of mine.'

'Smoking now, are we?'

'For years. You can't *not* have known.'

'Oh, I knew.' She lit one of Wade's cigarettes and coughed. 'Wade – these are more like cigars. Oh, God, I'm feeling dizzy.'

'You'll get used to them.'

For a brief moment the sun cut through the daily drizzle outside. Wade did a double-take: 'Aggh! That yellow orb up there – it burns my eyes – what *is* it?'

'It's about time we had a spot of sun,' Janet said.

'Sun – you called the golden orb the "sun" – what else do your people know that I do not?'

Janet giggled, and the two of them enjoyed the sunshine. Wade asked, 'Mom, what was the happiest moment in your life?'

'What? Oh, Wade – I can't answer that.'

'Why not?'

Well, why not? No reason, really. 'Well, I suppose I *could* tell you.'

'Do.'

It took Janet a little time to isolate the moment. 'I wasn't much older than you. I was eighteen and such a dumb bunny. My father shipped me off to Europe for a month the summer before I met your father – Daddy was starting to make real money then, and the dollar – I can't *tell* you how far it stretched in Europe.'

Janet noticed Wade sipping coffee. *Oh – Wade is drinking coffee now.*

'I had a lovely tan, and I'd thrown away my frumpy Canadian tourist clothes, and I bought these lovely light summer dresses in Italy. Like the woman on the Sun-Maid raisin box. The whistles and attention I got – I loved it. And I was paired with these two gals from Alberta who were fearless, and I sort of absorbed their strength. I was so bold.'

'You're a beautiful woman, Mom. You should accept the fact. But what about your happiest moment?'

'Oh yes. In Paris, near the end of my trip. Some American boys were flirting with us, and we'd been out to dinner and then we'd gone dancing at a nightclub.'

'American guys?'

'They were *such* fun! In the end, that's probably why I married your father. He was American, and Americans are always *doing* things, and I like that in people.'

'But your story—'

'There's not much more to it really. It was three in the morning and I was walking along the Seine, just beside Notre Dame cathedral with Donny MacDonald, and he was singing songs from *Carousel* to me – I felt as though my heart would burst! And then there was this chill wind – so cool that I developed goose bumps even though the evening was hot and sultry. I had this premonition that my youth and carefree times were about to end – and it filled me with sadness and resignation – I mean, I'd only just begun to feel like a newly minted human being, entertaining all sorts of life options – or as many as a 1950s girl could entertain. So that was my little moment of happiness. Before I could digest anything I was back in school, and then marrying your father and having you kids, and it's as if the entire universe of possibilities that might have been mine ended right there on the Seine with Donny MacDonald.' Janet dried her eye with a paper napkin. 'What about you, Wade? What's your happiest moment?'

Janet hadn't expected Wade to have a happiest moment; he was too young to even *have* moments, let alone good or bad ones, but he caught Janet off guard. 'It was with Jenny. About two months ago.'

'Jenny?'

'Yeah. We were in the hammock out behind her house. We

both knew she was pregnant, and we thought we could pull the whole thing off. I'd get a job and we'd find an apartment, and we'd raise the kid and be a family. She let me touch her stomach and suddenly I wasn't me, Wade Drummond, any more – I was something larger and better and more important than just myself. We felt as if we'd made a planet. We felt like the mood would last always.'

Janet was silent. *This is Wade's way of filling in the blanks for me.*

A police car with sirens whistled by on the street below. The sun went behind the clouds. 'Wade, why don't you come home?'

'To visit? Sure. Soon. Maybe next week, depending on my delivery shift.'

'No. I mean come back and live at home. I'm sure your father regrets the fight and the scene at the party.'

'Mom—'

'It could be different this time around.'

'Mom, I've left home.'

'Wade?'

'I can't come back, Mom. I've gone.'

Yet again Janet felt as though she were falling through time, and now she was back in the lineup in a Texas airport, where she was paying for her snack. She ate it while sitting on a railing near a vent, and once finished, she had an hour and fifteen minutes to kill. Across the way she saw a booth selling Internet access. A spot had just come vacant, and so she took it. She looked up Donny MacDonald, and learned he was an ophthalmologist living in New Lyme, Connecticut. She thought of contacting him, but then realized she'd never dream of doing such a thing.

And then the falling stopped, and Janet and Wade squelched into a warm pudding of mud. She felt no fear. Lloyd and Gayle's car simply floated away down the bridge, and that was that. Her body bumped into Wade's. The warm swamp water was only technically knee-high, but as they stood up, their legs squelched down into the bottom sludge as though they were dock pilings.

'Oh, Christ,' Wade said. 'Sorry, Mom.'

'Sorry?' The two of them were doing an awkward do-si-do trying to achieve stability. 'It's my fault we're here. I got us into this.'

'Are you hurt?' Wade asked.

'I think I am. My wrist and ankle – from the handcuffs. But pain doesn't always mean damage. You?'

'Yeah. My arm.' They righted themselves, and by then their eyes had adjusted to the moonlight. The only man-made light was at least a dozen miles away, hotels along the Atlantic, their lights seemingly waiting to be untethered so as to float heavenward.

Janet said, 'I think I actually cut my arms pretty badly.'

'My arm's broken, Mom.'

'Are you sure? How can you tell?'

'Look—'

His unshackled left forearm dangled in a disturbing manner. Something was protruding from within.

'Good God, honey, does it hurt?'

'Nope. Not really.'

Janet didn't believe him – there was no time to quibble. 'We're dripping blood into the water. What about alligators?'

'People worry about alligators, but they're not the big deal you think they are.'

'You're lying.'

'I was trying to make you worry less.'

Janet looked up at the silvery gray poles that held up the road above. 'Can we climb up to the bridge? It doesn't look too high.'

Wade looked at it: 'No.'

'OK then, can we walk out of here?'

'Theoretically, if we weren't hurt or handcuffed together, I'd piggyback you a few miles in either direction. But like this? No.'

'What about attracting other cars?'

'What other cars? This is a semiprivate road – or a government road.'

'Stop being so *negative*. There must be *something* we can do. Wade—?' Janet became aware that Wade was trying not to cry. 'Shoot. Oh, honey, I'm sorry, I didn't mean to snap at you. I didn't mean to sound angry.'

'It's not that. It's me. Everything I touch turns to ratshit. All the people whose lives I touch turn to ratshit. I've had a nothing life. A zero. Wasted.'

'What about *my* life, honey?'

'*Your* life? You've had a great life. You had three kids. You were the center of the family. You—'

'Stop. You said "*were* the center." '

'Sorry. You *are* the center.'

'Whoopee-gee. Look what it got me.'

'Your life isn't meaningless, Mom.'

'I'd debate you on that point.' Wade's face calmed down. Janet could only imagine the pain his arm must be in. 'Are you comfortable? How can I make you more comfortable?'

'Why don't we both just sit on our knees in the mud. I think it's more stable that way.'

'Ow! My wrist . . .' Janet was stabbed with pain on her wrist. Wade looked at it and could see what Janet saw, how badly she had been hurt in the fall, strips of skin sheared away.

'Mom, I'm so sorry.'

'Wade, it's six hours until sunrise, and even then . . . What are we going to do?'

'Let's just sit and stay calm. Let's just breathe.'

So they sat in silence; the moon shone down; insects flickered about; and Janet thought she saw egrets asleep in the dense thickets of swamp grass. She tried not to feel any pain, but the pretending was hard. From high above, she heard a jet, which soon passed, and they were returned to the rich protean silence.

Janet felt like a bacterium. She felt like a reptile. She felt like meat. She didn't feel human.

A cell phone rang.

Huh?

It sat in Janet's right pocket. 'Wade. Oh *dear* – I assumed . . .' She slipped her hands into moist, muddy pocket folds. '. . . it'd be dead from the water.'

Wade looked on, alarmed. 'They're waterproof these days.'

Frantically, awkwardly, Janet opened the device's flap. 'Hello? Help!'

'Mom?' Sarah was on the line.

'Sarah, call an ambulance. Wade and I have been hurt. We're in a swamp.'

'A swamp? Where?'

'I don't know – inland, south of Daytona Beach.'

'How are you hurt?'

'Wade's arm's broken like it was kindling wood. And we're handcuffed together – my skin is in ribbons.'

The phone's low battery noise kicked in with piercing beeps. 'Mom,' said Sarah. 'Listen to me: hang up. Now.'

Eeep eeep eeep

'The battery—'

'Hang up. Then wait a minute. I'll phone back.'

. . . *click*

Janet's line went blank. 'What do we *tell* her, Wade? Where *are* we?' For the umpteenth time that week, Janet felt as if she were back in time; in no way did she feel as if she were in the United States.

'Mom, I hope that battery lasts us a few more seconds. Christ, to be at the mercy of a *battery*.'

'I'm scared, Wade.'

'Don't be scared, Mom. We'll work this out. We will. Please don't be afraid.'

They sat in silence. Palmetto beetles hummed, whippoorwills

trilled and crickets chirped. The phone rang. 'Hello, Sarah?'

A cool, detached and technical male voice was on the other end. 'This is NASA triangulation. Do you read me?'

Janet said, 'Yes!' but the question was meant for another technician. 'I read you, NASA. Signal source confirmed. Location is—'

Eeep eeep eeep

The phone was dead.

'Wade, what did they mean? Triangulation? They didn't find our location.'

'Mom, you don't know that.'

'What if they didn't?'

'You don't know that they did or didn't. Sit tight. At the very worst we'll have to wait until morning.'

'Wade, your arm's broken like a cracked broomstick. The morning comes, and then what?'

'It gets light out.'

'Don't be silly.'

'You're the one being silly, Mom.'

'No, *you're* the one being silly.'

'You're silly.'

'No, *you're* silly.'

'Silly.'

'How's your arm, Wade?'

'It feels perfectly silly.'

'We'll stick this out until morning.'

'We will.'

They sat for a while and heard more little noises – creatures jumping in and out of the water; buzzing sounds; a hoot from the dark distance.

'So you gave Florian the letter in the end.'

'I did no such thing.'

'But he said . . .'

'He said it *wrong*. I had the real letter with me in the restaurant but I told him it was a fake. The genuine letter is actually here in my pocket still – in its little Baggie.' She pulled it out, grimacing with pain. 'Here – you take it.' She slipped the document into Wade's shirt pocket.

'Mom, what did you tell Dad and Nickie back at the house?'

'What do you mean?'

'You said something to them – and they *changed*. They became . . . younger. Dad even looked relaxed. What did you tell them? You know something.'

'Yes. I do.'

'What do you know? Tell me.'

Janet wondered how to explain it to Wade. The news had been so easy with Ted and Nickie. She'd felt like a Mafia *capo* dispensing life-transforming benedictions with one breath, asking for a carafe of red with the next. But with Wade the telling of the news was somehow more complex, and she hadn't anticipated this. 'Wade, say you didn't have AIDS. Say you weren't sick, that you learned you had a false positive the way Beth did.'

'Mom, you've seen how far gone I am. Sitting in this swamp with our open wounds is probably going to be the death of us both.'

'Answer my question, Wade. Pretend.'

'What would I do?'

'Yes.'

Wade considered this at same length. 'I wouldn't have any excuses, would I?'

Janet kept silent.

'I'd—' Wade paused again.

Janet herself thought about this question. She'd had no time to herself since Cissy had transformed her life at the restaurant. What would be the difference between death at sixty-five and death at seventy-five? – those ten extra years . . . what could they possibly mean? Or eighty-five – twenty extra years. She'd wanted those years so badly, had mourned for their loss, yet now she had them again, and she couldn't decode their implication. *Well, for that matter, what was the purpose of my first sixty-five years? Maybe the act of wanting to live and being given life is the only thing that matters. Forget the mountain of haikus I can write now. Forget learning to play the cello or slaving away for charity. But then what?*

She thought about her life and how lost she'd felt for most of it. She thought about the way that all the truths she'd been taught to consider valuable invariably conflicted with the world as it was actually lived. How could a person be so utterly lost, yet remain living? Her time with the disease had, to her surprise, made her feel less lost. That was one thing she knew was true. Sickness had forced her to look for knowledge and solace in places she might otherwise not have dreamed of. Sickness had forced her to meet and connect with citizens who otherwise would have remained shadows inside cars that idled beside her at red lights. But maybe now she'd continue looking for ideas she'd never dreamed of in places once forbidden – not because she had to but because she chose to – because that had proven to be the only true path out of her brittle, unlivable life-before-death. Now she could seek out the souls inside everybody she met – at the Super-Valu, at the dogwalking path, at the library – all of these souls, bright lights, blinding her perhaps . . .

'I suppose—' Wade said.

'Yes?'

'Well, look at my situation this way. Right now I'm technically dead. Don't say I'm not because I'm a goner for sure. All those protease inhibitors and reverse transcriptase inhibitors ever did was give me an extra year with Beth – and they gave me the time to come down here to be with the family for the launch.' He turned his head to his mother. 'It's been a hoot, hasn't it?'

'The hootiest.'

'There you go.' He turned and looked at the yellow hotel lights far away. 'But if I learned I wasn't going to die, I don't think I could go on being Wade any more.'

'How so?'

'I'd have to start from scratch. I'd be like a scientist in a comic book who gets horribly maimed in an accident, but who gets a superpower in exchange.'

Janet asked Wade, 'What superpower would you get?'

'You go first. Tell me yours.'

'OK, I will. You know what it would be?'

'No.'

Janet said, 'Remember back around 1970 when we added the two new bedrooms and the new bathroom to the house? There was this period during the construction – a week maybe – when the framing of the walls was in, but not the walls. I'd go out there at night, by myself, and walk from room to room, through the walls, like a ghost. It made me feel so superhuman – so powerful – and I don't know why it affected me so much. So I'd like to be able to walk through walls. *That* would be my superpower.'

'Good one.'

'And you?'

'Huh. Funny. Beth and I discussed this once. I told her I wanted to shoot lasers from my eyes – no, from my fingertips – and when the beams hit somebody, they'd make that person see God. I'd be Holy Man – that'd be my name. But I don't know. A super power like *that* is almost too much power for mere human beings. But then maybe I could try and see God myself, and maybe once I did, I'd be firing lasers in all directions all the time, a nonstop twenty-four-hour God transformer.'

'So if you were cured, you'd really try and do that?'

'I would.'

'Is that a solemn promise?'

Wade said, 'I don't make solemn promises too often. Just once before. To Beth. But I'd make a solemn promise for that.'

'Give me your arm.'

'Huh?'

'Your broken arm.'

'Why?'

'Wade, *do it.*' Janet grabbed her shackled wrist and placed it on to Wade's open wound.

'Mom! You shouldn't be doing that.'

'Wade, shut up.' Janet held her wrist closely to Wade's wound:

'*One Mississippi, two Mississippi, three Mississippi*'

'Mom?'

'Shut up, Wade – *four Mississippi, five Mississippi, six Mississippi*'

'Mom, what are you doing?'

Janet counted on: '*Twelve Mississippi, thirteen Mississippi, fourteen Mississippi*'

'Did Florian—'

'*Twenty-five Mississippi, twenty-six Mississippi, twenty-seven Mississippi . . .*'

'Oh, dear God—'

'*Thirty-seven Mississippi, thirty-eight Mississippi, thirty-nine Mississippi . . .*'

'He *did.*'

'*Forty-two Mississippi, forty-three Mississippi, forty-four Mississippi . . .*'

'Mom—'

'*Fifty-six Mississippi, fifty-seven Mississippi, fifty-eight Mississippi . . .*'

'I . . .'

'*Sixty Mississippi, sixty-one Mississippi, sixty-two Mississippi. There.*' Janet pulled her wrist away and separated their mingled bloods, slightly clotted. Janet felt as if she were removing her hand from a patch of slightly tacky drying paint.

'He fixed you, didn't he?' Wade said.

'Yes, he did, dear. He did.'

'And now I'm—?'

'Yes, dear, you're reborn.'

'I'll . . . I'll be able to see my child grow up.'

'So will I.'

From the south came the thundering of choppers, and with them a beacon of light that shone down from the sky, on to the swamp and on to mother and son.

29

An hour before final boarding, Sarah was shown a monitor where she'd been able to view her family in the VIP bleachers – and what a decrepit crew they were: Bryan and that creepy Shw, both bruised and black-eyed, with Bryan also slathered in zinc ointments, and Shw on crutches. Dad was there with his hand on Nickie's tush, and at Nickie's side was a man with a forearm swaddled in bandages – *who on earth?* Howie was nowhere to be seen. *Big deal.* Mom and Wade, meanwhile, were both testimonies to the nurse's craft, trussed and slinged and wrapped and becrutched. Beth still looked as if she'd been plucked from a rerun of *Little House on the Prairie*. And lastly there was a suave Europerson – *why are Europeans always so easy to spot?* – next to Janet with his arm around her. The European was whispering something evidently quite funny into her ear. Her family stood beside the Brunswick family, Fuji-film bright, wearing matching polo shirts and chunky necklaces made of binoculars, recorders and cameras.

Her own family looked so . . . *damaged* beside the Brunswicks, and yet they were – well, they were *her* family. And even with all of her genetic studies, she'd never been able to figure out how she'd sprung from this lot.

Well, nature conspires to keep things interesting, doesn't she? Back to business . . .

Sarah knew that if she were to die during liftoff, she'd die quickly. She knew the odds. She'd heard the NASA lore – bodies soaked in jet fuel morphing into walking lava; technicians on the tarmac, eating a sandwich and accidentally straying into colorless invisible streams of burning hydrogen – vaporized in a blink – and of course the *Challenger* crash, 1986: she'd heard about it on the car radio while on the way to give a lecture at Pepperdine University, and she'd had to pull her car off on the freeway's shoulder and grab for air as if she'd been kicked in the gut. But *now* – now snug in her seat, the liftoff had begun. To her surprise, the shuttle's rumble was so loud and wild and hungry it sounded instead like a color, a shade of white lightning crackling around Frankenstein's head – a puking nuclear reactor.

Finally, after all these years, I'm leaving. My arms . . . my head – they feel so implausibly heavy, like cartons of textbooks – or river rocks. I can barely blink.

She tried to clear her brain, to enjoy the moment as if it were sex, to blot out her mind, but she was only partially able. Her perception was invariably invaded by images from two nights before, of medics lifting her mother and brother from a Volusia County swamp as if they were insects being spooned from a chowder. They'd been dripping with a batter of mud and leeches; their skin was ripped and bloody, and a bone was sticking out of Wade's arm while his legs were polka-dotted with lesions – and oddest of all, the two had been handcuffed together.

'Mom! Wade! Good *God*, how did this happen?'

'Long story, baby sister.'

'Dear, now's not the time to go into this.'

Medics dowsed the two with fresh water, plucked away the leeches, cut away their garments, all the while injecting them with painkillers and drying them off with crumpled veils of gauze and a hot air blower. A female medic had cut apart the cuffs with a jaws-of-life.

The sequence of events leading to their rescue had been bizarre – the quick phone call to apologize to her mother – the horrendous news – then sprinting down the antiseptic white gantry screaming for a radar technician to pinpoint the phone's location – grabbing a helmeted quarantine body suit, and then busting out of the quarantine zone to flag down a golf cart, which then raced her to the medical pavilion. *Damn, I'm good! I feel like a* M*A*S*H *rerun.* She knew it was too late in the mission to have an understudy replace her. She knew she'd be reprimanded, but not punished, and this had turned out to be the case.

Blink . . .

Liftoff continued. Sarah knew she must be miles above the earth's surface – and she hadn't blown up yet – but she remained frozen by extra gravity and was unable to turn and catch Gordon's eye.

Blink . . .

She was in the chopper, landing on a wooden bridge the dry silvery color of a moth's wing. The bridge saddled a vast swamp, but the chopper's searchlights had found her mother and Wade right away. *God bless radar*. The pilot, on seeing their handcuffs, asked, with no trace of humor, 'Are they prisoners?'

The rotors slowed to a stop and Sarah hopped out of the copter and looked over the bridge's edge. She was backlit, and she knew she could only appear to her family like an astral visitation, a uranium angel with a head shelled in Plexiglas, crackling with power and the Word.

Blink . . .

The shuttle was arcing now, the G-force dwindling. *We must be over Africa*. She turned to Gordon at the same moment that he turned to her. They were a pair of space virgins thinking they'd discovered the weightless world all by themselves. Gordon winked.

Blink . . .

'Mom, for God's sake, tell me what happened here.'

'Not now, dear, it's too . . . messy. You need full use of your noggin for the launch.'

'Mom, I can *see* that it's messy.'

Wade, stuffed into a plastic evacuation sled, winked at Sarah. 'Trust me on this one, Sarah. Wait until the mission's over.'

Sarah was furious. 'I won't be able to wait.'

'Sure you will,' said Wade. 'You were always the coolest cucumber on Christmas morning.'

'Only because every Christmas Eve I went down in the middle of the night and unwrapped all the presents to see what they were.'

'Did you really?' Janet asked. She was being tucked into a plastic evacuation manger like Wade's. Neither Wade nor her mother seemed the least bit fazed by their bizarre predicament. If anything, they were utterly at peace with the world. 'Thanks for coming to fetch us, dear.'

Sarah repeated these last words: '*Thank you for coming to fetch us?*'

'Yes. It was risky for you.'

'No, not really. I'll catch flak, but the flak will pass.'

Wade asked, 'You won't be . . . calling the *cops*, will you?'

'I don't think this is the sort of thing NASA likes John Q. Public reading about in the paper.'

The enormous copter lifted off. Once airborne, Wade asked, 'Is that quarantine suit you're wearing germ-proof?'

'It is.'

'So if a person, say, had no immune system, they could wear one of those and never be sick or anything?'

'Maybe. But all of us have so many creepy-crawlies inside us that it'd be like shutting the barn door once the horse has fled.'

Wade said, 'Remember that old movie – *The Boy in the Plastic Bubble*?'

'Of course.'

'What was it about?' Janet asked.

I can't believe I'm flying above a swamp at 4:30 in the morning with Mom and Wade discussing a 1970s made-for-TV movie.

'This guy,' Wade said, 'John Travolta. He's born with no immune system – so he lives in a bubble inside his parents' house. But then one day he gets fed up with the bubble and punctures it, and he walks out into the real world.'

'Does he die?' Janet asked.

'What do you think? Of course he does. But at least he was able to see the real world.'

Janet thought this over.

Sarah thought: *These helicopters certainly are noisy.*

Janet then said to Sarah, 'Dear, you know that once the flight's over you'll be off the hook.'

'Off the hook?'

'That's right, dear. There'll be nothing left to prove. You'll be able to have a life. You won't have to live out someone else's vision of your life.'

'Meaning Dad?'

'Meaning *everybody*.'

'That's true, isn't it?'

'It is.'

Blink . . .

Now I'm up in space. I'm in free float. No nausea. No dizziness – me and the planet and Gordon and my experiments. If this were all there were to life, then life would be perfect.

The four other crewmembers were methodically performing their shuttle tasks. Gordon signaled Sarah into a corner and they . . . sat? . . . stood? . . . floated? face to face.

'T-minus-fourteen hours,' said Gordon.

'I copy you, Commander Brunswick.'

In fourteen hours she and Gordon would couple, but the act itself wasn't what thrilled Sarah. What thrilled her was the knowledge that if everything worked out, she'd conceive a child during the flight, the first child ever conceived up among the stars. A child conceived in space would be a god. The child's very existence would be proof of human perfection – proof of human ability to rise above the cruel and unusual world – flawless, golden, curious and mighty.

She looked out the window at brave, blue Earth. She put out

her hand and squinted her eyes, and briefly, before her mission duties claimed her, she held it in her palm.

Blink . . .

As the chopper pulled into NASA, Sarah remembered something and mentioned it to Janet and Wade: 'Guys, I'm allowed to bring twelve ounces of personal belongings up into space with me. Do either of you have a lightweight object you'd like to be able to present at a show-and-tell in 2020 and say, "This was once up in space"?'

Wade and Janet looked at each other, then Wade removed a letter from his shirt pocket, but before he handed it to Sarah, he asked her, 'Sarah, are you going on a spacewalk on this trip?'

'Outside the craft?'

'Yeah.'

'Yes, I am.'

'So if you were to leave something out there, that thing would circle the planet for ever?'

'For a pretty long time.'

'Take this for me.' He gave her the letter. 'But don't bring it back, OK? Leave it out there, out in orbit.'

Sarah looked at the letter and made no historical connection. 'Sure.'

'You promise?'

What's he up to? 'I promise.'

'Good.' Wade made a face that might have been made by pioneers crossing the continent, dropping a piano off the Conestoga wagon onto the wheezy Oklahoma dirt – a burden relieved.

'What about you, Mom?'

'Could you pass me a pair of those scissors there, dear?'

'Scissors? What for?'

'Please, I need them just for a second.'

Sarah handed them to Janet who, regardless of the state of her arms, reached back, pulled her hair into a ponytail and quickly snipped off the large lock.

'There.'

'Mom!'

'Oh shush, girl. And these are excellent scissors. I'd like to get a pair for myself.'

'Mom, why did you—'

Janet quickly tied the severed ponytail into a neat knot.

'Mom, you're scaring me.'

'Sarah, answer me this – if you were to be out in space, and if you threw an object down to Earth, it would burn through the atmosphere on reentry, wouldn't it?'

'Sure.'

'Good.' She handed Sarah the ponytail. 'Do that for me, dear.'

'What – throw it down to Earth?'

'Yes, dear.'

'But why?'

'Because people will look up to its trail when it falls down. They won't know it, but it'll be *me* they're looking at.'

'And—?'

'*And* they'll think they've just seen a *star*.'